the Land
BEYOND
the
PORTAL

the Land

BEYOND

the

PORTAL

J.S. BAILEY

TATE PUBLISHING & Enterprises

Published by Tate Publishing & Enterprises, LLC
127 E. Trade Center Terrace | Mustang, Oklahoma 73064 USA
1.888.361.9473 | www.tatepublishing.com

Tate Publishing is committed to excellence in the publishing industry. The company reflects the philosophy established by the founders, based on Psalm 68:11,
"The Lord gave the word and great was the company of those who published it."

Book design copyright © 2011 by Tate Publishing, LLC. All rights reserved.
Cover design by Amber Gulilat
Interior design by Nathan Harmony

Published in the United States of America
ISBN: 978-1-61777-311-2
Fiction / Christian / Suspense
11.03.21

DEDICATION

This book is dedicated to Nathan, who encouraged me to finish writing this story even when it seemed doubtful that I ever would.

ACKNOWLEDGMENTS

I would like to thank my mother, Janel, for helping me work out some problems with my original plot; my husband, Nathan; father, Bill; and siblings, Billy and Raquel, for their continuing love and support; all of the great authors big and small whose works inspired me to write; and God for giving me the gift to create this novel.

CHAPTER 1

A charming brick house sat in the mountains like a mother bird in her nest. It usually looked cozy and welcoming to motorists who happened to pass through, admiring the beauty of the Appalachians. However, the house had become almost invisible from the powerful snowstorm that was dumping inch after inch of icy precipitation on the range. Entire trees leaned to one side, their limbs drooping under the weight of the snow. The lane leading to the house was completely buried. A howling wind ripped through the air and sculpted the snow into mighty drifts.

Inside the dwelling, a girl paced back and forth, biting her nails. She was expecting a very important phone call from her parents. She could hardly bear to think about it. It had been such a dreadful accident. And it had been all her fault! Would he live?

She needed some medicine for the pounding headache she had developed within the past few nerve-racking hours and started up the steps to the second-floor bathroom, where such items were kept. When she was halfway down the hallway, she heard her cell phone ringing in the living room. Her heart pounded even harder. They were finally calling her back! The teenager wondered for the thousandth time why her grandparents didn't have their own phone and raced back down the steps, not looking where she was going. She tripped over her grandfather's pair of house slippers, tumbled down five steps, and landed headfirst on the slate floor below with a sickening thud. This was met with blinding pain and abrupt darkness. She was falling, falling…

The girl regained consciousness a short while later. As she opened her eyes, she realized that her legs were lying on the steps and the upper half of her body was sprawled out on the floor. Her whole face hurt.

"What the heck did I do to myself?" she wondered aloud before sitting up.

Suddenly, a sharp pain sliced through her head, and the girl had the overwhelming urge to throw up. Struggling to control herself, she carefully rose, walked to the nearest chair, and sat down. She took some calming breaths.

Her next thought was, *Where am I?*

Panic coursed through her as she realized that she had no idea *who* she was either.

What was she doing in this strange house? Whose house was it? To make matters worse, she kept feeling like something terrible had just occurred.

A nearby bleeping sound made her jump. She saw a small black cell phone sitting on the coffee table and picked it up with interest. "Low battery," was the message displayed on the glowing green screen. She put it back and began to ponder her strange predicament.

It was apparent that she had fallen down the steps and crashed headlong into the hard floor. But why she had been going down in the first place was beyond her. She felt like she had to go to the bathroom. Had she been headed for a bathroom? The girl gingerly rose up from the armchair, but her head felt so bad that she considered calling 911. After all, head injuries were never something to be taken lightly. She picked up the cell phone only to discover that it was now completely dead. Frustrated, she threw it down and went off to locate a bathroom.

On the first floor, she found a bathroom with very pink, flowery wallpaper that smelled strongly of potpourri. The odor was nauseating. She saw a full-length mirror hanging on the back of the bathroom door and gazed at her vaguely familiar reflection. A girl with dark brown hair looked back at her with hazel eyes that were full of worry. She wore a pair of khaki pants, a light purple knit sweater, white gym shoes, a pair of hoop earrings, a gold necklace that had a letter *L* on the pendant, and a class ring. She pulled the ring off of her finger and saw that the name *Laura* was engraved on one side, opposite the words *Class of* 2005. A beautiful light green stone was in the center.

So, my name must be Laura, the girl thought.

Laura sounded right. The only problem now was that she had no idea what her middle or last names could be. But that thought could wait until later, as she had more pressing matters to attend to.

Laura returned to the living room and sank dejectedly into the chair, wondering why on earth she was all by herself in a big, lonely house with nobody there to tell her what had happened. And how her head ached! It was so eerie knowing that she was all alone. It seemed like invisible pairs of eyes were watching her every move and some hidden being would suddenly jump out at her from behind a corner when she was least expecting it.

Above her, the roof creaked. She twitched. *Stop being so paranoid*, she ordered herself.

Her stomach rumbled, and instinctively she got up to go find the kitchen. To her great surprise there was a pair of sodden white boots sitting on the mat. Closer inspection revealed that they were just her size, but she couldn't recall having ever worn them before.

Just as she was pondering this, the lights flickered. At first, Laura had the impression that somebody had been fiddling around with the switch; but then every single light and appliance in the house shut off. She was left in total darkness, and her nervous and jittery feelings increased tenfold.

Well, she thought, frowning, *so much for me finding something to eat!*

She groped her way out of the kitchen and back into the living room, where a log was smoldering in the fireplace. After tossing a few medium-sized sticks on the meager flames, she grabbed a blanket, curled up on the couch, and went to sleep.

She was awakened by a startling flash of light when the electricity came back on. A quick glance at the clock told her that it was nearly midnight. She had slept for almost six hours. She sat up, and a searing pain shot through her injured head.

Man, I need an icepack, she thought.

Laura went to the kitchen once more and removed the desired first aid from the freezer, which luckily was still cold inside. She wrapped the icepack in a dishtowel and returned to the couch in front of the dying fire. She added a few more sticks and a log for good measure just in case the power would go out again in the middle of the night. Then she turned out the lights and went back to bed, gently pressing the icepack against the lump on her head.

Her dreams were filled with unearthly horrors. She kept seeing the image of a huge icicle hanging precariously from a drooping tree branch, waving like a dagger in the breeze. There came a crash, and then all she could see was bright red blood splattered on the snow. A young man lay sprawled out on the ground, gasping in pain. Laura screamed.

"No!"

She awoke with a start, her heart pounding.

Laura, just calm down, she said to herself. *It was just a dream, a freaky, weird dream.*

She leaned back and shut her eyes, thinking how odd the dream had been. It was almost as if she had seen it before. Why couldn't she remember? The more she thought about it, the more obscure it became until she disregarded it altogether and dozed off once again, only to have even more bizarre dreams.

She got up at nine o'clock in the morning with brilliant light streaming in through the frosted panes and dancing across the tan, carpeted floor. She sat up and rubbed her tired eyes, glancing at the date on the wall-mounted satellite clock, which read "1/12/2003." It was a Sunday. It was also freezing. The fire seemed to have extinguished itself at some point during the night, and she was out of logs. Why wasn't the furnace running? Laura reluctantly put on her boots and coat and ventured outside to get some wood. Around the back of the house was a shed; and luckily, it was unlocked. The building was filled with logs of varying sizes, and it dawned on her that the owners of the house had a wood burner instead of a regular furnace. For the next half hour, she carried in wood and set it on the floor near the fireplace. Then she relit the fire.

After some much-needed breakfast, Laura sat in the armchair and switched on the morning news, hoping that something on the television might trigger her memory. A woman in a business suit sitting at a news desk appeared on the screen.

"…have said that they received at least another foot of snow during the night in addition to the eighteen inches that fell between eight a.m. and eight p.m. yesterday. And they'll certainly be getting more later this evening due to a large cold front pushing down our way from Canada. At least fifty thousand homes in the area are currently without power from the storms."

The screen changed, and there were several red and blue temperature bars with numbers labeled on them.

"Today's forecast high is around thirty-three degrees at noon. By evening it will have plunged to a freezing eleven degrees Fahrenheit. Experts advise the public to dress with many extra layers while outside but to only remain outdoors for short periods of time. Now we have Jane Eldridge, reporting live from East Millersburg."

Next, it showed a windswept woman wearing a trench coat standing by a huge snowdrift. She gripped the microphone with a red-gloved hand and spoke, her breath forming little clouds of mist around her head.

"Yes," she said. "It has been dreadfully cold these past several days, but that doesn't stop snow-lovers from attending the fifth annual Snow Fest that is currently taking place here in East Millersburg."

The camera panned around and showed a view of warmly clad people constructing sculptures despite the cold snow stinging their rosy faces. Laura was glad she was indoors where it was warm, unlike them.

"Today is the second day of the weeklong gathering, and it is estimated that it might receive crowds as large as fifteen hundred. Yesterday, seven-year-old Jorie Landon from East Millersburg won the Most Creative Snowman contest. The prize-winning sculpture stands eight feet tall and has four body segments."

The woman proceeded to interview a girl who wore a bright purple coat and neon pink earmuffs and gloves.

After the brief interview, the other news reports dragged on. A local man had been accused of beating up his ex-girlfriend and a semi carrying hazardous material had overturned on an icy highway, according to anchorwoman Heidi Pelzman. Laura grew bored as she watched a segment about two "hot" new ways of keeping your car engine from freezing. She switched off the television in disgust.

During an excavation of the kitchen later that day, Laura found a well-used deck of playing cards in one of the drawers and sat down at the table for a nice game of Solitaire. After three consecutive losses, she built a house of cards; but a sudden draft toppled the structure onto the floor just as she was about to place the top two cards on the last level. She let out a mild curse and put the cards away. By that time it was rather late; so she went to bed.

She went to sleep once more on the comfortable sofa in the living room. In the morning, she opened her crusted eyes only to find herself lying on the cold floor with the blanket twisted in a knot around her body.

"Rrr," she grumbled as she pulled it off and slung it over the back of the couch.

After a sparse breakfast of graham crackers and water (the milk had spoiled), she leaned back in the chair to think. It had been two days now since she had awakened at the bottom of the steps. At least the lump on her head had reduced considerably in size. She worried for a second that she might have a hematoma somewhere in her aching skull but dismissed the idea, as she would have most likely been in much worse of a condition if that had been the case. But she did know without a doubt that she'd had a fairly serious concussion.

How do I know all of this? she wondered.

Bored, she went upstairs to see if there was anything interesting she could do. At the top of the steps, there was a short hallway with four doors leading off of it: two on the left, one on the right, and one straight in front of her at the end.

The first room on the left was almost bare. In one corner stood an empty set of shelves that needed dusting; and an old, black trunk leaned against the back wall with its lid open. Uninterested, Laura proceeded to the next room. It appeared to be a young man's bedroom since there was an expensive-looking drum set filling up half the room and the walls were covered in heavy metal rock posters. Laundry covered most of the floor, and there were multiple cigarette burns on the white carpet. She wrinkled her nose and moved on.

The room on the right side of the hallway turned out to be an enormous bathroom, and the last room contained a king-sized bed and some dressers with ugly little knickknacks sitting on them.

Okay, Laura thought. *It really doesn't look like anybody my age lives here. So, why am I here? How the heck did I get here?* She eyed a pair of slacks that had been draped over the end of the bed and realized that she had been wearing the same clothes for an unknown length of time. It couldn't hurt to look for a different outfit.

She searched through all the dressers and the cramped closet, but all she could find were clothes like men's golfing pants and tent-sized olive green sweaters. She let out a groan when she realized that she'd have to wear the same clothes until someone came back to the house. Besides, she had no idea when the owners would—or could—return. The roads were probably completely impassable.

Next, Laura went back downstairs and was searching through a closet when she found something that greatly interested her: it was a light blue coat just her size, hanging sloppily on a clothes hanger. It had to have been hers since the garment did conjure up a few obscure memories. A quick search of the pockets revealed nothing except that she had recently eaten a small chocolate candy bar. She looked around for a purse to see if she had some kind of identification, but there wasn't one to be seen anywhere.

In the living room, she investigated a writing desk buried in stacks of envelopes addressed to someone named Clarence Berger, but the name didn't seem very familiar. Laura knew that her name couldn't have been Laura Berger. It just seemed wrong. She pulled out drawers and rummaged around through their contents, but they contained mostly pens and pencils and a large amount of dust. On the wall above the desk were several photographs of an elderly couple as well as baby pictures of four girls and one boy. She grabbed them each down and took the pictures out to see if names had been written on the back; but to her disappointment, they did not. She replaced the pictures and tried to hang them neatly back in their places.

She saw that the sun was shining brightly outside and light was glinting off the freshly fallen snow like a million sparkling stars. Laura thought of venturing out there to find a person to talk to but decided that it was a bad idea. If she didn't freeze to death and actually *did* find someone, they would probably think she was insane. She sank down onto the ottoman and chewed her fingernails.

Later that same day, she discovered a door in the back of the pantry while searching for a snack.

How odd, she thought. *I wonder what's behind it.*

She carefully stepped over some bags of angel hair pasta and canned vegetables piled in the back. She found the doorknob to be coated in grime, as if no one had used the door in a very long time. She wiped her hand off on her jeans and pushed the door open. It swung inward at her touch, exposing a flight of stairs descending into the blackness. To her dismay, there wasn't a light switch to be seen. Luckily, there was an orange flashlight sitting on one of the pantry's shelves. The weak beam would have to do. As Laura went down the creaking staircase, she wondered what kind of person would have the entrance to their basement hidden behind used plastic store bags in a pantry.

She shined the light all around when she stepped out onto the floor and saw that she was standing on an old, moth-eaten green rug. There were deteriorating cardboard boxes stacked all along the walls with things like "Grandma's Wedding China" and "Tom's Baby Clothes" written on them in black permanent marker. She saw the only light fixture hanging from the ceiling. She pulled the rusty chain dangling loosely at its side, but it didn't work.

Along the same wall as the entrance and behind the steps was another door, although it was smaller and less noticeable. For lack of anything better to do, she decided to see what was inside. She had to strain to push it open and was very surprised to see another flight of stairs leading downward into who knew where. Shrugging, Laura walked down the new flight of steps into what at first appeared to be a perfectly ordinary empty room.

That's when everything went wrong.

As she placed her left foot on the floor, something very bizarre started to happen. All of a sudden, something clicked and a low, humming vibration filled the room. It made Laura's insides feel like they were shaking. A small amount of light appeared from nowhere, and she felt her heart racing in fear. She turned to leave as fast as she could but found that some invisible force field was preventing her from getting past the first step. The air began to crackle, and a considerable amount of static electricity raised all the hairs on her arms and scalp.

Her mind whirling in panic and confusion, Laura tried running back up the stairs, determined to get out of there as fast as possible. This time, it felt as if she was actually getting through.

Laura started to lose consciousness as she climbed, trying to escape the strange phenomenon behind her. Suddenly, she was surrounded by an intense, blinding white light and she was gone.

Chapter 2

Something rustled nearby, like a small creature scuttling through a bed of dry leaves. Laura absentmindedly rolled over to ignore the intruding sound; but then she felt a sharp, pointy object like a stick digging painfully into her side. Startled, she sat up with a slight yelp and opened her eyes. She let out a choked gasp when she saw where she was.

Somehow, it seemed, she had transported herself to the middle of a dense forest. Not only was there no trace of snow on the leaf-and-stick-strewn ground but it was warm, *very* warm. Laura stood up, taking note that she was in a small clearing and that there was a dark hole in the ground inches away from her. Had she come out of that?

She began to panic, her heart pounding in her chest. What was going on? How could this have happened? *Maybe I'm dreaming*, she wondered, although everything seemed a little too lifelike to support that theory. But she pinched her arm just in case. Nothing happened.

"Darn!" she muttered aloud.

"You'we a funny pewson," said a youthful voice directly behind her.

Laura nearly jumped out of her skin, wheeling around in a mixture of fright and surprise to see a pair of cute young children standing less than four feet away. Both wore dirty clothing made of coarse, brown cloth. The older one, a boy of perhaps five years, looked amused.

"Hello," he said amiably. "What's youw name?"

Laura, her heart still hammering, was too surprised to speak.

"Can't you talk?" he asked, beginning to appear perplexed. "Mommy told me some people don't know how." He paused. "But you did just say, 'Dawn,' didn't you?"

"I…I can talk," Laura said, wondering what on earth was going on. "You just scared me a little. That's all."

The boy giggled and swatted at his tiny little sister (at least Laura assumed that's who she was), who had a finger buried up to the knuckle in one of her nostrils. "Bad Natalie! Mommy said you'll get youw fingew stuck and nevew get it out!"

The toddler removed it grudgingly and wiped something green on the front of her shirt. Laura tried to ignore this and said, "Didn't your mommy ever tell you not to talk to strangers?"

The boy blanched. "Please don't tell hew!"

Laura felt herself grin at his reaction in spite of her unexplainable situation. "Okay. I won't."

"Fank you vewy much!" He paused. "Uh, what's youw name again?"

"I'm Laura. Who are you? Wait! Let me guess. Is it Bobby?"

The little boy giggled and shook his head. "No! Guess again!"

Laura pretended to think very hard. "Is it Sammy?"

"No!" he squealed. "It's Wade Yelton, and *she*"—he pointed to the little girl, who was now tasting a round, shiny rock she had found— "is my baby sistew, Natalie."

"It's nice meeting you, Wade and Natalie. But what did you say your last name was? I didn't quite catch it."

"It's Yelton, and you can't catch a name, silly."

"Yelton?" Laura hadn't heard of that surname before—at least not that she could remember.

"That's it! It's funny you don't have a last name like us. Did you fowget it ow somefing?"

Laura nodded halfheartedly. "I suppose that's it."

She noticed that the child was scrutinizing her outfit with a confused expression on his face, as if he had never seen anything remotely like it before.

"What's the matter?" she asked him.

"You weaw funny clothes," he stated. "Whewe did you come fwom?"

"I don't know," she replied in all honesty.

"Well, my mommy says sometimes people come out of twees and holes in the gwound weawing funny clothes. She said Wochelle Pelteeay came weawing a bwight pink shiwt!"

"I think I just came out of a hole in the ground," Laura said, wondering who this Wochelle Pelteeay person was. She turned to point at the spot. "It was right over there."

"What hole?" Wade asked.

"The one right—" Laura broke off, confused. Where she had seen a gaping black hole just a minute before there was nothing but broken sticks and dead leaves. "Never mind," she said hurriedly. Was this some kind of bizarre hallucination?

Wade had an odd look on his face. "Well," he said, "it's pwobably about time fow lunch. Mommy can cook somefing fow you. Just follow me. It's not too faw."

The dark brown-haired youngster called to his sister, and the pair wandered off into the trees. Laura trailed behind them as she dodged the thick trunks and spiky brambles untouched in their wake, still trying to comprehend what had just happened to her and realizing this whole situation was obviously too vivid to be a product of her imagination. She thought about asking Wade where exactly they were, but she suspected that she'd never get a straight answer out of him.

"Huwwy up, Lauwa!" called Wade as she began to slow her pace. "Even Natalie's walking fastew than you!"

"Sorry," said Laura. She jogged to catch up, but her shoelace got caught on a protruding stick and she fell painfully to her hands and knees.

"Aw you all wight?" asked Wade, who had stopped to untangle his sister from a thorn bush.

"I'm fine," she grumbled as she brushed the dirt off her pants and trudged onward.

Soon, they turned left onto a little-used dirt road, a decomposing mound of horse manure being the only indication that anybody had traveled it in recent weeks. After several minutes, the trees thinned and eventually stopped at the edge of a grassy hillside dotted with small, wooden houses. A few scattered trees below reached their ancient limbs up to the azure sky. A quaint village sat at the bottom of the hill like a collection of miniature dolls' homes. To Laura, it looked similar to the pictures of pioneer settlements that she recalled from somewhere in the forgotten life she had left behind.

Wade appeared nervous when the threesome strolled by the first building on their left: a very great, two-story, stone house resembling a small castle. It even had a little tower at the top, which was probably used to overlook the town.

"That's the Owenses' place," he said in a low voice.

She could see mild fear in his eyes.

"Let's huwwy by."

"Owens?" Laura was puzzled, and she didn't even know why. "What's the matter?"

"I'm a little bit afwaid of them," the boy replied. "That mean ol' Wotanev punched me a few days ago. My mommy says they should have named him Wotten Eggs. He's about as nice as wotten eggs." He paused. "Oh. I bettew be quiet. Hewe comes Spica."

A pretty little girl with two dark brown pigtails and a blue dress came running out of the enormous house, calling to Laura's young guide. "Wade!" she hollered, kicking up dust in the lane as she ran. "Wait! Daddy says your folks can come over for lunch today! Isn't that great? He's awful mad that Rotanev hit your arm. Who's this?" She stared at Laura with one eyebrow raised.

"I found hew on the gwound in the cleawing," Wade said proudly. "Hew name's Lauwa. She don't know hew last name."

The girl spoke, her eyes fixed on Laura's. "Your name's Lauwa?" She seemed baffled.

"Um, actually it's Laura, but he couldn't say it right."

"I know what you mean," said Spica with a haughty laugh. "He calls Rotanev Wotanev and Alcor Alcow and Tabitha Tabifa. He never calls my parents anything because he's too afraid to talk to *them*."

"Why?"

Spica seemed to have an odd glint in her eyes as she held up her left hand so Laura could see the palm. She tapped a blue tattooed dot in the center about the size of a quarter. The sight of it looked vaguely familiar, but Laura did not know where she could have seen such a thing before.

"See, Laura," she said with a hint of smugness, "this is the mark of the royal family of Sparkling Falls. If you ever see someone with this, you'd better be really nice to them."

Laura was somewhat taken aback by this young show of opulence. *A royal family!* she thought. *No doubt it's full of royal brats like this. But maybe they can tell me what's going on!*

Wade thankfully broke the awkward silence by saying, "Uh, what aw we going to eat fow lunch? Mommy would want to know."

"Chicken and vegetables," said Spica, turning to go. "Freshly picked. They smell wonderful! We'll see you in a while."

"Fanks!" Wade called after her, grabbing his sister's arm and continuing down the dirt road.

A moment later, they arrived at a considerably smaller stone house also on the left-hand side of the road that was just as nice as the one next door, although its roof was made of thick, golden brown thatch. A flagstone path led up to the door, and the yard was surrounded by a primitive picket fence. Some unusual orange and pink flowers gave the place a welcoming touch.

A woman in her midthirties stood on the doorstep with her hands planted firmly on her hips and a wooden spoon clutched in her right fist. "Wade Yelton!" she yelled, brandishing the utensil at the boy as he approached. "Where in the blazes have you been for the past half hour? I thought you two'd been lost! Your father even went out looking for you!"

"I-I'm sowwy, Mommy!" Wade wailed as Natalie went chasing after a butterfly, oblivious to the fact that her brother was in trouble. "I found this giwl lying on the gwound in the cleawing, and I fought she might be huwt but she wasn't and I took hew with us. Hew name's Lauwa. She don't know hew last name."

"Really," the woman said, squinting at Laura with interest. Suddenly, a look almost like recognition entered her eyes. "Wade," she said, "please go into the house. It'll be time for lunch soon."

"But Mommy! Spica Owens said hew pawents invited us to lunch! She says it's chicken."

"Did they now?" The woman was thoughtful. "Well, you can still go in to put on some clean clothes. You look like you've been rolling around in a pigsty. Go on. You don't have to wait for your friend here. I'd like to talk to her alone for a few minutes."

Wade slumped into the house, followed by Natalie, whose butterfly had just soared out of sight. Mrs. Yelton let out a heavy sigh.

"So," she said, "you were lying on the ground in a clearing. Do you have any idea how you got there?"

Laura tried to explain as best she could, but it was difficult keeping her thoughts straight. "I was all alone in a house, and I just went into this room in the basement. And all of a sudden, something started vibrating and everything got really weird and I woke up on the ground a few minutes ago in the middle of nowhere! I can't make any sense out of it. It was winter there, with snow on the ground and practically a blizzard going through. But I can't have just gone out a secret tunnel or anything like that. It's really hot here." She looked around at the nearby houses. "And so primitive."

The woman nodded with surprising understanding. "I see. Was there any sort of hole in the ground that disappeared when you walked away, without a trace of it ever having been there?"

"Yes!" Laura couldn't believe that this woman already knew what had happened. "How did you know about that? Can you tell me what it was?"

Mrs. Yelton cocked her head to the side. "I wish I could, but I don't really know for certain. I've never seen it. It's just one of those things you hear about from time to time."

"I just wish I knew what was going on!" Laura exclaimed. She reached up and rubbed the painful knot that had hardly shrunk in size since she'd awakened at the bottom of the stairs. Her eyes began to fill with tears.

"There, there. Don't cry," said Mrs. Yelton as she handed Laura a white handkerchief from inside the pocket of her brown, homespun dress. "Don't worry. I haven't used it. But anyway, this is definitely not a dream. This has happened to others before you. The most recent time was only three or four years ago, believe it or not. The poor girl was even more hysterical than you when she first arrived. But she adjusted just fine, and now she's as content as can be."

Laura looked up with wide eyes. "You mean she's still here? Why didn't she go back to wherever she came from?"

The woman shrugged, shaking her head. "I'm not sure if a person *can* go back, Laura."

She gave a weak smile that somehow made Laura feel ten times worse. Her heart sank.

"Nothing is easy. I know," Mrs. Yelton continued, reading her feelings. "We just need to see what happens. Maybe you will find a way back. But right now, we need to get you into some different clothes. It looks like you're melting in that thing! Then, if Wade is correct about lunch, we'll all go over to the house of Owens. Maybe they can tell you more about your situation."

"You mean you'd take me with you?" Laura wiped her eyes and sniffled.

"Of course! I wouldn't have you wandering around all alone in a strange village, would I? Besides, you can get to meet Lord Arcturus and Lady Capella. They're the rulers of this village. Now do come in!"

Inside the cozy abode was a homely living room containing a huge, green, braided rug; a sort of loveseat made of cushions sitting on a wooden frame; and a handcrafted coffee table with a thick candle burning on a dish in the middle. Mrs. Yelton showed Laura a small closet where she could change into a bottle-green dress the woman offered to her. Laura took the candle in with her so she could see. As she tried to figure out how to tie the sash properly, she could hear footsteps enter the room beyond and a masculine voice began to speak.

"Evelyn, did the children come back here? I can't find them anywhere."

"They just got back a couple of minutes ago."

"Good!" He sounded relieved. "Oh! I almost forgot to tell you something. Arcturus wants us to come over for lunch today. He mentioned something about an apology." He paused. "Is there someone in the closet?"

"Yes," Mrs. Yelton replied, lowering her voice.

Laura strained to listen in as she examined herself in the mirror, realizing how dumb the dress looked with her gym shoes on.

"It's a girl. She looks about sixteen years old, though I could be wrong. She turned up in the middle of the woods and has no idea how she got here. It sounds just like the Rochelle Peltier incident a few years back, doesn't it?"

"It does. Where did you find her?"

"*I* didn't. Wade and Natalie did. He said that she was lying on the ground in Maribu Clearing, apparently unconscious. The poor thing must have fainted from the shock."

"It sounds like there must be a portal near there," said the man. "Hmm. I never heard of one existing in that part of the woods. I think they can only be seen at certain times. Some old legend said the moon has to be full or something. I'll have to go investigate sometime. Wade and I can go out tomorrow to see what we can find."

"Frank, the moon has been a waning crescent for the past week! You know that. We were just looking at the stars the other night. Don't you remember commenting on how well we could see them because of how thin the moon was?"

There was a pause. "Oh. I forgot. Oh well. Whoever said that old legends had to be true?"

His wife didn't answer. Laura, having finally completed her change in attire, stepped out of the dressing room. The dress was made of a soft, lightweight material that felt good against her skin. It was clearly made for a person to withstand the heat of summer. "Did I put this thing on right?" she asked.

"Yes. It looks wonderful!" exclaimed Mrs. Yelton, smiling. "You can keep it for all I care. It hasn't fit properly since before I had Wade. Oh, and this is my darling husband, Frank Yelton."

"Hello," Laura said to the tall man standing before her. He wore black pants and a long, gray shirt with a black belt clasped around the middle. Laura couldn't tell if his tan complexion was the result of being outside in the hot sun on a regular basis or if it was his actual skin tone. She smiled. "I'm Laura."

The man nodded politely. "And I suppose you have already been introduced to my wife, Evelyn."

"Well, not formally. We didn't really get around to—" She broke off upon noting how the man scrutinized her with an air of unusual curiosity. "What?" she asked.

"Are you sure you haven't been around here before?" Frank Yelton inquired.

Laura furrowed her brow. "I really don't think so. Why?"

The man shook his head. "Oh, nothing. You just look a little familiar. That's all." He shrugged. "I must be going mad. Think nothing of it."

After the Yelton children had been forced at spoonpoint to change into some finer attire, the party of five left the house and walked up the road to the large stone edifice overlooking the quaint village below. Wade and Natalie's faces were still red from shrieking at their mother. Laura smiled inwardly, not wanting to show any approval or amusement from their naughty behavior.

There was an enormous stone sundial on the great house's front lawn that had beautiful blue flowers growing in profusion all around it. The shadow it cast pointed to an engraved 12 at the top. Laura wondered if the owners would ever know the time in cloudy weather, when the sun could not shine.

Frank Yelton rapped on the ornately carved wooden door; and it was immediately opened by the little girl named Spica, who spoke a cheery, "Come in!"

It was immaculately clean inside the house. Laura blinked in amazement at the polished stone walls that seemed to glitter as she passed by, as if they had been scrubbed a thousand times. In the center of the room was a long, wooden table and about twelve chairs already occupied by two adults and three chattering children of varying ages. The man at the head of the table rose when they entered, his arms spread wide in welcome.

"Good afternoon, Yeltons!" he said, coming over and giving Frank Yelton a hearty slap on the back.

Laura stared in awe at the man, whose appearance was quite stately in his brick-red robe. To increase this effect, he wore a gold ring with a ruby in the center and a thin, golden chain around his neck. He grinned.

"How are you, Frank?"

"Not bad," the man replied with a smile. "I hope you and the family are well. Some folks in town have been coming down with upset stomachs. Something to do with bad meat, I think."

The red-robed man, whom Laura assumed to be Lord Arcturus, shook his head. "No. The only problems we've had lately deal with poor behavior," he said, glancing back over his shoulder at his three older children, who suddenly became very quiet.

Frank laughed. "I think I know what you mean."

"Sit down and get comfortable, everyone," said the woman at the table, who was probably Lord Arcturus's wife, Lady Capella.

She appeared to be quite tall for a woman even while sitting and was very slender and pale in complexion. She had jet black hair shot with little wisps of gray tied back out of her face and wore a cerulean dress that made her eyes stand out like sapphires. Laura imagined her as having once been a beautiful princess who had been hardened from the trials of life. The lines and dark circles around her eyes made it seem even more so and gave her a very tired look.

"Rochelle will be out with the food in a few minutes."

She smoothed out a wrinkle in her skirt as Laura and the Yeltons sat down at the end of the table. Laura parked herself between Frank Yelton and an empty place reserved for someone not present at the moment, feeling about as uncomfortable as she would if she had been dining with the queen of England. It wasn't a pleasant feeling.

"And who's this you've brought with you?" inquired Lord Arcturus, returning to his original seat and drawing the chair closer to the table. "Is she related to you?"

"No. This is Laura," said Evelyn Yelton, shaking her head. "Wade found her lying unconscious on the ground in Maribu Clearing just a while ago. She has no idea how she got there. My guess is that there's a portal in the area that nobody knows about."

"That's interesting," the royal man said. "It sounds like what happened to Rochelle. You know, my father knew somebody who came here through a portal decades ago. I'd have him tell her about it, but he left earlier this morning to go visit relatives in Upton. He and Mother should be back tomorrow or the next day if the weather holds. Ah. Thank you, Rochelle. That smells delicious."

A dark-haired young woman had entered the dining room as he spoke and began setting down trays of steaming chicken; hot, buttery rolls; and cooked vegetables on the table. She served the food onto wooden plates, which she then distributed to everyone present. Then she poured some chilled water into each person's cup.

"Would you like anything else, Lord Arcturus?" she asked, glancing curiously out of the corner of her eye at Laura.

"No, no. It looks like we have everything we need. Thank you."

Rochelle took the emptied trays and carried them into what Laura supposed was the kitchen. Seconds later, she returned carrying an additional plate and utensils; and only when she took the remaining seat at the end of the table next to Laura did anyone begin to eat. Lord Arcturus's wife started to raise her fork to her mouth, stopped, and set it back down on her plate.

"Now, Evelyn," the elegant woman said to Mrs. Yelton, "the main reason we decided to invite you here is because we felt horrible about what Rotanev did to your boy. We are so sorry and assure you it *won't* happen again."

A teenage boy who looked possibly a year or two older than Laura stared down in humiliation at his plate. Laura saw his cheeks flush and his jaw stiffen.

"Rotanev," continued his mother, "please tell the Yeltons why you punched their son. It had better be a good explanation."

Rotanev gulped. "I-I didn't mean to hurt him that badly."

"That's beside the point." His mother looked cross.

"Well, you see, I caught him picking some of the flowers out by the sundial. And when I told him to stop, he got angry and said they were for Spica. I said I didn't care *who* they were for and that he'd better stop right then or I'd smack him. He bent over and picked one more, so I did. I didn't mean to give him a bruise. Honestly."

"Now what do you say to Wade?"

"Sorry." Rotanev's face turned about as crimson as his father's robe.

"That's okay, Wotanev!" little Wade piped up. "I fowgive you! Mommy always says to fowgive people."

"Thanks," the older boy muttered, quickly looking away.

"Very good. All seems to be reconciled," said Lord Arcturus, somewhat relieved. "Capella, will you please pass the salt? Thank you."

While all this was going on, Laura heard a soft knock at the front door. No one else seemed to take notice, but she was too shy and nervous to mention it. After all, it wasn't her house. When the visitor's knocks remained unanswered, he must have given up and tried another method of communication, for suddenly, the face of an auburn-haired man with a short beard appeared at the open window.

"Pardon me for interrupting your lunch," he called into the house, "but I have some important news." He wiped sweat from his forehead, appearing quite distressed.

"For goodness' sake, Andrew," said Lord Arcturus, rising, "why don't you come in?"

"I knocked, but nobody ever came. I didn't think you'd like it if I just barged in."

"If the news is *that* important, there's no need for knocking! Come on in here!"

The man named Andrew muttered something and vanished from view only to show up seconds later on the rug just inside the front door. He slumped down onto an empty chair leaning against the inner wall and sighed.

"So, what happened?" Lord Arcturus asked, frowning. "Nothing too bad, I hope?"

Andrew shook his head. "No. And actually, now that I think about it, it isn't really important at all, but you're not going to like it anyway. It's about Miss Matarna."

"What has she done *now?*" The lord's face contorted into an expression of incredulity.

"Well, she decided to break into the storage building earlier this morning and made off with some of your glowstones. Luckily, I caught her heading down the road with them. She said they were a present for someone or something like that. She didn't say whom."

Lord Arcturus let out a groan. "Did she take any of the medicines? You know how she is with the stuff."

"None of the medicines were reported missing. I had everything checked and double-checked. Young Mark helped me."

"Good. What did you do to the girl?"

"I shut her up in the jail after promising to leave her in there for a week. Stupid child. One would almost think she *likes* getting punished. Such a shame."

"Well, when you look at her upbringing…"

"Or lack thereof…"

"It's too bad."

"Too bad indeed." Andrew blinked a few times and stood up. "Well," he said with a sigh, "*I* need to go give Miss Matarna some lunch. Mark will certainly never remember to. I'll be seeing you later."

"Take care, Andrew," said Lord Arcturus as the man left.

After their delicious meal was consumed and the once-full platters had been emptied of their contents, Rochelle began clearing away the soiled dishes and utensils, and the Owenses' guests were ready to leave.

"Evelyn," said Lady Capella as the Yeltons and Laura made their way to the door, "where do you suppose Laura should stay? She shouldn't be left all alone in a strange town."

Mrs. Yelton frowned. "I hadn't really thought about accommodations. She can't exactly stay with us. We don't have any extra bedrooms, and I'd hate to force Wade to share his room with his sister."

"She can stay here with us," said Lord Arcturus without hesitation. "We do have a spare bedroom upstairs at the end of the hall. You don't mind if you stay here, do you, Laura?"

Laura shook her head, feeling awkward from all the stares she was receiving. "I guess not. I-I wouldn't be intruding, would I?"

"Goodness no!" cried Lady Capella. "Everyone is welcome in our home! We have plenty of room and are always glad to help out those in need! Don't worry. We've done it before. You certainly aren't the first and probably will not be the last. Come on! Rochelle can go help you prepare your room."

CHAPTER 3

Laura followed the young servant up the stairs to the second floor as soon as the Yeltons had left, and the woman kept casting strange looks at her over her shoulder as they went along, making Laura feel even more nervous. They stopped in front of the fourth door on the left in the upstairs hallway, and Rochelle turned the tarnished knob with a pale, white hand. The door swung open with a loud *creak* that made Laura cringe.

"Look out. It could be nasty in here," the dark-haired woman cautioned, lighting a match she withdrew from a pocket in her apron. "We haven't had it open in about a year. The Owenses don't seem to like it used much. I think it must hold too many memories for them."

Without bothering to explain, Rochelle entered the room with the lit match and proceeded to light a tall, yellow candle sitting on a small stand just inside the door. Laura took note of the neatly made wooden bed covered in an old, green-and-blue checkerboard quilt and dark blue pillows with the letter *P* embroidered on the cases with red thread. Whoever had made the set had certainly taken a lot of time making it so precise.

A dresser with a mirror stood against the wall opposite the bed, as did a sturdy set of shelves and a writing desk. The walls were light brown paneling. The whole room had a very stale, dismal feel to it until Rochelle threw back the dusty drapes and pushed the window open, sending in a welcoming breath of fresh air.

"This place needs lots of work," the servant said, placing her hands on her hips and looking around as though trying to figure out where to begin.

Laura approached the desk and ran her finger across the top, uncovering a line of shiny, polished wood that would have looked wonderful had it been cleaned. Someone had carved the initials P. O. deep into the surface with something sharp, and the old grooves were caked with thick dust and grime.

Rochelle was already lighting more candles she had pulled down from the shelf so Laura could see better. "Well," she said, "I suppose we could begin by taking all the bedclothes and rugs out of here to be washed. I can put up a new set of curtains for you. Those things look about a hundred years old. Then we've got to dust like crazy and sweep the floor. Hopefully once the air starts circulating it'll be more tolerable. This place reminds me of a tomb."

Laura sighed and sank onto the bed, sending up a swirling cloud of dust particles that tickled her nostrils. She sneezed.

"Aren't you feeling well?" Rochelle asked in concern.

"I feel so lost," Laura said, gazing in despondence at the filthy floor. "I wish I knew what was going on."

The servant nodded in understanding and sat down beside her. "I overheard some of what they were saying when you and the Yeltons first came by," she said in a low voice, "but I wasn't entirely certain of what they said. Did you really come here through a portal?"

Laura shrugged. "I guess I did. I'd been in a house in the middle of nowhere in the winter, and I was looking around in the basement. And suddenly I was surrounded by some kind of energy field or something. I got scared and must have blacked out. I woke up lying on the ground in that clearing, and that's when those little kids found me." She frowned. "You probably think I'm nuts."

"I don't at all." Rochelle looked serious. "Whose house was it that had a portal in the basement?"

Laura knew that tears were forming in her eyes again, but she couldn't help it. "That's the thing! I don't know! I can't remember anything before a few days ago. I must have fallen down the steps and hit my head really hard, because I woke up not knowing who or where I was. I was completely alone in that house, so no one could tell me what happened. It's so scary." She started to cry and swiped away a tear that began trickling down her cheek.

Rochelle patted her gently on the back. "I'm so sorry," she said, her eyes full of pity. "That must be awful for you. But tell me, how do you know your name if you can't remember anything else?"

Laura held up the hand containing her class ring. "I looked at this. And my necklace has an *L* on the pendant."

"May I see that?" Rochelle pointed to the ring.

Laura slid it off her finger and passed it to the young servant. "It's engraved on the side."

Rochelle turned it over in her fingers. "That's a really pretty stone you have. Green is one of my favorite colors. Let's see. Yes, it does say *Laura*, doesn't it? Ridgefield Local High School. Class of—" She broke off with a strange expression on her face. "Laura, how old do you think you are? Just take a guess."

Laura wiped her eyes and thought for a moment. How old *was* she? "Probably about sixteen."

"Then you wouldn't have graduated yet."

"I guess not. Why?" Laura couldn't see where this was going.

"Let me show you something you'll probably find very interesting." Rochelle reached into the collar of her dress and withdrew a chain with a different class ring strung onto it. She unfastened it and handed the ring to Laura. "Now you look at mine. And keep in mind that I am twenty-two years old."

Laura brought the piece of jewelry close to her face and studied the violet stone. "La Salle High School," she read. "Rochelle Marie Peltier." She paused. "Class of *twenty seventeen*?"

"And you were in the class of two thousand and five," Rochelle finished. "Laura, I was *born* in nineteen ninety-nine. And I am obviously several years older than you and have been here much longer. It was twenty seventeen when I came through a portal—and it's been about four years since then."

"But it was January two thousand and three where I came from!" Laura exclaimed. "I saw it on a satellite clock on the wall! You would have been only four years old!"

"Three," Rochelle corrected. "My birthday is in June." Then, in a softer voice, she said, "My parents would have still been alive."

They were both very silent for several minutes. Laura fell only slightly short of being terrified out of her wits, because the more and more she thought about her impossible situation the more and more her mind seemed to spin with the world around her. After all, it had been 2003 that morning, at least to Laura. If she had met Rochelle before going through this supposed portal, she would have been little more than a toddler. *That very morning…*

Her head started throbbing again.

"Maybe we should just start cleaning," she suggested. "I really need to focus my mind on something else. Otherwise I think I might go insane."

"Good choice!" said Rochelle with a smile, snapping out of her grim state. "There's nothing like fumigating a deplorable room to keep your mind off of unpleasant things! Instead, you can think about how we can decorate it to suit your own tastes when we're done! We can go into town and get you some furnishings better suited for a girl your age. We can get you some nice clothes too. In the meantime, you can borrow some things of mine since we're about the same size. But first, let's get these blankets and things out of here…"

For the rest of the day, Laura helped Rochelle wash the bedclothes and hang them on a clothesline in the sun to dry, thoroughly beat the rugs, dust all the furniture, and sweep and wash the floor. By the time evening came around, she had a terrible headache. Rochelle immediately recognized that she didn't feel well.

"What's the matter, Laura?" she asked, hanging the old curtains back on the wooden rod and closing the window. "Too much stress for one day?"

"You bet," Laura replied, kneading her forehead with her fingers. "My head hurts really bad." She was sitting on the edge of the bed again, which had been covered in a newer pink and yellow quilt that thankfully wasn't very dirty.

"You should drink some of Lord Arcturus's best pain reliever medicine, as he calls it. It's always worked for me."

Laura lifted her head in interest. "What's it made of?"

Rochelle gave an embarrassed smile. "To be honest with you, I have absolutely no idea! But I will be right back with some. You just wait."

She left and returned moments later with a brown glass bottle and a ceramic cup, handing each to Laura and instructing her to fill the glass until it was a third of the way full. Then, Rochelle went off to locate some comfortable clothes for Laura to sleep in.

When she had gone, Laura pried the cork stopper from the bottle and poured the bubbling liquid into the cup. It tasted terrible.

That night, Laura lay wide awake until well after midnight, her mind buzzing with wonder. Who was she? Where was she? How had she gotten there? Could she ever return?

Suddenly, she felt a terrible sense of loneliness and began to weep. Oh, how she longed to hold something close to her for comfort! She thought of how nice it would be to have a cute, furry cat snuggled up against her to keep her warm; but the Owenses didn't have any as far as she'd seen. Instead, she rose and crept over to the shelf, where she spotted the silhouette of a stuffed bear. She curled up on her side with it clenched closely to her body. She started to relax a bit and smiled weakly to herself. For some reason, resting like that felt right, as if it was the way she had done it for her entire life.

When Laura did finally doze off, she once again saw terrible visions of a deadly icicle and splashes of warm blood on a snowy lawn.

In the morning Laura awoke to the appetizing aroma of cooking meats that made her mouth water. She sat straight up and saw sunlight streaming in through the open window, noting that Mrs. Yelton's green dress lay neatly folded on top of the dresser along the opposite wall. She assumed that Rochelle must have been in already and was surprised that she hadn't been awakened by her coming and going.

She climbed out of bed and slid her feet into a pair of soft slippers that were lined with fuzzy brown rabbit fur on loan from Lady Capella. She stretched her arms and gave a huge yawn before plodding down the hall and stepping into the dining room, where most of the house's occupants were already seated. Laura sat down quietly in a vacant chair across from Lady Capella.

"Good morning, Laura," the woman said politely from behind a small newspaper. The front page read *Sparkling Falls Weekly Messenger*, and Laura saw that it was dated 14 June, 241. It appeared that everything on it had been carefully written by hand; and she instantly felt very sorry for whoever had to make all the copies. The headline read "Holy Valley Day Celebration will be led by Adalbert Wang for Third Year in a Row."

Rochelle hurried into the room from the kitchen carrying a large, wooden tray heaped with sausage, bacon, and scrambled eggs. Lady

Capella moved a mug of what Laura assumed to be tea out of the way, and the servant set the food down in the center of the table.

"Mm-mm!" exclaimed the Owenses' older daughter, a brown-haired girl of roughly thirteen years. "That smells like it was made by angels!"

Rochelle smiled and laughed. "Thank you very much, Tabitha. I thought that I would make something extra special this morning to make the newest member of the household feel more at home. Isn't that right, Lady Capella?"

Lady Capella folded up the newspaper and stuffed it away. "That's right," she said with a warm smile. "We want you to feel welcome here just as if you were a member of our own family. Laura Owens. Doesn't that sound lovely?"

Laura found herself blushing. "Thanks so much for letting me stay here. But actually, I don't know what my last name is. I don't remember who I am or where I came from."

The woman looked aghast. "You mean to say that you can't remember *anything*?"

Laura shrugged, frowning. "I remember that George Washington was the first president of the United States and other facts like that. I remember how to read and write and talk, obviously. I just don't remember anything about my own life, where I was born, where I grew up, that kind of thing."

"Not even your family?"

She shook her head. "No. I don't even know if I had a family! So you might as well call me Laura Owens since nothing is going to make me know who I really am."

"My goodness," Lady Capella said, still in mild shock. "I was only kidding when I said that. But by all means, take the name. After all, you do bear a slight resemblance to our family. I think you have the same beautiful eyes that my dear little Procyon once had."

"Hey," said Rochelle with a deadpan expression, "why didn't I get to be Rochelle Owens when I came here? My hair is the same color as yours, and I have the same build as Tabitha."

Lady Capella laughed. "I suppose if you really want to ..."

"Nah," Rochelle said thoughtfully. "It wouldn't sound right. The only way I'll ever be Rochelle Owens is if I marry either Rotanev or Alcor. What about it, boys?" She winked at Laura, who couldn't help but smile.

The two Owens sons began making painful retching noises as Spica giggled merrily.

"I think I'll look for someone closer to my own age," the younger son, Alcor, said.

Rochelle gave a melodramatic sigh. "Oh well. I should have known I'd never have a chance with such strapping young gentlemen as yourselves."

Suddenly, the front door banged open and Lord Arcturus stormed into the house. He slammed the door shut and stood fuming on the mat.

"Dear, what's the matter?" asked his wife, whose face had become very pale. "Has something happened in town?"

Judging by the looks of shock on the children's faces, Laura guessed that this behavior in Lord Arcturus was quite uncommon.

"No," he replied in a voice ready to crack. "It's just people spreading more and more rumors about me that are completely untrue. It makes me so angry! To think that someone would have the gall to make up these lies in the first place!"

He wiped his feet on the mat and sat down at the table, placing his head in his hand and glaring off into the distance. Laura noticed that his other hand was clenched into a tight, trembling fist.

"Daddy, what kind of lies did people say about you?" Spica asked curiously but with a worried expression. "Did they say you did something bad?"

Lord Arcturus lifted his head a little to look at his daughter. "Yes, Spiky, they said some *very* bad things about me."

"How did you find out?" asked his wife, still concerned.

"I heard about everything from Andrew and Frank," he explained. "They were having a drink in the tavern last night and overheard groups of specific individuals talking about me. They said that apparently half the town thinks that after Eliza Matarna is out of jail I'm going to send her away to Upton so she can be permanently locked up in the home for the insane! But the thing that really set me off was that supposedly I'm going to enact a new law that will put a strict limit on childbirth, leaving only two children per family, and that any additional children will be killed. Something about keeping the population down in the valley to prevent overcrowding. *Overcrowding*, for Litch's sake! And the fools ate it up like it was candy!"

Lady Capella, Rochelle, and the children looked utterly flabbergasted.

"That's ridiculous." Lady Capella shook her head. "Children are our town's greatest gifts. Didn't Andrew and Frank try to do anything about those people?"

Lord Arcturus actually chuckled. "Andrew told me that they told the bunch to stop the slander or he'd order the Woodland Youth to go after them with their bows and arrows!"

"But Andrew is the chief of police! Why didn't he just arrest everyone who was saying those things?"

"Nobody actually did anything wrong, which is good. And if he sent the whole crowd to jail, there would almost certainly be some sort of riot. I don't want there to be more trouble than necessary. I say things are best left alone."

"But, dear, they're going to completely ruin your reputation."

Lord Arcturus shrugged, seeming a little calmer than before. "I'm afraid they already have. But there's nothing I can do about it. Nothing at all."

He rose and slunk slowly out of the dining room through a doorway into the back of the house, shutting the door behind him and leaving his steaming breakfast abandoned at the table. To Laura, he looked completely defeated.

The remainder of breakfast was spent in total silence, broken only by Lady Capella's sighs and the occasional clatter of dishes. Laura wanted to do something to make these people cheer up but didn't have any kind of idea what to do. Besides, she barely knew them and would have felt a little awkward. In the end, she decided that she would just be nice by helping Rochelle clean up after the meal; but when the family had finished eating, Lady Capella announced that Rochelle was to take Laura into town to purchase some items for herself, such as clothing and maybe some room furnishings.

"But who's going to do all the dishes?" asked Rochelle, who was already carrying an armload of plates off to the kitchen.

"The girls and I can get them done," the royal lady replied. "Don't worry about it!"

Excited to have something to do, Laura ran upstairs to her new room and quickly changed out of Rochelle's pajamas, putting on Mrs. Yelton's old, green dress. She chose to leave her gym shoes behind since she didn't want to have to endure any additional stares once she got into town. Luckily, Rochelle had placed an old pair of leather shoes at the bedside just for Laura to wear. Glancing at herself in an ancient mirror that looked to be at least two centuries old, Laura grinned in spite of herself. Who would have thought that a twenty-first-century girl such as herself would end up living in a pastoral valley in an unknown land?

She met Rochelle by the front door a minute later after brushing out her tangled hair and tying it back with a shiny blue ribbon she had found in a drawer. Rochelle was holding a brown sack about the size of a purse, and Laura suspected that it contained a large sum of money.

"Come on," Rochelle said with a smile. "We'll want to get your shopping done before the whole town wakes up all the way and starts bothering you with questions! The people around here are horrible about gossip."

They set out and turned left onto the dirt road, walking down the large, grassy hill toward the little village of Sparkling Falls. The wind felt refreshing as it billowed past Laura, whipping the skirt of her dress around gently and making her feel as light as a feather. In fact, it was the best she'd felt in days.

"You seem a lot more cheerful this morning." Rochelle laughed as Laura began to skip along the way.

"I sure do," Laura replied, smiling. But suddenly she felt extremely dizzy, as if the world was rocking viciously back and forth beneath her feet, unsettling her. She stopped, putting a hand to her forehead. Something began to throb.

"Are you okay?" Rochelle asked worriedly, looking Laura closely in the eye. "Do you need to sit down?"

"I-I think I'll be fine," Laura replied, shaking her head. What had caused it to start hurting again? "I'll just walk a little slower, I guess. I can probably make it to the store."

Rochelle stared at her with a raised eyebrow. "Are you sure you'll be fine? Your face is all gray."

"I'm pretty sure I'll be okay." Laura blinked, feeling the earth settle down. "Maybe it was just one of those head rushes people get when they move too fast."

Rochelle shrugged. "Well, if you insist. Let's go."

Laura was impressed at the charming village with its quaint, log-style homes and small shops that sold fresh fruit, produce, meat, and handmade furniture. When she and Rochelle arrived in front of a larger store called Litchfield's S.F. next to a tavern, they stopped.

Rochelle peered in through a grimy windowpane beside the wooden door. "I'm not sure if he's opened it yet this morning. Wait a minute. Yeah. He's in there. Never mind."

Laura gathered her skirts and followed Rochelle through the door, eager to see what lay inside.

CHAPTER 4

Litchfield's S.F. was very pleasant inside, as Laura noted immediately after entering the cozy shop. The place seemed to give off a strong smell of cedar and cornbread as well as numerous herbs and spices that stirred some elusive memories of an elderly woman's kitchen that she couldn't quite place. The whole room was lit by a pair of brilliant, gleaming balls of light suspended from the ceiling by what looked like rope hangers for potted plants.

Laura stared up at the lights in deep curiosity, wondering what in God's name they could have been, when a cheerful voice said to her, "You like the glowstones, Laura? Miss Peltier was equally fascinated by them when she first came here."

It was Frank Yelton, who sat on a high stool behind the counter, eating a slice of freshly baked cornbread that dripped with butter.

Laura smiled. "They're really neat! I've never seen anything like them before. What exactly are they?"

Frank Yelton gave a shrug. "They're just stones that glow."

"What makes them light up?"

"Water, of course. They glow for a few hours once they get wet. They usually need rewetted several times a day."

"Well, how do you make them?"

Frank's expression turned blank. "Nobody makes them. They're just here. They've all been around for as long as I can remember."

"Okay. So who made them?"

The man shrugged. "Who knows? But why are you asking so many questions? After all, they're just lights."

Before Laura could answer, Rochelle laughed and said, "I don't know if you remember, but she hasn't asked nearly the amount of questions as I did when I first came here!"

Frank chuckled as he shook his head. "How could I possibly forget? You drove the village half mad asking about every single little thing!"

"Hey, I was curious about this place. I still am, actually." She paused, changing the subject. "By the way, Lord Arcturus told us about what happened in the tavern last night. He was in a rage. Wasn't he, Laura?"

Laura nodded dumbly, not knowing what to say.

Frank sighed. "It really is unbelievable what people can cook up around here. Andrew and I were appalled by the things they talked about. Killing children ..." He shuddered.

"Who were the ones talking about it?" Rochelle asked.

Frank lowered his voice, and Laura took a half step closer to the counter so she could hear him. "It's the Wangs," he said. "Louise and that pathetic husband of hers, as well as their oldest daughter, Clarissa. You'd have been shocked if you'd heard what they had to say."

Laura saw Rochelle's lips form a straight line. "Rotanev is courting their second daughter, Nicole. I wonder if Lord Arcturus will force them apart because of this."

"No. I'm sure he'll understand. Nicole's a great kid. I always did think she was the most decent of the bunch, although we have yet to see how the younger four will turn out."

Just then, a middle-aged man traipsed into the shop, nodding politely to Laura and Rochelle as he approached Frank at the counter.

"Morning, Kelley," Frank said to him. "How's the new house coming along?"

"Fairly well," the man replied, "but I need some more nails and an extra axe, if you have any. My oldest son decided to start helping us so we can move the job along faster."

"You're lucky. We just got a new supply in from Upton yesterday. I think Evelyn put them along the back wall. If not, they could still be in the storage room."

"Thanks. I'll go see," Kelley said as he went off to locate the things he wanted.

Frank turned back to Laura and Rochelle. "But anyway, as I was saying…" He trailed off, glancing out the window with an expression of tremendous distaste painted across his face. "Well, if it isn't the devil herself," he muttered.

A second later, an extremely conceited-looking woman with long, dark hair woven into a thick braid entered the shop, wearing a tidy blue dress with white lace stitched around the edges of the sleeves and skirt. The front of her dress was cut low, and she wore a very expensive-looking silver necklace with a sapphire pendant. The woman had slightly Asian features and high cheekbones and gave off an aura of arrogance. Laura found herself automatically stepping back out of the way as she approached the counter.

"Good morning, Mrs. Wang," Frank said icily as he crossed his arms. "What can I do for you today?"

"Actually, believe it or not, I came in to apologize about yesterday," the woman said in a harsh tone.

Frank blinked. "Apologize?"

"Yes," she replied. "I'm sorry that we caused such a big uproar in the tavern last night. It made my husband and I look absolutely foolish. We shouldn't have spoken like that around people's children. It probably scared them to death. Although, I am *not* sorry about the things we said." She stopped and looked piercingly for a brief instant at Laura, who was already discovering an intense dislike for the woman. "Could you please leave the two of us to talk in private, girl? This is a matter of strict confidence between Frank and myself."

Not wanting to be impolite, Laura promptly moved toward the back of the shop so she might be out of earshot and wouldn't be rudely accused of listening in. She couldn't believe how nasty this Mrs. Wang was.

"I'm just letting you know that this could get ugly fast," Rochelle warned in a low voice, pretending to examine a beautiful ceramic bowl and pitcher that were on sale for six coins, whatever that meant.

Laura gulped. "Maybe we should leave and come back later," she whispered while glancing toward the counter, where tension between Frank and the unfriendly woman seemed to be heating.

Rochelle's eyes became as round as golf balls. "Are you crazy? We'd have to walk right by her to get out!"

Suddenly, the little shop was filled with the sound of angry shouting that rattled Laura's nerves. She peered above a display of women's shawls to see that Rochelle's prediction had indeed been correct.

"And just how in Litchfield's name do you expect me to believe that garbage?" Frank Yelton roared a foot away from Mrs. Wang's seemingly impassive face.

The woman appeared to be quite unfazed by his fiery display of emotion and simply crossed her arms in front of her and tapped her foot on the floor as if patiently waiting for his outburst to pass.

"I've known the man for my entire life! I just cannot believe that he'd order people's children to be killed if they have more than two. He's had five himself!"

The woman allowed herself a tiny smirk. "But he doesn't have five *now*, does he?"

Frank stiffened. "If you mean to say that he *killed* his own son, you—you're insane!"

"But am I? Don't you remember how he just *mysteriously* vanished one day as their family was traveling to Upton? A four-year-old child should have had proper supervision. But according to Lord Arcturus, they had all fallen asleep in the carriage along the way. And when they awoke, the boy was gone. Don't you find it somewhat strange that not even a *trace* of him was found, not even with half the valley out looking for him?"

"Louise, it poured down rain later on that day. You really expect footprints to show up after that?" Laura could tell that Frank knew he was losing his argument, for the volume of his voice had lowered considerably.

"No. But if a wild animal had gotten him, there would have been bits and pieces left behind. You know, a scrap of clothing here, a fragment of bone there. If I recall, the search parties found *nothing.*"

To Laura's surprise, Rochelle marched boldly forward and said, "Mrs. Wang, Lord Arcturus loved that child and was completely devastated when he went missing. Do you really think a man could fake such grief?" Her hands were trembling in rage.

Louise Wang wrinkled her nose. "How would you know, *servant?*" she snapped. "You hadn't even shown up from your precious Canada yet when all that happened. Unless, of course, you've lived here longer than you claim you have."

Laura admired Rochelle for keeping her composure in front of such an unpleasant person. Rochelle stared directly at her in a manner of defiance and continued in a firm tone of voice. "It might have happened seven years ago, but the man has still never recovered from his loss. I've heard him and Lady Capella talking about how much they miss him late at night when everyone else is asleep. Sometimes, when Lord Arcturus thinks no one is around, I hear him praying to the heavens for his son to return. He even has a drawing that little Procyon made for him and keeps it in a frame on the wall in his private study."

"What does this really have to do with anything?" Louise asked impatiently. "It seems we've gone a bit off topic."

Rochelle put her hands on her hips. "No, Mrs. Wang. I'm telling you that Lord Arcturus wouldn't kill a child even if his life depended on it, not his own or anybody else's. Stop trying to smear his reputation with such stupid lies. And why don't you just leave since you're obviously not here to shop?"

Mrs. Wang looked like she had the overwhelming desire to slap Rochelle as hard as she could in the face. Instead, she simply said, "Fine," and stormed out of the shop, slamming the door behind her.

"Woohoo! Go Miss Peltier!" cheered the man named Kelley, who was applauding from the far corner of the room, partially hidden by a rack full of garden tools.

Rochelle turned around. "Thanks, Kelley," she said, her cheeks slightly flushed. "But I probably shouldn't have talked to her like that. I just couldn't take her bashing Lord Arcturus anymore."

"You did fine," said Frank. He was still standing behind the counter, his slice of cornbread lying abandoned on his plate. "I certainly wouldn't have been able to do it. It isn't proper for a man to yell at someone else's wife." He shook his head hopelessly. "That woman's poison."

"I think we should give Miss Peltier the citizen of the year award for being the only one brave enough to stand up to her," said Kelley.

"I really hope I never end up getting on her bad side," Laura worried aloud.

"Listen, kid," Kelley said to her. "They say you're living with the Owenses. That automatically puts you on her bad side."

"Oh no." Laura grimaced. Would she have to endure the woman's nasty disposition again?

"Well, Laura," Rochelle said, thankfully changing the subject, "I've got to go run a few errands. I'll leave you here while you pick out your stuff. If I'm not back by the time you're finished, just wait outside for me, okay?"

"Sure," Laura said. "You won't be long, will you?"

"No. It'll only be a little while," Rochelle said reassuringly. "I promise I wouldn't ditch you in any town with Louise Wang in it."

Laura smiled at the young woman's levity and wondered how she could have retained it after being whisked away from her home to a strange land. She decided she'd ask her about it later if she remembered. But most of all, she thought about Louise's argument about Lord Arcturus. Had his son really vanished, leaving behind no trace? Now she knew why the family had had a spare bedroom available and shuddered to think that it had once belonged to a little boy who no longer existed.

When she had finished shopping, Laura sat down on a wooden bench outside to wait for Rochelle's return. It had taken her a full half hour to search through the women's clothing rack before she finally decided on a lilac dress with pale cream edging; a mint green dress with a soft brown, leather belt embroidered with flowers that fastened around the waist; a bright blue dress with small, white flowers stitched around the sleeves and hem; a shorter-sleeved, light brown dress; a few pairs of knitted stockings; some colorful hair ribbons; and another pair of dark leather shoes.

Laura peered into the sack of coins and was dismayed to see that there were only five left. Had she really spent almost all of it? Guiltily, she remembered that the total had been sixty-seven coins. Mr. Yelton had certainly seemed pleased with her large purchase.

Sighing, she leaned back and watched with interest as some of the other villagers began to go about their day's work. She felt her face heat up when she noticed all of them staring at her as they passed. A few of them seemed to be disgusted by her presence. *Am I really that much of an oddity?* she worried.

As she looked closer at them, she began to notice that these people tended to have slightly darker skin tones than her own and almond-shaped eyes. One or two people had extremely fair skin and freckles or blonde hair, but not many. So maybe she was in the minority. The strange thing was that no matter how hard she thought about it, she could not place what nationality these people resembled.

She shut her eyes and listened as the people went by. *What could Rochelle be up to?* she thought to herself. *If she was going off to do errands, I could have at least helped her! No wonder she became the Owenses' servant. She probably had nothing else to do.*

Laura thought about what kind of things people might do for a living in a town such as this. Of course, there would be farmers and butchers and probably a seamstress or two; but what on earth could a teenage girl like herself do to keep busy?

Suddenly, she heard the clip clopping of horses' hooves approaching from the right. She opened her eyes and saw Lord Arcturus's friend, Andrew, and a younger man slowing their sleek, black mares to a halt directly in front of her. She stood up, not knowing what else to do.

"Hello," she said politely.

Andrew swung out of his saddle and held out his hand. "Why hello, newcomer! I hope you forgive me for not having introduced myself at the Owens place yesterday. My mind wasn't quite with me. I'm Andrew Walker, the chief of police."

Laura shook his hand and smiled. "I'm Laura...uh, I guess Owens. At least for the time being. Lady Capella said I could have their last name." She began to feel embarrassed since she could tell that some of the passersby were making obvious efforts to eavesdrop on their conversation.

"That's certainly an honor," Andrew replied. "But why? Why try to make yourself even *more* famous?"

She shrugged. "I don't know my real one, so I might as well use theirs." She paused for a moment. "So I'm famous, huh?"

The man laughed. "Of course you are! It isn't every day that someone appears from nowhere in the woods!"

"I sure hope not," Laura muttered, feeling vastly sorry for anyone else who had.

"So it's true, then," said the other man, dismounting from his own horse and joining the group. "You really came through a portal?"

"I guess so."

He too held out his hand for Laura to shake. "I'm Mark Ericson, by the way. I'm Andrew's assistant."

Now that he was much closer, Laura saw that Mark was actually quite a bit younger than she'd thought, probably only two or three years older than herself at the most. Not only that, but he was extremely handsome. He had shiny, chin-length, light-brown hair that was bleached blond in places by the sun; and his almond-shaped eyes were blue-gray with a faint rim of brownish green around the edges of the irises.

"Hi," she said, blushing in spite of herself.

Suddenly, she realized that she was holding his hand much longer than necessary and quickly jerked it back. Mark, however, didn't seem bothered at all. He was actually very busy scrutinizing her face, much to her surprise.

"Have you been here before?" he asked, his eyes lingering on hers. "You look really familiar."

"I'm pretty sure I haven't," Laura said, noting that he was the second person to say such a thing. "Otherwise, someone would have recognized me."

Mark shrugged. "Oh well. Maybe I saw someone in Upton who looks something like you."

"Maybe." Laura didn't know what else to say, and the two men turned to leave.

"Well, we've got to go," said Andrew, starting to hop back up onto his horse. "I'll be seeing you around."

"Wait a minute," Laura said as something occurred to her. Andrew halted in mid mount and looked at her. "Since you're the police chief, would you know if there's anything I can do around here?"

Andrew's eyes brightened. "You mean a job?"

"Yeah. I mean, when Rochelle came here, she became a house-keeper, but the Owenses probably don't want another one. I just don't want to die of boredom sitting around doing nothing while I figure out how to get out of this place!" *And while I try to get my memory working again,* she thought.

Andrew laughed. "Around here, there's so much to get done that you'll probably never have to worry about being bored again! Is there anything you have in mind?"

Laura shook her head, unable to think of anything in particular. "Not really," she admitted.

"Hmm…" Andrew looked thoughtful. "Well, there are at least three job openings in town that I can think of off the top of my head. One family is planning to build a house in the woods about a mile outside of town and need help clearing space for it, but that's more of a man's job. I think they're offering two coins an hour and free meals. Also, the town's main garden needs a couple of extra hands, and that's two or three coins an hour. Now the last one I know you probably wouldn't want to do."

"What is it?" Laura asked warily.

"Well, it would be a very temporary, part-time job that you could do until I find something better for you. I need someone to bring Miss Eliza Matarna her meals for the next six days while Mark and I help get the town ready for the Holy Valley Day Celebration on Saturday."

Laura almost laughed. "That doesn't sound so bad."

"Yes, but you don't know Miss Matarna," said Mark from atop his horse. "She really isn't like other people. Her mind is normally somewhere else. And she's a bit, um…"

He looked to Andrew, who said, "Deformed."

Mark nodded and turned back to Laura. "She tends to make people very nervous."

Laura formed a mental picture of a girl with several extra arms and a few heads and grinned. "I think I can give it a try. I might as well start somewhere!"

Andrew sighed with relief. "Thank you! I was worried that I wouldn't have been able to find anyone to do it."

"*I* could have done it, you know," said Mark, furrowing his brow.

Andrew gave a short laugh. "Not after you practically starved the Melbourne boy the day he was locked up for trying to steal one of Lord Arcturus's sheep. His mother just about murdered me for that one."

Mark's cheeks turned pink. "Do we really have to go into this again? I believe I learned my lesson, so you don't have to try to humiliate me further in front of a stranger."

"Don't worry about it, Mark. I won't. But right now I need you to go tell your grandfather that I'll be a little late getting to the celebration grounds. I need to show Laura where the jail is."

"Yes, sir," Mark said, nudging his horse into motion.

Laura noticed that he kept stealing glances at her over his shoulder as he rode off, and she felt herself smile. Maybe being stuck in a strange village wouldn't be so bad with people like him around.

She turned to Andrew. "What should I do with my things? I was supposed to wait for Rochelle to come back."

"You don't have to wait any longer. Here she comes now."

Sure enough, Rochelle was jogging right up to them, looking rather winded. Laura explained to her where she was going, and Rochelle picked up the cloth bags containing Laura's purchases.

"I'll put them up in your room, okay?" she said, turning to go. "See you in a while!"

"Let's go, Laura," Andrew said, gesturing for her to hurry. "I don't have all day."

CHAPTER 5

Laura gripped the man's waist tightly as they rode out of town, the horse's hooves kicking up a huge cloud of dust behind them. When the road split off in two different directions near the edge of the river, they made a left and followed the river until it veered away in the distance. Laura noticed a sign hammered into the ground that read *Upton: 12 miles.* A minute later they reached a very grimy stone building on the left side of the road, which was situated at the bottom of a large, sloping hill.

"This is it," said Andrew as he got down from the saddle. Laura leapt to the ground, careful not to twist her ankle on the uneven soil; and Andrew tied the black horse to a wooden hitching post. She then followed him to the door.

The building was surprisingly small for being a jail. It was only about thirty feet wide, and it looked as if each side of it had a door. Andrew pulled out a rusty old key from his shirt pocket and unlocked the door facing the road. It swung inward with a screeching noise that made Laura cringe.

She noticed a small, circular window in the wall above the door, which was probably there to let in some fresh air and a little bit of light. She had no idea what to expect within the cell when Andrew bade her to step inside.

It was filthy in the little room. Chunks of dried mud and pieces of straw littered the floor, and a pit toilet nearby buzzed with blowflies. A few squealing mice skittered across the ground before disappearing into a gap between the stones in the wall by the toilet. Laura had the overwhelming urge to throw up. Being imprisoned in this jail would be an absolute nightmare.

Directly across from the door was a bunk bed, and on the bottom lay a girl who was curled up in the fetal position and sleeping peacefully. She had long, messy, brown hair and wore a dirty, blue dress that had been patched in several places. As far as Laura could tell, there was nothing greatly unusual about the inactive figure at all.

"I don't see anything wrong with her," Laura whispered, trying to determine how this innocent-looking girl could make a person nervous. And why had Andrew said she was deformed?

"That's because she's not awake yet," he said, not bothering to keep his voice down. "She has something wrong with her. How old do you think she is?"

Laura stared at the girl's freckled face and shrugged. "I don't know. Younger than me?"

Andrew shook his head. "No. Eliza just turned twenty-three. She's older than your friend, Rochelle."

Laura's jaw dropped open, but she immediately clamped it shut in fear of tasting the foul air. Besides, some of the flies were starting to become overly friendly; and the thought of one accidentally flying down her throat was enough to make her stomach lurch.

"Oh, Eliza," Andrew was saying, "wake up! Somebody's here to see you!"

Laura watched closely as the girl stirred and muttered something unintelligible before sitting up and rubbing her eyes.

"Hi, Andy," she said in a voice like that of a child. "Did you come to bring me a friend?"

She blinked, and Laura almost cried out in astonishment as she stared at the girl's eyes. They gave her the chills—not because of the vibrant blue color, but because of the fact that there were two pupils in each one.

"Eliza," said Andrew, "this is Laura. She's going to bring you your food each day that you're staying here."

Eliza walked up to Laura and stuck out an arm. "Hi, Laura," she said as she shook Laura's hand with unnecessary gusto. "I'm Eliza. Will you really be my friend?"

"Uh, sure." What else could she say?

Eliza clapped her hands and jumped up and down with obvious glee, shouting, "Hooray! I have a friend! I haven't had a friend since I met Joey, but he went away and never came back. He really liked me a lot. I wish he was still here."

"Um, we have to go now," Andrew said quickly. "Laura will be back at lunchtime with something delicious for you! See you later!"

"Bye-bye, Andy and Laura," said Eliza, looking sad that they were leaving so quickly. She waved furiously as they stepped out the door.

As soon as she got outside, Laura took a deep breath of wonderfully fresh air and brushed a few stray flies from her sleeve. "You know," she said as Andrew untied the horse, "I don't think she's all that bad. She just has some kind of mental disability. And those eyes! I've never seen anything like them before. But I don't understand why people are afraid of her. She's like a little kid!"

"I've noticed that people around here don't really like things that seem to be out of the ordinary because they can't find a way to explain them," he said as they climbed back onto the leather saddle and rode back toward town. "One year, a relative of my wife's had five babies all at once, and everyone thought she had done it with magic. Unfortunately, only three of them survived. But even to this day, she and her children are treated differently because of it."

"Do you think people would consider me to be out of the ordinary?"

"What do you think? You appeared out of nowhere in Maribu Clearing, not knowing where you were or how you had gotten there."

"Oh. I see your point." Just then, a thought popped into her head and she asked, "Who's Joey? Eliza said something about him having been her friend. Was he a real person, or did she make it up?"

To her surprise, Andrew seemed to stiffen. "No," he said softly. "He's a real person. He's my son."

"But she said that he went away and never came back."

The man let out a heavy sigh, and his shoulders slumped. "Three years ago this past spring, Joseph was swimming out in the river with a group of friends when he got caught in the current and was carried over the waterfall. His neck was broken by the fall, and he almost drowned. But miraculously, he survived." He paused to lift a hand from the horse's reins, and he dabbed it at his eye. "Anyway, it paralyzed him, and he doesn't seem to know me or my wife when he sees us. He can't speak either. It's like he's brain dead. Sometimes I think it would have been better if he had died."

"I'm so sorry to hear that!" Laura said, feeling horrible. *Why* did she have to ask?

"Don't worry about it. After it happened, I told Eliza that Joseph had gone away forever and that she wouldn't be able to see him again. It killed me to see how sad she was, but I didn't want her to see him like that. She wouldn't have understood if I had tried to explain what really happened. Late one night, I had my wife take Joseph to Upton, where they moved in with my sister-in-law. I go to see them several times a week."

"How old was your son when it happened?"

"Seventeen. He and Eliza had been friends since they were both very young. He was one of the only people who ever showed her any kindness in spite of her disability. Her own parents never even cared for her. They abused her. And when she was eight, they both committed suicide. Nobody ever knew why, but I suspect they were insane."

By that time, the pair had reached the center of town; and after an awkward farewell, Laura walked back up the hill toward the house of Owens, immersed in a sea of unpleasant thoughts.

The next morning, Laura rose early so she could go for a refreshing walk around the village and spend some time racking her brain to remember who she was. It was unlikely that anything in this town would be a trigger for her memory, but it was worth a try! Maybe later she could even enlist Rochelle or one of the Owenses to take her back to the clearing to help find the portal. After dressing, she quickly scribbled a note on a piece of scrap paper she had found in the nightstand drawer, saying where she would be. She left it on the dining room table and quietly crept out the door.

A heavy fog hung over the valley like a shroud. Through the mist, she could see blades of grass spotted with droplets of dew and tiny, glistening spider webs. The sun was just starting to rise above the mountains in the distance across the river from her. Just as she considered going down to the riverbank to relax and maybe skip a few stones, she heard a strange, eerie blast echo across the valley. It sounded like some kind of horn. Then she noticed a few young people close to her age leaving their houses and running down the road toward the river. Apparently, the horn was some kind of signal.

When she had reached the village's edge, she thought she heard someone calling her name. Confused, she turned to see Mark Ericson jogging down the hill toward her.

"Hello, Laura!" he said when he had caught up with her. "Are you going to the meeting?"

Laura blinked. "What meeting?"

"The Woodland Youth meeting, of course. Didn't Rochelle tell you about it?"

Laura thought hard, trying to recall yesterday's events. "I don't think so. Why?"

"She thought you might have been interested in joining. That's where she went yesterday, to go tell Yvonne Harding, the leader, that you might be a possible recruit."

So that's *where Rochelle had gone for her errand.* "But what exactly *is* the Woodland Youth?" she asked. "And why would Rochelle think I'd want to join it? In case you haven't heard, I don't plan on staying here for long."

He gave a slight shrug. "It would be something for you to do for fun. It's basically a club for young adults like us that teaches us how to survive in the woods and things like that. We learn archery, how to make fires, how to recognize edible and poisonous plants, and so on. Sometimes we go hiking. But mostly we just sit, talk, and have a good time. Everyone there is really nice. You might want to go just to meet some people and make friends."

Laura pondered this for a few moments and nodded. It *did* sound like fun. Being stuck at the house of Owens all day had become dull almost instantly. "Could I go later on today?" she asked, noting that there were now some other townsfolk out and about. "It's about time for me to get Eliza her breakfast. I don't want to make her wait too long."

"Certainly!" he said with a smile, obviously glad that she had chosen to see what the group was like. "I can meet you down by Litchfield's S.F. around lunchtime so I can show you the place. I think you'll probably enjoy it. But right now I need to hurry and get there or Yvonne will be annoyed. She hates it when people show up late!"

"You'd *better* hurry, then!" Laura laughed, feeling cheerful for the first time in days. "I don't want to get you into trouble!"

"Yvonne will get over it. It isn't every day that I get to speak to a nice girl like you."

Laura blushed. "Thanks," she said, feeling silly.

Just then, there was another echoing blast that came from the hills across the river. "Uh oh," Mark said with mock seriousness, "I need to get out of here! See you later, Laura!" He broke into a swift run as she bade him farewell.

When she turned to walk back up the hill, she nearly collided with the one and only Louise Wang, who was carrying a wicker basket full of bread and carrots under her arm. Luckily, Laura hadn't caused her to spill them.

"Watch where you're going, girly," the woman said nastily as Laura halted in her tracks.

Laura was absolutely mortified. "I am *so* sorry!" she exclaimed. "I really didn't mean to! I didn't see you there!"

"Sure you didn't. You're the new girl, correct?"

"Yes." Laura began to grow tenser.

"And what might your name be?"

"Laura."

Louise nodded. "Laura. Such a lovely name. Laura *who*, might I ask?"

"It's just Laura." She was beginning to feel upset and knew that the woman could tell too, judging by her smug expression. Why wouldn't she just go away and leave her alone?

"Oh, don't be ridiculous," Louise tutted. "Everyone has a last name. Or have you somehow *forgotten* yours?"

Laura didn't say anything as she tried to blink a shameful tear from her eye. Louise smiled cruelly and abruptly turned to stroll into the small tavern located next door to Litchfield's S.F. She was astounded to see how incredibly unkind this woman was, especially to a perfect stranger.

After she went and got a fresh bowl of steaming oatmeal and a pitcher of chilled goat's milk from Rochelle for Eliza's breakfast, she forced the thoughts of Louise Wang to the back of her mind and tried to focus on the beauty of the valley in the morning. The fog had at last begun to lift, and rays of sunlight splayed themselves across the valley floor, giving everything a fresh, new look. However, when she passed the tavern, she could hear the harsh sound of boisterous laughter coming from inside. It seemed like they were laughing at her, but she knew she was just being paranoid.

Feeling miserable again, she hurried off to the jail, thankfully encountering no curious townspeople along the way.

"Good morning, Eliza," Laura said in what she hoped was a cheerful voice as soon as she entered the wretched cell. "How are you?" She propped the door wide open with a rock lying on the ground to ventilate the room. At least she didn't see any more mice, although there were still a few lazy blowflies hanging around.

Eliza, who had been sitting on the bunk playing with what looked like a doll with a head made from a dried-out, carved apple, blinked her peculiar eyes two or three times as if she wasn't used to the sunlight. "I'm fine!" she said happily. "Did you bring me food again? I really like food. What is it?"

"Fresh oatmeal and milk. I hope you enjoy it." Laura set the dishes down gently on a wobbly legged table by the wall. She noticed that the only chair had one of its legs busted off at the bottom, and both it and its leg lay askew on the floor.

"I fell over the chair in the dark last night." Eliza giggled, seeing what Laura was looking at. "I think I crunched it. Now I have to stand when I eat!"

Laura stood near the open doorway as Eliza hovered over the table and dug hungrily into the oatmeal. "Wow! This is yummy!" the girl exclaimed through a mouthful.

Laura smiled to herself as she watched Eliza eat. Why did people seem to think she was some kind of criminal? She seemed so child-like and innocent. This made Laura wonder what kind of thing had possessed Eliza to steal Lord Arcturus's glowstones in the first place.

"Eliza," she said, "why did you try to steal somebody's glow-stones? You know it isn't nice to take other people's things."

Eliza paused in her eating and raised an eyebrow. "I never, *ever* stole anything from that storage place. Why would I do that?"

"But you were put in here for trying to steal, weren't you?"

"Yeah. But I *didn't*. Somebody told me to get them. They said they'd give me a neat present if I got some glowstones out of there for them."

Now Laura was genuinely interested in the matter. "Someone *told* you? Who was it?"

"I don't know her name."

"What did she look like?"

"A person." Eliza giggled again. "What did you think she'd look like? A tree?" She continued eating and began to hum a little tune to herself.

Laura couldn't help but think that the mysterious person who had told Eliza to break into the storage building was Louise Wang. It wouldn't have surprised her.

After Laura had delivered Eliza's lunch later on that day and then eaten some herself, she walked back down the hill into town to wait for Mark. She had stood out in front of Litchfield's S.F. for only a minute or two when Mark arrived, wearing a clean, brown, button-up shirt and a pair of knee-length gray trousers. His hair was dripping wet and smelled faintly of soap.

"Sorry I'm late," he said, panting. "After the meeting this morning, I had to help set up chairs for the celebration on Saturday. It took about three hours, but we got it all done!"

They began to walk down toward the river, where Laura could see a sturdy, wooden footbridge spanning across. She wondered if it was as safe as it looked.

"So, are you ready to see the training camp?" he asked.

"What's that?" He hadn't mentioned anything about a training camp before.

"I didn't tell you? It's just what we call the area where we meet. There's a building where we have meetings, a storage shed, a target practice area, and an obstacle course we run through twice a week to help us stay in shape." He paused. "Well, we *used* to have an obstacle course. A few weeks ago we had a bad storm and it blew a huge, old tree down right on top of it. Now half the equipment needs to be rebuilt. Some people think the Woodland Youth is a big waste of time and that we should be laboring in the fields all day instead, but I think it's quite enjoyable."

"How long have you been in it?"

"Almost three years. Yvonne Harding had pestered me to join for ages, so I finally did when I was sixteen. It was probably one of the best decisions I'd ever made. I was always really lonely at home, and my grandfather was always complaining that I wasn't good enough for anything. He hasn't said it since then and especially since I started helping Andrew out too."

"You don't have any siblings?" Laura asked, supposing that this had been the cause of his loneliness.

Mark let out a sigh. "Sadly, no. My parents died when I was very young, and I had been their only child. My father's father has raised me ever since."

"I'm sorry. I shouldn't have asked," Laura said, her feelings of excitement about the Woodland Youth reverting to ones of gloom. It seemed like nearly everyone she had spoken to in this town had had awful things happen to close family members.

"Don't be sorry about it!" Mark chided, giving her a teasing smile. "It was such a long time ago. I think I was about five when it happened. I can just barely remember them. Isn't that terrible? For some reason, they believed that other lands existed outside of our valley, which I suppose there must really be, since *you're* here. And one day they left to go find out if there were or not. A few days later, that idiot Adalbert Wang found what was left of them when he was out hunting. Apparently, they'd been attacked by a bear. Grandpa said it was horrible and wouldn't even let me see them. I was really upset. But thinking back, I know he did the right thing. I was too young to understand what they would have looked like after a bear attack."

He chuckled. "It took the town almost three weeks to hunt it down and kill it, and nobody's been that far up into the woods since!"

Laura was mildly confused. "Do you mean that you don't believe there's more to the world than this valley?" she asked in amazement. She stopped in her tracks to face him. "This is a big planet!"

As had Frank Yelton's when she had asked about the origin of glowstones, Mark's face went utterly blank. "What's a planet?" he asked, seeming puzzled.

Laura was astonished by the young man's lack of common knowledge. "Well," she said, trying to explain, "a planet is a huge ball of rock in space that orbits the sun and rotates, which is what causes night and day."

She might as well have been trying to teach quantum physics to a third-grader. Mark looked as bewildered as she had been when she found out that Rochelle was born some twelve years after her.

"I have absolutely no idea what you're talking about," he said with a sort of half chuckle, "but it certainly sounds as if *you* do! Maybe things are that way wherever you came from. But here, we have only the valley and the mountains on either side of it. Nothing exists outside."

"But where do you think *people* came from?" *And where do you think I came from?* Laura was beginning to feel frustrated.

"Litchfield created us."

"Litchfield?" she repeated blankly. That was the name of the general store. "You mean like where Frank Yelton works?"

"The store is called Litchfield's Sparkling Falls, or S.F. for short. There is also one in Upton called Litchfield's Upton. Litchfield made this land for us, his children."

"So Litchfield is the name of your *deity?*"

"If a deity is someone who created the world, then yes, you could say that." He paused and glanced up at the golden sun, which was now directly overhead. "Well, let's get going. We don't want to make Yvonne wait all day."

He immediately resumed walking without a backward glance. Laura practically jogged to keep up with his long strides, wondering what on earth poor Mark—as well as the rest of the town—had been brainwashed into believing.

CHAPTER 6

When Laura and Mark crossed the bridge, she could tell that the village of Sparkling Falls was situated at the southern end of the long, narrow valley. She saw the river tumbling over the edge of a small cliff before vanishing at the foot of a low mountain about a mile or two away. She remembered Andrew's story about his son and shuddered. She wondered if the river flowed underground as it traversed the range. The whole scene reminded her of another mountain range she had once known, but she couldn't really think of which one it was. The Smokies? No, those were in Tennessee, and she was sure she had lived farther north than that.

This side of the river seemed wilder than the other. She saw no houses or buildings of any kind here, and the forest grew right down to the water's edge in places. A man fishing with his small son along the bank waved politely as they passed, and Laura responded in kind. At least there were *some* people in town who chose to treat her with some courtesy.

The hard dirt road wound its way up the wooded hillside, and soon the village had disappeared from sight behind them. Up ahead, the hill flattened out for quite a distance; but beyond that it continued to slope upward into a decently sized mountain. Laura could see a cleared area off to the right that was obviously a graveyard, judging from the slabs jutting from the ground in neat little rows. A minute or so later, several small buildings came into view through the trees, as well as what must have been the remains of the obstacle course Mark had mentioned earlier. A pile of splintered wood had been placed against the outer wall of a shed, and the tree that had been the culprit lay scattered on the ground in sawed-up pieces the size of dinner tables.

"That *was* a big tree," Laura commented, marveling at its size.

Mark nodded. "We're very lucky it didn't fall on one of the buildings or on one of us."

He led her to the largest of the three buildings that had a sign above the door reading, "Meeting House," and politely held the door open for her. They stepped inside, and Laura saw about twenty chairs arranged in a lopsided circle in the center of the room. Mounted deer heads lined the walls, and above a stone fireplace mantle was a large painting on canvas in a polished wooden frame. Laura took a few steps closer to try to see it more clearly, but in the semi-darkness she had trouble making it out. It looked like a portrait.

"Hey, Mark," she said, "isn't it dark in here? I can barely see."

Mark, who appeared to have been lost in his thoughts for a moment, jerked his head up. "Sorry. What did you say?"

"I said it's really dark. Are there any candles in here that we can light?"

Mark shook his head. "No, but we have something that's much better."

He walked over to a table along the same wall as the fireplace and picked up a dark, round object that was roughly the size of a grapefruit. Laura heard a splashing noise as he lowered it into a ceramic pitcher of water that had been sitting there; and when he withdrew the object, she saw that he had just activated a glowstone.

"Here," he said, placing it in her hand. "Go over there and put it in the hanger in the far corner." He pointed to the opposite side of the room.

Laura turned the gleaming ball of light over in her hands, noting that it was slightly heavy for its size and cold to touch. It was almost too bright to look at directly. She carefully made her way around the ring of chairs and slipped the glowstone into the rope hanger that was just like the ones she had seen at Litchfield's S.F. By the time she returned to the front of the room, Mark had already activated a second stone and hung it up. Now the room was fully illuminated.

Now Laura gazed up at the portrait on the wall, feeling a peculiar sense of unease. It was a very detailed painting of an elderly man with a long, gray beard and a balding head and cold, blue eyes that showed no hint of kindness. His bony, angular face was as emotionless as that of a statue. He wore a black, long-sleeved shirt that was buttoned neatly up the front; and in his arms, he held a serene-looking infant wrapped in a pale blue blanket. The child stared up at the man in what looked like supreme love and adoration.

Laura felt an unexplainable chill go up her spine. "Who is that man?" she asked.

Mark gave a chuckle. "That's Litchfield, of course. The baby in the picture was my great-great-grandfather. His parents were so honored that Litchfield chose him to be in the painting with him."

Laura turned and stared at him with a raised eyebrow. "You mean people have actually *met* Litchfield in person?"

"Well, yes. Why wouldn't our creator come to see us? He isn't among us very often. But from time to time he makes his appearance to check on how we're doing."

Laura was skeptical. "How many years ago was this painted?"

"Ninety-nine, I think. There might be a date down at the bottom." He leaned closer to the painting and nodded. "Yes. This was done in the May of one forty-two. Now we're in the year two forty-one."

"So when was the last time anyone has seen him?"

"I think it's been seven years. It was right after Lord Arcturus's son, Procyon, went missing. I can remember seeing Litchfield storming down the main street of town like he was furious about something. I saw him go inside the tavern. And according to Grandpa, he ordered a whiskey and sat off in the corner, muttering to himself for hours! Later on, they all looked and he had vanished; although he did leave a large sack of coins on the table in payment. The family who owns the tavern was thrilled."

Laura was speechless. She had no idea what to make of this Litchfield entity and didn't feel like asking anything more about him. After all, she was already developing another headache.

Instead, she wisely chose to change the subject and asked, "So, where's your leader? I thought she was supposed to be waiting for us."

"She was," Mark said, looking perplexed. "She must be running late for some reason." He paused. "We could go up to the signaling platform to see if she's on her way."

Without bothering to explain, Mark strode out the door. Laura trailed after him around to the side of the building, where there was a large, old tree towering above most of the others. Hammered into its trunk at two-foot intervals were boards, forming a crude ladder. Mark immediately began climbing straight up.

"You want me to follow you up there?" Laura asked, incredulous. The tree had to have been at least sixty feet high.

Mark stopped and looked down at her. "Why not? I'm sure you won't regret it. Just don't look down."

"Whatever you say."

Laura was about to begin climbing; but when she glanced up at the branches above her, she had a brief vision of that large, dangling icicle that she had dreamed of before her journey through the portal. She remembered a lot of blood and gulped. There had been a man lying there too. Had the icicle fallen and stabbed him? She didn't know. She reluctantly began the ascent, holding onto the rungs with a death grip. At least it wasn't winter and there were no icicles to worry about. One step, two steps, three steps... At around the fifteenth rung, it seemed as if the tree was swaying gently back and forth in the breeze. She felt her muscles tighten from pure instinct, but she forced herself to keep going up. Soon, the tree branched out and she reached a thick, wooden platform that had been nailed securely to the surrounding branches and looked fairly new; so she didn't have to worry about it collapsing under their weight. She was also relieved to see a railing going around the edge of the platform.

Mark was standing a few feet away, gazing out over the valley; and she approached his side with care.

"What do you think of the view?" he asked her.

Laura was amazed by the beautiful sight she beheld through the branches. They were so high up that she could see almost the whole town below like a little doll's village, complete with miniature people walking around, doing their daily tasks. Along the outskirts of town, she could see huge, plowed fields that were growing all sorts of vegetables and grain. Herds of brown and black cattle grazed on a grassy knoll just south of the village; large, wooden barns and stables dotted the landscape; and on the opposite hill next to the house of Owens, she could see the Owens family's flock of sheep that she had yet to meet in person. Down in the town there were women beating rugs thrown over clotheslines; young girls going along picking pretty yellow and white wildflowers; and a few men and women milling about in what had to have been the Holy Valley Day Celebration grounds, judging from the hundreds of chairs that had been set up near the cow pasture.

"It's beautiful," she said.

"You should see it in the fall when the leaves are all changing color. That's when it looks the best."

They were both silent for a brief length of time; and Laura said, "So, do you see that Yvonne person coming from up here?"

Mark peered down at the distant village and shook his head. "No. I can't think of what could be keeping her. Normally she'd be here way before anyone—"

His voice was drowned out by the sudden, deep wail of the same horn that had summoned the Woodland Youth to their meeting that morning; but this time, the sound came from directly beneath them.

Laura looked down at the ground to see a blonde woman wearing dark, gray pants and a paler gray shirt like a man's, blowing with all her might into an enormous pink conch shell. Laura didn't bother asking where it had originally come from.

When the woman saw the pair staring down at her, she stopped and said, "I thought that would get your attention. What in the world are you two doing up there?"

"Trying to see if you were ever going to show up," Mark said defensively.

The woman, who had to have been Yvonne Harding, shook her head with an air of hopelessness. "Mark, I *told* you I was going to be late because I was helping bake snacks for the celebration."

"Oh." Mark looked embarrassed. "I forgot."

"Sometimes you really worry me, Mr. Ericson. Now get down here and introduce me to that lovely young lady!"

Laura found that going down the ladder was much easier than going up, and she soon found herself shaking hands with the leader of the Woodland Youth.

"I'm Yvonne Harding," the woman said, brushing a few stray locks of her braided hair out of her face and tucking them behind a sunburned ear. "But you can just call me Yvonne. Everyone does."

Yvonne looked to be in her early thirties and also had almond eyes, like the many others Laura had seen in the town. However, unlike the cold, cruel ones of Louise Wang, these eyes were warm and friendly.

Laura nodded and gave her a smile. "I'm Laura. It's nice meeting you."

Yvonne looked delighted. "And the same to you! But let's not talk out here. Let's go inside, where we can sit down and be more comfortable!"

She and Mark followed the woman back inside the meeting house, where they each took a seat.

"So, Laura," Yvonne began, crossing her legs and leaning forward in her chair, "what do you know about the Woodland Youth?"

"Not much," Laura admitted. "Mark told me a little, though, like how you learn to survive in the wilderness."

"That is correct. Every member of the Woodland Youth eventually learns the names and uses of most wild plants, how to make temporary shelters in the woods, how to collect water from dew if water is scarce, and so on. We also have a campout once a month when the weather permits. And occasionally we go for long hikes."

"How many people are in the group?" Laura asked.

"There are currently twenty-one members ranging in age from little Amy Marsh, who is twelve, to your friend Mark here, who is nineteen. We like to call him our senior member."

Laura saw Mark squirm uncomfortably in his seat.

Yvonne continued without pause. "Now, the Woodland Youth has been around for eleven years and was founded by my father, Joseph Lee, who has since passed away. The idea behind the group was that our village's young people would have some of the training and experience to create a new settlement of their own somewhere in the forests north of Upton. No one ever has, but the group still is quite popular since it is something fun for the young to do when they're not busy working. I've tried to convince some of the Upton folk to create their own Woodland Youth for years, but they're such a stodgy bunch that they've never found the idea remotely appealing! Now, are you still interested in joining?"

Laura nodded. "Sure. Just don't expect me to be a permanent member. I don't even live here."

"Nothing wrong with that!" Yvonne seemed pleased. "But in order to be an official member, you have to go through an initiation."

Laura gulped, beginning to feel nervous. "What kind of initiation?" she asked. "It's not anything dangerous, is it?"

The woman laughed. "That really depends on who you talk to! You see, almost everyone spends the night alone in the cemetery for their initiation. Many people are terrified of spirits attacking them while they sleep. But in reality, the biggest worry one might have would be wild animals. And if you keep a good-sized fire going the whole night through, chances are they'll probably leave you alone." She paused thoughtfully. "Except for maybe the raccoons. Didn't you cross paths with a particularly friendly one during your initiation, Mark?"

"Well, yes." He looked embarrassed. "I'd been asleep, and I woke up to see one about three inches from my face. It was sniffing me." He chuckled. "I'm just glad no one was there to see my reaction."

"You see?" Yvonne turned back to Laura. "You might have some wet pants, but I assure you that you'll be perfectly safe!"

"So that's it? All I have to do is sleep out in the graveyard?" Laura still wasn't quite convinced that it would be that simple. What if someone tried to play a practical joke on her?

"Yes. There's nothing more to it. The reason we have the initiation at all is to see if our potential members have enough courage and willpower to be a useful member. I figure that if someone is too afraid to set up a blanket on the ground and camp out among rows of headstones, then they have no business being a part of our group."

"And I'll be alone?"

"I can *promise* you that you'll be alone, Laura. The members of the Woodland Youth would never stoop so low as to try to scare somebody during their initiation, if that's what you're worried about. After all, we want to recruit new members, not frighten them away! So, are you still interested?"

Laura nodded, hoping that everything the woman had said was correct. "I guess so. When will the initiation be?"

"Next Monday evening would be fine with me. The celebration will be over by then, so I shouldn't have too much to do. Meet me here right before dusk, and don't forget to bring all the supplies you'll need. And let me tell you, you'll be needing a lot."

That evening during supper, a million thoughts were swirling through Laura's mind. Not only did she still have the issue of trying to figure out who and where she was (and finding the time to locate the portal), but now she had an initiation and the mysterious Litchfield to occupy her thoughts as well. She also couldn't help but wonder why the people in this valley were so narrow-minded as to believe that nothing existed outside of what they could see with their own eyes. She really wanted to talk to somebody about it, like Rochelle. Maybe she would have found out more about the villagers' belief system, having lived there for several years already.

Then there was the issue involving Eliza. When she had brought the girl her dinner, Laura tried to question her further about the person who had bribed her to steal the glowstones but got absolutely nowhere. All she managed to learn (if it could be considered that) was that it had been "a woman with long hair wearing clothes." Frustrated, Laura had returned home. She made a mental vow to herself that she would find out the person's identity if it was the last thing she did.

"What's the matter, Laura?" Lady Capella asked as the Owens family ate, pausing to take a sip from her mug. "You look as if something is bothering you."

Laura sighed and looked down at her plate of stewed apples laced with cinnamon, which, while it had seemed quite appetizing at first, had long since transformed itself into a gooey, brown mass. She really wished she had a slice of hot meat lover's pizza in its place; but since she might never get to eat pizza again, she tried to push that thought to the back of her mind.

"I've just been thinking about too many things today," she admitted, stabbing halfheartedly at her dinner with a fork.

"Well, look at what all has happened to you these past few days!" the woman said, her eyes full of pity. "I don't blame you for feeling overwhelmed."

"But it's not just that! This woman named Louise Wang said some mean things to me today, and I think she might be the one who made Eliza steal those glowstones."

Lord Arcturus, who had been busy cutting up a steak with a knife the size of Laura's forearm, lifted his head and stared at her. "Louise Wang? What makes you think that?"

"Eliza told me that a woman told her to go get them out of the storage building and she would give her a present in return. I just figured it was her since she doesn't like you and they were your things."

Lord Arcturus snorted. "That's jumping to big conclusions, isn't it? Louise Wang is not the only person around here who is hostile toward our family. And besides, Eliza probably just invented the whole story to impress you. Don't always take the things she says seriously."

"Why not? She seemed honest to me."

"Listen, Laura. I'm not trying to sound unkind, but Eliza isn't exactly what you'd call normal. She behaves like and has the intelligence of a child. And therefore, she is fully capable of creating her own foolish stories like any real child would."

"But you can usually tell if someone is lying by the look in their eyes, can't you?" Laura said, thinking how unfair it was for Lord Arcturus to automatically dismiss anything Eliza said as fiction.

"But her eyes aren't really like yours and mine, are they?"

He resumed cutting his steak, his face impassive. He seemed strangely different from the cheerful man Laura had met a few days ago. Perhaps it had something to do with those unpleasant rumors.

"Daddy," Spica piped up suddenly, "when are Grandma and Grandpa going to be home? You said they'd be back today."

"They *were* supposed to be here by now," her father said darkly, as if this had been weighing on his mind for a while. "I can't think of what would be keeping them away for so long. I actually thought they would come back last night. I hope nothing has happened that would detain them."

"I wouldn't worry about it, dear," Lady Capella said soothingly, placing her pale, white hand over his tan one. "They're probably just sitting around, playing cards with Leo, Bjorn, and Sedna right now, enjoying themselves! After all, they won't be here for the celebration on Saturday, so your parents are probably spending as much time with them as they can before they come home."

The man sighed. "I hope you're right. I don't know what I'd do with myself if I found out they'd been hurt on the way home."

Following dinner, the Owenses' son, Alcor, suggested that they all go outside and look at the stars; so the whole family, including Laura and Rochelle, made their way out a back door onto a stone patio, where at least ten wooden chairs had been set up around a large, circular table complete with a primitive canvas umbrella for shade. Laura was looking at the setup in mild amusement when she was startled by a row of waist-high plants that were blooming before her very eyes. At first she thought her eyes were deceiving her, but upon closer inspection she saw a flower head unfold into a large, yellow bloom. She reached out her hand and touched its petals, considering picking it and tucking it behind her ear.

"Those are our night-blooming primroses," Lady Capella said as she sat down at the table. "They open up very quickly. But when morning comes, the flowers all die. We had them when I was a little girl in Upton."

Laura nodded but left the flower untouched. She decided to let it live while it still could.

"Wow! Look at all the stars!" she heard Tabitha Owens say as she and her other siblings plopped down in the grass several yards away from the patio.

Rotanev Owens sat under the umbrella with his arms crossed, looking sullen as usual.

Laura looked up at the sky with awe, impressed by the incredible number of stars she could see even though the sky wasn't yet completely black. The lack of city lights gave each individual pinpoint of light a striking clarity, the likes of which she knew she had never seen before. She sat down in one of the chairs next to Rochelle, who had brought out a ball of gray wool and was beginning to crochet something with a wooden hook. She had lit a small candle that she had brought with her to see by. Almost ironically, the woman began humming a tune softly to herself that Laura recognized as "Memory" from the Andrew Lloyd Webber musical *Cats*.

Laura pictured herself driving a car accompanied by a faceless woman in the passenger seat who was giving her directions: *"Slow down, turn on your left turn signal, get into the turn lane…"* This song was playing on the radio. It was the Broadway station. *"Memory… all alone in the moonlight. I can smile at the old days, I was beautiful then,"* sang Elaine Paige's voice. Laura was so engrossed in the music that she rear-ended a pickup truck that had stopped at the light.

In the present, Laura sighed. Of all the things she could have remembered, it had to be a car accident! But it was a start.

Rochelle was still humming. Laura found herself envying her for being so content. Didn't the woman have any worries or cares to bother her?

"It's beautiful out here, isn't it?" Rochelle said, never taking her eyes off of what she was making.

Laura looked all around her and silently nodded. There was something so peaceful about the quiet village at night. Most of the houses had a faint, yellow glow in the windows and thin swirls of smoke rising from stone chimneys. The one word the scene conjured for her was *cozy*. It looked as if nothing terrible could ever happen there in Sparkling Falls—no crime, no evil, no war. Over the sound of the cool evening breeze, Laura heard the gentle bleating of sheep coming from the Owenses' fenced-in pasture and the relaxing chirps of tiny tree frogs.

"Well, what *do* you think?" Rochelle said, looking up this time.

"It *is* beautiful," she said. "I mean, it's so ... quiet. And dark."

"I know." Rochelle paused as she undid a row of what must have been messy stitching. "I like it that way. One thing I definitely will never miss about my old home is the noise and bright lights."

"Where were you from originally?" Laura asked her.

"Ottawa. That's in Ontario in Canada, if you didn't know. The summer after I graduated from high school, I came up with the marvelous idea to go on a solo backpacking expedition through the Appalachian Mountains in West Virginia. I don't really remember what had possessed me to do it! So I was hiking along the road when nature began to call. And I hiked way up into the woods, where I stumbled into a portal. I can remember that I was walking and suddenly I saw a gaping black hole in the ground at my feet. And before I could figure out anything, I saw that I was surrounded by a strong field of static electricity. You can guess what happened next." She laughed. "Imagine the stares I got when I showed up in town wearing a huge backpack and the neon reflective clothes I'd put on so vehicles would notice me better."

"Don't you miss where you came from at all?"

Rochelle shrugged. "Not really. I mean, there's times when I'm really hungry and all I can think about is a big, juicy cheeseburger! And I miss hot showers and going to the mall and movie theaters and listening to my music. But other than that, no. I didn't really have any friends or close relatives, so I had very little emotional attachment to my home."

"When you came through the portal, didn't you try to go back through it?"

"Yeah, about that ... At first I didn't realize that I had transported myself to another forest. Trees all pretty much look the same to me. I walked back to where the road should have been, and it was gone.

I started to panic and ran back to where the black hole had been, but I couldn't find it anywhere."

She fell silent and continued stitching. Laura looked up at the beautiful, twinkling stars in the sky that was growing ever darker and said a prayer that she might have her memory return soon so she would know what kind of life *she* had left behind.

Suddenly she heard the steady thumping of horses' hooves on the hard ground approaching at a rapid speed; and Lord Arcturus rose from his seat in alarm. A moment later, a wooden carriage rumbled around the side of the house led by two dark brown mares; and it came to an abrupt halt as soon as the man at the reins spotted Lord Arcturus. It looked like there were about five people sitting in the carriage in all, along with several duffel bags that had been heaped in the back. The silhouette of a man probably in his sixties hopped down from the front after handing the reins to a short, gray-haired woman.

"Father?" Lord Arcturus said in a questioning voice, sounding more concerned than happy to see the man, despite the fact that he had been worrying about his well-being during supper. "What's going on? Why have you brought Leo and the others with you?"

"Because," said the man, sounding grim, "Upton will not accept us anymore. They have turned us all away."

CHAPTER 7

"I can't believe this is happening."

Lord Arcturus paced back and forth across the living room floor in front of the fire. His hair was tousled from the many times he had run his hands through it, and he kept gesturing wildly with his arms. He looked like he was about to have a nervous breakdown.

The entire family had gathered inside the house, where Lord Arcturus's father had begun to explain what turmoil was going on in their neighboring village twelve miles up the river. Everyone was very tense, and Laura could tell that whatever had occurred had definitely never happened before.

"Me neither, Son," the older man said with downcast eyes. "It came as a shock to us all."

"But what I don't understand is why they would have sent Leo, Bjorn, and Sedna back with you since they support me. There's enough resentment of me here. Why would the anti-Owens idiots make you leave town? I just…Ugh!" He clenched his hands into fists and took a deep breath, trying to calm himself.

"Arcturus," the man said softly, his bluish eyes full of sorrow, "it was our own relatives who made us leave."

Lord Arcturus stopped pacing, his face draining of color. He looked completely dumbfounded. "You're kidding. You can't mean *Rudyard...*"

The man nodded. "And Ulric. And their wives and children. They all have suddenly chosen to loathe us because we're on your side. Rudyard informed me that he was ashamed to have us as relatives, especially since we don't buy into all this muck people have been saying. Apparently, they've heard a terrible rumor about you and taken it to heart; although I don't know why they'd believe *that* and not us. Something about killing children to keep the population down. I tell you, the fools will believe anything."

"What about my parents and sisters, Sualocin?" Lady Capella asked, shaken. "Don't tell me they believe all of this too."

Sualocin Owens shook his head. "No, but they haven't admitted their allegiance to us yet. I think they're trying to lie low for as long as they can to see if this crisis passes. But the way things are going, I won't be surprised if they join us here before too long. People aren't likely to change their minds about something like this, and we have no way to prove them wrong."

"It's probably those cursed Wangs!" Lord Arcturus shouted in fury. "They were the ones spreading lies about me in the tavern the other night! The whole lot of them can burn for all I care! I never did one single blasted thing to them, not one little thing! And here they go, making me look like some kind of murderer." He started shaking.

Rotanev Owens, an enraged expression frozen on his face, silently rose from his seat in the corner and left the room, banging the door shut behind him. Laura heard him stomping up the stairs and slamming the door of his room as well. A couple chips of gray mortar broke loose from the wall and fell to the floor.

"The poor boy," murmured one of the older women sitting on the couch, shaking her head sadly. "This ordeal won't be easy for him."

Laura remembered hearing Rochelle mention to Frank Yelton that Rotanev and one of the Wangs' daughters were dating. She wondered if the Wangs were even aware of it.

"Daddy, you should put all those mean, nasty people in jail and never let them come out!" Spica said, sitting on the floor, constructing a house out of colorful, wooden blocks. "That's what I would do. And then I'd make them eat lots and lots of asparagus and broccoli. I *hate* asparagus and broccoli."

"I'm not sure that would make much of an impression on people like the Wangs, Spiky," Lord Arcturus said, his voice trembling. "I can think of a few more effective ways of dealing with them, but then I *would* be a murderer."

"What are you going to do about it?" asked one of the other members of Sualocin Owens's party, a gray-haired man probably around four or five years younger than Sualocin himself. Laura could see a strong family resemblance between the two men and decided that they must be brothers.

"I don't know, Leo," Lord Arcturus replied. He kept biting his lip. "I've never dealt with anything like this before. I just want to know what's possessed them to do this. Now that they've turned my own family against me, I'm terrified about what they'll try to do next."

His daughter, Tabitha, suddenly gasped. "Dad, maybe they want you to look bad so they can take over and become the rulers themselves!"

Her grandfather gave a slight chuckle. "Lord Adalbert and Lady Louise? I doubt it."

"I agree," said Lord Arcturus. "Adalbert Wang doesn't know the first thing about being in charge. You should see him at town council. He likes to make himself sound big and important, but really, to put it simply, he's an idiot. I'm almost certain that Louise would have to be the one coming up with all of these rumors. I don't think her husband is quite that creative."

"It should be interesting having him lead the celebration again, what with this going on," Lady Capella mused. "He'll have to pretend that he likes you."

Her husband nodded. "You're right, but hasn't he been doing that for years?" He was silent for a moment. "I wonder if our Uptonian relatives will still come to the celebration. I really don't want them to cause an uproar. That's the last thing we need."

"Don't worry, dear," Lady Capella said. "I'm sure the celebration will run smoothly, even if your relatives arrive. Litchfield would never allow something to disrupt his day of honor, would he?"

Laura thought she saw a strange look pass over Lord Arcturus's face when this was spoken, but it was gone in an instant.

"I mean, what could they possibly do?"

Lord Arcturus let out a short, hollow laugh. "I'm almost afraid to find out."

Later on, after sleeping arrangements had been made in which Lord Arcturus and Lady Capella had surrendered their spacious bedroom to their relatives (who, Laura learned, were indeed Sualocin's brother as well as Sualocin's wife, Tara; his cousin, Bjorn; and Bjorn's wife, Sedna), Laura found Lady Capella sitting alone on the couch with her stocking feet propped up on an ottoman. She had let her long, black hair down; and she bore the look of someone unimaginably tired. She was crocheting what looked like a thick doily, humming softly to herself.

"Lady Capella?" Laura entered the room, hoping that nobody else was around. "May I ask you something?"

The woman looked up from her work and smiled, although she did not appear to be in the least bit happy. "Of course you can! Just ask quietly. Arcturus has shut himself in his study, and I don't know if he's gone to sleep yet."

Laura sat down in a padded chair across from her, trying to come up with a good place to begin. "Well, it's kind of complicated," she admitted. "It has to do with something Mark told me today."

Lady Capella set her doily down on the end table and gave Laura her full attention. "Oh?"

Laura tried to remember everything the young man had said. He hadn't known what a planet was, didn't believe that there were lands beyond the valley, and was under the strange impression that a deity named Litchfield who looked like a creepy old man periodically visited the village.

She said, "He told me that he believes that nothing exists outside of this valley."

To her surprise, Lady Capella nodded. "That is true, although I wouldn't say *nothing* exists beyond the valley walls. We are surrounded by a vast mountain range with miles and miles of unbroken wilderness."

Laura was amazed. "Then how do you account for people like me and Rochelle? Where do you think we came from?"

"You came from a different world, not a different land," the woman explained enigmatically. "Do you follow what I'm saying?"

Laura shook her head. "Not really." As a matter of fact, what Lady Capella had just said didn't make much sense at all.

"It is a difficult thing to describe," she continued. "Imagine that you decided to travel beyond our valley. You would travel for days or even years and never find your home. That is because it doesn't exist here. And likewise, if you were in your homeland and tried to find our valley, you would be unsuccessful. The portals are the only way to travel from one world to another."

"But Rochelle and I both came from the same world, but she came through a portal fourteen *years* after I did! How can you explain that?"

Lady Capella shrugged. "Evidently, two different portals connect your world to ours, only through different years."

"And what *are* the portals? What are they for?"

"Nobody knows. Not even Litchfield has been able to tell us. Perhaps it is his secret. We generally try to steer clear of them since once a long time ago a little girl wandered into one and never returned."

Laura was suddenly rapt with attention. "So people *can* go back through them?"

The woman narrowed her eyes. "Of course they can, if they would care to find them. Evidently, they can only be seen when you're practically standing in them. But at that point, I think it would be too late. I don't know how it is possible for one to travel between worlds. The portals were created by something far more powerful than a mere human being, and none of us truly understand them. But nobody has ever had the desire to venture purposely into one. We have no idea what would lie on the other side and don't know how easy it would be to return home. Besides, I think we all like it here well enough to not want to leave. This is our home! From what Rochelle has told us about her native land, I will gladly stay here!"

"So that little girl who went through a portal, didn't anyone go in after her to bring her back?" Laura thought it would have been awful for someone to see a person vanish and not do anything about it.

"According to the child's mother, the girl disappeared in the blink of an eye when they were out picking blackberries in the woods. The mother didn't know what had happened and ran back into town for help. She was raving like a madwoman, and we all gathered that it had been a portal, possibly the one from which Rochelle later arrived, if Rochelle was correct in naming the location. But when the search party went back with her, none of them were able to find the precise spot. The child was gone forever." Lady Capella let out a long, melancholic sigh. "And I know *exactly* how she felt."

Laura felt sorry for the woman but decided that it was too late to be up talking since Lord Arcturus was probably trying to sleep in the next room. Besides, she was beginning to feel depressed hearing about everybody's woes and wished to escape from it all for the night.

"I think I'm going to try to get some sleep now," she said, rising from her seat.

Lady Capella smiled. "Sleep well, Laura. I'll see you in the morning."

When Laura had changed into her nightgown, she pushed open her window to let in some fresh air. Why did this room keep getting so stuffy? It was probably the lack of a central air conditioning system, which would be impossible to have in this primitive land.

The soft nighttime breeze blew in and swirled around her as she stood gazing down at the quiet lawn. She sighed. Somewhere out there was her home, somewhere beyond. Beyond what, she did not know.

The chirping of the crickets and tree frogs off in the woods nearby began to lull her to sleep, so she carefully made her way through the darkness and slipped beneath the covers. She clutched the stuffed bear against her chest, closed her eyes, and fell fast asleep.

The next day passed by in a flurry of activity as the villagers scrambled to get ready for the celebration that was to be the following day. In addition to bringing Eliza her meals, Laura helped Rochelle; Lady Capella; Tabitha; and Lord Arcturus's mother, Tara, bake pies and cakes for the festivalgoers. It was expected that as many as two thousand people would show up for the event; so most of the women in the village were frantically baking their goods and hauling them down to Litchfield's S.F., where they would be stored overnight. The men and boys were down at the celebration grounds for most of the day, setting up additional chairs and stalls for the food and putting up last-minute decorations.

Lord Arcturus had spent the better part of the morning trying to find a nicer place for his displaced relatives to stay, where they would have more room for themselves. Luckily, Andrew finally agreed to take them in; so Leo, Bjorn, and Sedna packed up their things and headed off across town in the carriage.

Later on, when Laura was alone in the kitchen with Rochelle, she decided to ask the young woman a question that had been bugging her all day.

"Uh, Rochelle?" she asked softly so that hopefully nobody in the next room would overhear. "May I ask you a really dumb question?"

"Oh, I love dumb questions!" Rochelle laughed and set down the bowl of cake batter she'd been mixing and turned to face her. "Fire away."

"I want to know exactly what this celebration is all about." Laura felt sheepish. "Well, I think I *sort of* know what it might be about. I guess I should have asked someone before. But, you know ..."

She left the sentence hanging; for suddenly, Rochelle began to look upset.

"What's wrong?" she asked her, worried that her new friend was feeling ill. "Are you okay?"

Rochelle just shook her head. "Nah. I'm fine. But, Laura, it's *weird*. I-I've always felt really uncomfortable when I've gone. I mean—" She waved her arms in the air, seemingly at a loss for words. "It just feels ... blasphemous or something. You see, everyone here worships this creepy deity named Litchfield. The celebration is basically the one day out of the year that is completely dedicated to him. It's their biggest holiday of all."

"Bigger than Christmas or Easter?" Laura found that she wasn't really surprised.

"But that's the thing!" Rochelle said, troubled. "They don't *have* a Christmas or an Easter or church, period. Laura, they don't have a *god*! That's one thing I don't like about this land. They place blind faith in Litchfield and nothing else!"

"But Litchfield can't be real, can he?" *Could he?*

"Oh, he's real all right," Rochelle said darkly. "And that's what scares me most of all. I don't know what he is, but I can certainly tell you one thing: he is no God."

Laura stared at her with wide eyes. "What do you mean? You've seen him?"

Rochelle let out a sort of nervous chuckle. "Oh, you'll find out tomorrow. Trust me." And with that, she grabbed up a tray of cooled pastries and strode out the door, leaving Laura staring after her in utter bewilderment. She felt another unexplainable chill go up her spine. What in the world could the woman have meant?

Around dinnertime that evening, a multitude of wagons and carriages began to roll into town from the north, laden with visitors who chose to arrive early and camp out the night before the big event. Tents appeared here and there between houses and barns on the hillside; and when it grew dark, Laura could see the light from dozens upon dozens of small fires.

When she had taken Eliza her supper, the girl had been afraid of the loud sound of wagons passing by outside and refused to eat until Laura had convinced her that everything was okay and not really a "herd of noisy monsters," as Eliza had initially thought. Luckily, the girl only had three more days of imprisonment; and after that, she'd be free. To do what, Laura had no idea. She assumed that Eliza would have to have a home.

Most of the family went to bed early after supper, so Laura walked down to the deserted living room, hoping for some quiet time to herself and maybe try her hand at some crocheting. After all, there seemed to usually be a few spare hooks lying around, and Lady Capella kept her balls of yarn in a large basket under an end table next to the couch.

The only light source in the room came from a small candle set on a dish in the center of the low coffee table, so Laura found it to be extraordinarily difficult to see as she made her way around the furniture, accidentally stubbing her toe in the act. Where was a glowstone when she needed one? She squinted, eyeing the dark form of a hook that had been left carelessly on the couch cushion. Now for some yarn.

Suddenly, a small noise coming from the opposite side of the room made Laura freeze in midstep. She wasn't sure what she had heard. Had it been the rafters creaking overhead? Or was somebody else in here? She strained her ears, and seconds later she heard it again. It was the soft sound of breathing.

Laura grabbed the candle and tiptoed across the cool, stone floor; and sure enough, she discovered that she was not alone. Tabitha Owens was sitting sideways in a padded armchair, gazing forlornly out the window, her knees drawn up to her chest. She was wearing a dark purple nightgown, which was probably why Laura hadn't been able to see her.

"Who's there?" the girl asked, not moving her head. She seemed to be focused on the canvas tents that had been set up in the field across the road.

"It's just me," Laura said. She sat down and placed the candle gently on the floor. "Is something the matter?"

Tabitha let out a morose sigh and turned away from the window. "I'm worried."

Laura was surprised. "Worried?"

The girl nodded. "Every year, Daddy's cousins from Upton come and stay with us for a few days when the celebration is going on. His cousin Ulric's daughter, Nerine, and I were always good friends and would play together a lot when we were little. She's just a year older than me. But everyone would always have a really good time and enjoy themselves. We'd light a bonfire out behind the house and sing songs and play games and things like that. It was so fun!" She actually smiled for a brief moment as if relishing the fond memory, but it immediately faded. "But now Grandpa is saying that they all believe those awful things people have been saying about Daddy. I think it's terrible. He hasn't ever done anything bad to anyone, so I just don't understand why people would say those things and believe them. Now Nerine will probably never want to talk to me again."

Laura pitied the poor girl. It would be sad indeed for a friendship to be ruined in such a way. "Do you think they'll still be there tomorrow?" she asked.

Tabitha nodded. "Probably. They're the rulers of Upton, and people would expect them to be there. Hardly anybody stays home when it's going on anyway, unless they're really sick. It makes Litchfield happy when everyone shows up."

"Well," Laura said, trying to ignore the statement about Litchfield, "maybe your cousin doesn't agree with her parents and will try to find time to talk to you away from them tomorrow."

"I hope so." Tabitha sighed. "I really hope so."

CHAPTER 8

For a brief instant after Laura awoke the next morning, she could not remember where she was. It was so early that it was still pitch black outside, so she could barely see anything. Where was she? This didn't feel like home. Why was it so chilly? Would someone really leave a window open in the middle of winter?

She sat up, the events of the past several days rushing back to her. Of course, this wasn't her home—at least not really. But for one fleeting instant, the image of a teenage girl's bedroom had stood out sharply in her mind. Pink, flowery curtains and bedspread; a pile of dirty clothes on the floor; posters of attractive male celebrities pinned up here and there on the pastel walls. She knew in her heart that it was hers. Was this a sign of her memory returning? She prayed that it might be true.

The sound of clanging pots and pans from down in the kitchen brought her back to the present. Today was the Holy Valley Day Celebration. She shuddered. Rochelle had certainly seemed uncomfortable enough about it. Maybe people offered live sacrifices to the

Almighty Litchfield. Maybe even *human* sacrifices. She hoped she was just letting her imagination run wild and stiffly climbed out of bed. In any case, she needed to get moving if she was to bring Eliza some early breakfast before the celebration began.

Luckily, someone had been thoughtful enough to light candles in brass sconces along the hallway so she could see as she made her way down to the kitchen. Her stomach growled. It would probably be a good idea to get a quick bite to eat before heading out.

Rochelle and Lady Capella were busy unwrapping packages of preserved sausage and dumping the meat into cast-iron pans sitting on the wood-burning stove that had already been fired up.

"Wow. You're up early," Rochelle commented when Laura plodded into the room. "What's the occasion?"

"I wanted to eat and then get Eliza some food before we all leave later on," she said, letting out a deep yawn. She paused. "By the way, what time is it?" She couldn't remember it having been so dark any of the other mornings when she had gotten up.

"It's around six," Lady Capella said, spreading out the sausage slices with a fork. "It's very, very cloudy, so it looks darker than it normally would at this time."

"I hope it doesn't decide to start raining when we're all down there." Rochelle frowned. "Last year it rained buckets during the celebration, and everyone was drenched. You'd think that this year they'd have had the sense to put up a huge tent over the seats."

"Do you think they would cancel the celebration and have it on a nicer day?" Laura asked.

Lady Capella stopped what she was doing and stared at her with a grave expression on her face. "We would *never* do such a thing," she said. "This is the day it has always been and always will be. Litchfield would not be pleased if we moved the date of the celebration around at our convenience."

"But what could he possibly do to you if you did?"

Lady Capella paused. "I do not know. But would you really want to find out?"

Laura hurried down the road as fast as she could, clutching a plate of eggs and sausage close to her chest. It had grown faintly lighter in the sky off to the east, but the wind was starting to pick up and whipped her hair around her face. She kept having to spit out strands that had blown into her mouth, which was aggravating since both of her hands were already in use.

Trees swayed violently back and forth. Couldn't this wind accidentally uproot those tents that people had set up? It looked like the pale blue pennants that had been raised around the edge of the celebration grounds were flapping like a flock of birds caught in a maelstrom.

Laura stumbled into a pothole she hadn't seen, and half the eggs slid off the plate into the dirt. She stood up, cursing herself for her carelessness, when suddenly she heard an all-too-familiar voice call out to her.

"Hi, Laura!" It was none other than Eliza herself, running merrily up the hill toward her. Andrew Walker followed her a short distance away. "Guess what!"

"What?" Laura replied, even though she was fairly certain what the girl was about to say.

Eliza caught up to her and started jumping up and down like an excited first-grader. "Andrew let me free!" she exclaimed. "Isn't he so nice?"

"He sure is!" Laura didn't know what else to say. Surely it wasn't normal to let people out of imprisonment sooner than they had been sentenced.

"I thought that I should have a heart for once and let her out for the celebration," Andrew said when he reached them. "Plus, she's been very well behaved, so this is a big treat for her."

"And now I get to go home!" Eliza skipped around as happily as could be, and Laura couldn't help but smile. "And I get to see Derek and Gina and Anna and David and Carla and Junie and..."

"She lives with her aunt and uncle and their ten children on a huge farm just south of town," Andrew explained as Eliza continued to rattle off a list of names. "They took her in after her parents died. But since they have so many children of their own, they have a hard time keeping track of her. They hadn't even realized that she wasn't home the day she took the glowstones, which reminds me..." He withdrew a small leather pouch from his shirt pocket and handed it to Laura. "I believe this is yours. Go ahead. Open it."

Laura carefully set the plate on the ground and undid the drawstring on the little bag. She peered inside and saw about a dozen perfectly round, wooden coins. "Thanks!" she said, stuffing it away in her own pocket. "But now I guess I'll need another job, won't I?"

"You sure do!" Andrew laughed. "But we can talk about that this next week after the celebration is over. We all have enough on our plates as it is." He paused, glancing up at the heavy rain clouds that hung ominously overhead like an evil shadow. "Curse this weather. It was like this *last* year. Half the town had caught colds by the end of the week from being drenched to the skin. If I had any say in the matter, I'd have postponed this thing for a day or two until this lets up. At least we need the rain."

Laura nodded in agreement, noting that Andrew hadn't mentioned the possibility of a displeased Litchfield if the date were to be moved. She looked down at the plate of food she'd set on the ground and picked it up. She needed to take it back home before she accidentally dumped the rest of it onto the road.

"I'd better get back home before it cuts loose out here!" she said just as a rather large raindrop splattered on her forearm. *Brilliant.* "See you in a bit! And thanks again for the money!" She began to sprint back up the road as a few more drops fell from the sky onto the dusty path.

Andrew laughed. "Good luck beating the rain!" he called. "We're all going to be *soaked*!"

Thirty seconds later, when Laura burst in the door, lightning crackled across the sky with a brilliant flash. The road outside was now speckled with droplets of rain. She stood panting on the mat, feeling sorry for the people who had camped out in the tents. Hopefully the people in this valley had developed a way to make their makeshift shelters waterproof.

After depositing the plate and what remained of its contents out in the kitchen, she met up with the Owenses, who were in the living room, getting ready for the celebration. Lady Capella was busy tying Spica's dark brown hair back into pigtails with pretty, mint-colored ribbons that matched the girl's dress. Tabitha worked her long hair into a thick but tightly woven braid, which she twisted into a bun. Alcor squirmed as his grandmother scrubbed behind his ears with a damp cloth, and Rotanev stood silently in the corner with his arms folded across his chest. Lord Arcturus and his father stood near the front window, conversing in low voices so Laura couldn't overhear.

"Laura!" Rochelle said as she entered the room holding a hairbrush and a ribbon in her hands. "Come here! You'll want your hair tied back out of your face in weather like this. You don't want it to get plastered all over you."

A low rumble sounded outside as Laura was forced to sit and have her hair done. She groaned. Why couldn't the storm just be nice and skip over the valley as it passed on its way?

"What if we get struck by lightning when we're down there?" she asked, wincing as Rochelle dragged the brush through a tangle of knots.

"I doubt that would happen," the young woman replied. "They set up flagpoles all the way around the celebration grounds. So more than likely it would strike one of those before it would strike one of us."

"I hope you're right!" It was beginning to look even more dismal outside, with the gray clouds above now tinged with a sickly, greenish hue. It thundered again, rattling the panes of glass in the windows. It sounded like the storm was drawing even closer.

"There. You're done," Rochelle said a minute later. "You look much better."

Laura stood up and patted the back of her head. Her hair seemed to be in a braided bun like Tabitha's. She hoped that it looked as pretty as hers did.

Lord Arcturus and Sualocin ended their hushed discussion at the front of the room and turned to face their family. All other talk ceased as everyone focused their attention upon them.

Lord Arcturus cleared his throat. "Father and I have decided to act as if nothing is going wrong in this town," he began. "There is no need to mention or make references to those rumors while we are at the celebration. We will proceed as we normally do and treat our opponents as we would anyone else. If anyone tries to confront any of you about those particular rumors, please do not do or say anything that will ignite an argument. This is a day of happiness and cheer, and the last thing we need is a fight to disrupt it all. Any questions?"

"What if our cousins *try* to pick a fight with us?" Tabitha asked in a small voice. She looked tired. "What should we do?"

"Try to be peaceful about it," her father replied. "And choose your words wisely with them. But let's just try to avoid such a confrontation as much as possible." He paused and glanced out the window. "Hmm. I think we should all leave as soon as we're ready. No sense in waiting until the last minute to face the inevitable."

Lady Capella looked around the room at each of her children. "It looks like we're ready now. But we'll be completely wet if we go down early."

Lord Arcturus shook his head. "Actually, I doubt we will. A little bird who should have kept his mouth shut told me that Litchfield had a surprise in store for us in case of foul weather. Let's just hope that that little bird isn't a liar as well."

His wife shrugged. "Whatever you say. Let's get going, then."

The clouds seemed to burst open above their heads the instant that the family stepped out the door.

"Arcturus, don't you think we should wait and see if this lets up before we end up drowning ourselves going down there?" Lady Capella asked, taking Spica by the hand and leading her around a mound of sodden horse manure she'd almost stepped in.

"No. We're going now," he said firmly, striding off toward the town.

Lady Capella shook her head hopelessly and followed with her children in tow. Lord Arcturus's parents brought up the rear of the group.

The road was turning itself into a squashy path of muddy rivulets that ran down the hillside, and Laura nearly got her shoes stuck in the glop.

"This is gross!" she shouted to Rochelle over the tremendous sound of the downpour. "Now I'm a mess!"

"Hey, you're definitely not alone!" she replied. Rochelle had been smart enough to bring along an old edition of the *Sparkling Falls Weekly Messenger*, which she held over her head like a soggy gray umbrella. She stopped walking and motioned for Laura to stay behind for a moment as the Owenses went on ahead.

"What is it?" Laura asked, concerned that her underclothes might get saturated with water if she stood out there much longer.

Rochelle leaned in close to Laura's ear, holding the newspaper over both their heads to keep dry. She looked very serious. "I just want to let you know that whatever happens, whatever you might see; try to keep your head. These are a strange and deluded people, and they have many customs and beliefs that I still don't understand and probably never will. But don't ever make snide remarks about the things they do. Because Litchfield is real. And when somebody makes him angry, he gets his revenge on them in some way or another. I've seen it. They might not realize that Litchfield is the source of their woes, but I've spent enough time here to notice that everything happens for a reason." She paused and glanced down the road to make certain that the Owenses were now out of earshot. "And that's why I know for a fact that Lord Arcturus has done something to make Litchfield angrier than he ever has been before. You mark my words. Rumors of that degree don't get started for no reason. Trust me."

Laura could hardly believe what she was hearing. "But what on earth could he have done to deserve something like that?"

"I have my suspicions," Rochelle said, gazing down the hill in the direction of the celebration grounds. "But in order to avoid spawning even more rumors, I will keep those suspicions to myself."

Laura and Rochelle made their way down the hopelessly muddy hillside and slogged across the fields to the celebration grounds. Laura's heart was thumping wildly in anticipation, not knowing at all what to expect.

About twenty flagpoles had been erected around the perimeter, their blue banners now as drenched as she was. The entire celebration grounds had to have taken up at least six acres of land. There was a wooden stage at the front with walls on three sides and a sturdy roof above it. Stalls for selling food had been set up between the flagpoles, and there were dozens and dozens of people milling around talking to one another.

But something seemed to be horribly wrong.

Rochelle seemed to have noticed it too. "Oh my God," she murmured.

Within the perimeter where all the seats, food stalls, and stage were, the ground was dry. Bone dry. Dry as if it hadn't rained in weeks. The chairs were all dry too. The people themselves, however, were still soaked from having walked through the downpour, but it was quite obvious that not a single drop of rain had fallen upon the celebration grounds.

Laura and Rochelle walked forward in total amazement; and the rain seemed to stop as if there were some huge, invisible roof above them. But it was still pouring down rain everywhere else.

"How in the world?" Laura couldn't help but gape in awe at the mysterious phenomenon. It was like magic.

Rochelle was actually laughing. "I don't believe it! Lord Arcturus was right! Litchfield really did have a surprise in store for us!"

The Owenses were already sitting down in the first row of seats on the left-hand side of the grounds, and Laura and Rochelle filed into the row behind them since they were not actual members of the royal family. Laura noticed that the two families in the front row across the aisle were making their best effort not to glance in their direction, so she assumed that they must be Lord Arcturus's relatives from Upton.

She began to see many familiar faces in the crowd as more people arrived. Mark Ericson waved at her from half a dozen rows back and winked. An old man who must have been his grandfather sat to his left. Laura also saw the Yeltons and their two children, Eliza Matarna, and Louise Wang. Louise was with her husband and four or five small children who trailed after them. Two girls in their late teens brought up the rear, one of whom was walking hand in hand with a young man. Her large belly made Laura assume she was pregnant. The Wangs sat down in the row behind the leaders of Upton, but the husband (Adalbert?) continued to the front and disappeared behind the stage with two other men who had joined him.

A great clap of thunder rumbled off in the distance, and Laura jumped. She glanced nervously up at the slate-gray clouds, praying that the lightning wouldn't strike anywhere near them. If it struck one of the flagpoles, as Rochelle had said, it would still be very dangerous. But maybe whatever mystical force that was keeping the rain from falling on the celebration grounds could deflect lightning as well.

It was an uncanny experience, sitting there with rain pounding the earth just yards away and not having a single drop fall upon her head. She nudged Rochelle in the side. "How do you think they can do that?" she whispered.

Rochelle shrugged. "If I had any idea, I would tell you. But it's funny; they never had so many flagpoles set up before..."

Over the next twenty minutes, more and more people filed into seats, gasping at the miracle that was blocking out the rain. Evidently, this had never happened before, which Laura thought to be odd. Why would Litchfield have hidden this power from them in the past if he was truly a god?

Again, Laura noticed that a good majority of the people had almond-shaped eyes, although the colors of their hair were as diverse as those one might have seen in any crowd, if her memory served her correctly. The Owenses were in fact one of the few families who had eyes anything like her own.

Soon, every single chair had been claimed; and many people stood in the back or sat in the grassy aisle between seats, holding small children in their laps. A mere thunderstorm obviously could not deter these people from attending this "holy" event.

Suddenly, the crowd grew quite hushed when the man who must have been Louise's husband strode out onto the stage. He wore a black, short-sleeved dress shirt with matching slacks. His dark hair had been slicked back out of his face and clasped at the base of his neck. His beady eyes scanned back and forth across the audience a few times before he began to speak.

"Greetings to all of you who chose to arrive today in spite of this inclement weather," he called out in a resounding voice. He sounded like a showman; and if Lord Arcturus had been correct in his description of him, that was all he really was anyway. "But as you can plainly see, out beloved creator had the foresight to prevent it from storming on his magnificent celebration. All hail Litchfield!"

"All hail Litchfield!" the crowd chorused.

Laura and Rochelle remained silent. In fact, Rochelle had her eyes clamped shut and her lips were moving; and Laura saw that she was praying on a crystal rosary that she had tucked between her palms.

Laura returned her attention to the man on the stage and gulped.

"Now I, Adalbert Wang, shall introduce to you the four illustrious rulers of our prosperous valley. Lord Arcturus Owens!" Lord Arcturus stood up and gave a stiff nod before sitting back down. "The former Lord Sualocin Owens! Lord Rudyard Obasanjo! Lord Ulric Obasanjo!"

The applause during the naming of the latter two men was incredible. When it had subsided, Adalbert Wang continued.

"These four men, by their divine right, have been granted the authority to govern these fertile lands. However..." He stared directly at Lord Arcturus. "Some feel that one of these men might be unworthy of his title and might need a replacement if certain things do not *change*. Let us hope that will never have to happen here in our valley!"

Lord Arcturus, who was sitting right in front of Laura, turned red with embarrassment; but fortunately, he followed his own advice and remained quiet.

"But let us not think of such things. Today is a celebration! A celebration of who and what we are; a celebration of Litchfield, the creator!"

Somewhere, some kind of flute began to play an eerie melody that seemed to be in no particular key. It was almost hypnotizing.

"In the beginning," the man said, "there was nothing. No sky above, no land below. No sun, no moon, no day, no night. All that existed was Litchfield and his magnificent power and intellect.

"Now Litchfield saw that there was nothing and began to feel lonely. Why should he spend the eternity of his existence in solitude? He decided to create human beings to be his comrades. Among them were Gertrude the Fair Mother, Sarah the Kind, Ira the Wise, and many others. But now these people needed a home, so he gave them this holy valley for them to live in. He taught them to farm, and to hunt, and to fish. He taught them to raise families so they may have children of their own. He helped them build the two villages of Sparkling Falls and Upton, and he taught them to govern. He taught them all, and the people passed down the knowledge from generation to generation. It has now been two hundred and forty-one years since this all began. Now we are here today to praise Litchfield for all he has done for us. Now it is time for me to step aside and let the Holy Valley Day Celebration begin."

Adalbert disappeared off to the left; and where he had been standing in the center of the stage, a mysterious ring of light appeared on the floorboards.

The flute continued to play but was now accompanied by the beating of drums.

Laura strained her eyes to see what was going on. She was only about twenty feet from the edge of the stage, so why couldn't she see correctly? It looked like the air above the ring of light was *shimmering*. Little wisps of golden light appeared and began to swirl together faster and faster like some kind of holographic kaleidoscope. The light began to take shape into an image (or was it solid? She couldn't tell) of what looked like a huge face the height of a person.

The face was old and wrinkled, with silvery gray hair around the temples and a thin beard. The skin was pale and sallow. The eyes were a shade of crystal blue and cold, with pronounced dark circles beneath them. However, they held a look of intense arrogance deep within.

To Laura's increasing shock, the face turned and stared directly at her, its demonic eyes burning into her skull. The lips began to move; and in a faint but audible voice, it said, "Welcome to my valley, Laura Owens. I hope you have enjoyed your stay so far."

CHAPTER 9

Laura was frozen with terror. How, exactly, was one supposed to respond to a giant, speaking head?

"Forgive me for my startling appearance," the head went on in a soothing voice that gave her the creeps. It looked almost amused at Laura's reaction. "You have nothing to fear from me. I am Litchfield, the father and creator, and mean you no harm. However, what you see here before you is merely a projection of my visage. I am, in fact, not present."

Then the head turned, and the celebration continued. Litchfield did not speak to her again.

Despite the initial shock of having a large, disembodied head watching over the proceedings, Laura found herself becoming more and more fascinated by the celebration. The people of Sparkling Falls sang a myriad of songs dedicated to Litchfield and all of his "wondrous works." A troupe of dancers performed an unusual ballet that lasted for about twenty minutes. It was hard to determine the exact length of time since nobody had a wristwatch. The men and women wore long, flowing robes that seemed to float about them as they twirled around and around, giving the dance a mesmerizing effect. Laura wasn't certain, but it appeared as if the dance was portraying some kind of twisted creation story.

Following the dance, Litchfield's giant head spoke again.

"And now, my children, we will have the annual blessing of expectant mothers and their husbands. Will all the said couples please rise?"

About thirty-five couples stood up, including Frank and Evelyn Yelton. But then, to Laura's surprise, Lady Capella rose hesitantly from her seat, followed by an equally nervous-looking Lord Arcturus. Laura assumed that the lord and lady had not previously told their children anything about this new pregnancy, since each one of them turned and stared at their parents with expressions of pure astonishment.

Animated whispers immediately broke out in the crowd behind them.

"Silence!" Litchfield roared. He looked irritated. "Is it not surprising that a happily married woman would be with child again? Show your respect and cease your foolish gossip!"

The crowd obeyed, but Laura could tell that the people were still feeling excited over this bit of news. Litchfield went on. "Life is the greatest gift of all, greater than any wealth one might find in the world. Children are a blessing and must be cherished or society cannot function. When a person is not valued, he or she becomes discouraged and prone to hatred. This erodes the fabric of society, causing it to collapse and ultimately fail.

"Parents, teach your children all that you know so they may grow into hard-working, virtuous, and responsible adults like yourselves. Love your children and show them all that is good. Be stern but do not abuse them. You are all blessed to have become parents. May you and your children experience the best in life."

Just as Litchfield was about to continue, a bolt of lightning shot from the clouds and struck one of the flagpoles behind the stage with the most blinding light Laura had ever seen. She could feel all of the hairs on her arms and scalp lift up from the electricity in the air. The image of Litchfield's face vanished in a shower of blue electrical sparks, and suddenly the rains came down upon them.

At first, Laura thought that the lightning had hit somebody, but then she saw with relief that nobody had been standing near the now-smoking flagpole. Children were screaming and running every which way while their parents struggled to keep them at their sides. Adalbert Wang had returned to the stage and was attempting to address the crowd, but nobody seemed to notice or care. They were too busy clearing the field to get out of the storm.

"Are you okay, Laura?" Rochelle asked, stuffing her rosary away. She looked pleased. Her praying seemed to have paid off.

Laura nodded. "Just a little spooked. That's all. That was so close it could have struck someone."

"Yes, but it didn't. See what the power of prayer can do?" Rochelle looked up at the dark, turbulent clouds and beamed. "Lightning struck that demon's image down, and nobody was harmed. My God is an awesome God." She turned to Lady Capella and Lord Arcturus, who were rounding up their children. "By the way, congratulations! I had no idea you were pregnant."

"Neither did we!" Tabitha said, looking positively joyful.

Lady Capella laughed and patted her abdomen. "Life is full of surprises, isn't it? Not many forty-year-old women get to have babies."

The throng leaving the festival grounds was moving as slowly as molasses, and the Owenses, having been seated at the front of the mass, were now stuck behind everyone.

Lord Arcturus cleared his throat and glanced around with concern. "Come on. Let's hurry up and get around these people. None of us need to get sick standing out here in this muck." He turned to the right and began squeezing through the thinner part of the crowd, leaving a wide enough gap in his wake for his family to follow.

Laura, bringing up the rear once more, happened to look down at her dress. It was plastered to her skin.

"Mommy, I can hardly see!" Spica complained, running to catch up with her mother. Her dripping pigtails flopped limply as she went. Laura noticed that the ribbon on one of them was coming untied.

"Spica, be careful," her mother cautioned. "If you keep running around like that in this mud you could slip and hurt yourself!"

"Sorry, Mommy." Spica slowed down. Suddenly, the wind gusted through the valley and the loose hair ribbon fluttered to the ground and began to blow away. "Wait! Mommy, my pretty ribbon!"

"Leave it!" the woman ordered. "We have more of them at home."

"No! It's one that Grandma and Grandpa got me for my birthday! I can't lose it!" The little girl turned and ran after it, oblivious to her mother's objections.

"Spica, you come back here!" Lord Arcturus called, nearly knocking over an elderly couple as he made an abrupt about-face.

"I will as soon as I find my ribbon!"

Laura had a rather peculiar urge to stop the child from running off after her ribbon, but before she could do anything, Spica slipped into the crowd and vanished from sight.

Minutes later, the Owenses (minus Lord Arcturus) had regrouped in the living room, and Laura went up to her room to dry off and change into a new dress. It was such a relief to be out of that soggy outfit! She sat down on the edge of her bed and started wringing out her braided bun with a spare pillowcase she'd found in the closet. If only she could have a hair dryer. She glanced down at her bare feet and saw that her skin was all wrinkly, indicating that a large quantity of water must have soaked into her shoes.

Rain spattered against the windowpane with a gentle *tapetty-tap*. Hadn't it been raining long enough already? Going at this rate, they might need to go out and build an ark.

She chose to join the rest of the family downstairs after she hung up her other dress to dry. But as soon as she entered the kitchen, Rochelle rushed in with a finger to her lips, gesturing over her shoulder with her thumb.

"What's going on?" Laura asked.

"They're all arguing," Rochelle said in a whisper. "Lord Arcturus just came back saying he couldn't find Spica, and Lady Capella is flipping out."

"You mean she's still out there, in *that*?" Laura frowned. Most little girls would have given up and come running home in that kind of weather. What could have been keeping her for so long? "Did anyone else go out to find her?"

Rochelle nodded. "Sualocin, Rotanev, and Tabitha went down about five minutes ago."

Just then, Lord Arcturus's voice blasted through the doorway. "And just how was I supposed to know she didn't come back here? I'd swear she isn't down there anymore!"

"You could have at least *asked* someone if they'd seen her!"

"But Spica isn't stupid! She knows her way home, for Litch's sake!"

"Yes! When it isn't storming!"

Laura gulped. "Maybe I should go back upstairs."

"No. Stay handy. Going at this rate, we might need you to be part of a search party." The servant peered out the window and sighed softly. "I only hope that the poor child hasn't hurt herself."

The two of them walked into the living room to warm themselves by the small fire that had been lit on the hearth and tried to ignore the angry tension permeating the atmosphere. Lord Arcturus stood with his arms crossed. His wife's face was red, and she drummed her fingers nervously on the windowsill, glancing out of the window every five seconds.

A few minutes later, Laura heard the front door open and close; and a dour-looking Rotanev entered the room. He had something clenched in his hand, but she couldn't tell what it was.

"Rotanev!" Lady Capella exclaimed the instant she saw her son. "Why are you back without the others? Couldn't you *find* her?"

He began to stammer. "I-I-they're still looking. Mostly everyone who was at the celebration has gone home to get out of the rain. We just saw some people moving the stalls and chairs off of the field, and Tabitha and Grandpa started asking if anyone had seen her go home with somebody." He paused and opened his hand. "I did find this, though."

It was the hair ribbon that Spica had so begged to retrieve, completely soggy and covered in mud.

Lady Capella grew pale. "You're certain Spica wasn't still down there?"

"I'm positive, Mother. The only people I saw were Adalbert Wang, a few of the Fentons and Patchells, and maybe two or three children. Tabitha and Grandpa and I asked *everyone* if they'd seen where she'd gone, but they said they'd been too busy clearing everything off the field to pay attention to anything else."

"Did you check to see if she'd come in with Frank and Evelyn?" Lady Capella asked. "They could have taken her in to dry off."

Rotanev nodded and drew up a seat. "I was just over there. The last they saw of her, she was chasing after this." He stared at the ribbon in his hand, looking troubled. "That's what everyone who'd seen her said. But the ribbon is here, so she didn't find it. So why didn't she come back?"

"Maybe her other hair ribbon fell out too," suggested Alcor.

"That still doesn't explain why she isn't here!" Rotanev threw the ribbon to the floor and stood abruptly. "That's it. I'm going back out there, seeing as her own *mother* and *father* aren't doing anything to help find her!" He threw his parents a dirty look and stormed from the room, muttering some kind of disrespectful profanity as he clomped out the door.

Laura hated watching this whole ordeal and feeling helpless. She slowly stood up. "I'll go too."

Alcor Owens rose from his seat. "Laura will need help. She doesn't know where Spica's friends live, so I'll show her the way."

Lord Arcturus looked somber. "We'll *all* go. But Mother, you should stay behind in case Spica comes back when we're all out there."

Tara Owens nodded. "I will."

"This weather is ridiculous," Alcor complained a few minutes later as he led Laura down a washed-out muddy path leading down the hill behind the sheep pasture. "I can't stand it anymore! Spica sure picked a great day to get lost, didn't she?"

"Uh huh." Laura could tell that underneath the youth's light-hearted façade, he was genuinely worried about his little sister. She knew that something had to have been wrong, because Spica didn't strike her as being the type to purposely upset her parents by going somewhere without telling them. "So, where should we stop first?"

"Hmm. I think Meggie's house. Spica goes there to play *dolls* sometimes." He rolled his eyes. "It's right over here."

Alcor walked right up to a small, wooden dwelling and knocked on the door. "You talk," he said. "I'll wait."

He stepped aside, leaving Laura shivering on the stone walk. She noted with dismay that her "dry" change of clothing was now just as thoroughly soaked as her other outfit had been. And her shoes! She wished she had a pair of rubber boots.

A flustered-looking woman opened the door, holding a wailing infant in one arm. "May I help you?"

"Yes," Laura began. "Um, we were wondering if Spica Owens might have come home with your family after the celebration. Nobody can find her."

The woman frowned and moved her baby to her other hip. "No. She's not here. Haven't seen her since that lightning struck a while ago. My husband and I just gathered up our children and ran."

Various pairs of eyes began to peer around the doorframe. A tiny arm reached up and tugged at the woman's dress. "Who's out there, Mama?"

"Who are you talking to?"

"Did Maria come over to play?"

"Mama, I'm hungry!"

The woman tried shooing her children back into the house. "I'm very sorry, but I honestly haven't seen her. She could have gone home with the Millers. They live just down the path. Might try asking at the Lawhornes' place too."

"Thank you," Laura said, gesturing for Alcor to lead the way again. "Hopefully she'll be with one of them."

The family at the next house told a fairly similar story. No, they hadn't seen her. They were too busy gathering up children and making a run for it. Try asking at the Marshes' house across the street. Sorry they couldn't be of more help.

It wasn't until Laura and Alcor had reached the fifth house they had been referred to that they learned anything new.

"Yes. I think I saw her running around after that lightning struck," an older woman said, looking thoughtful. "Then I just happened to see a woman stop her and say something to her. Then they started looking around at the ground like they were searching for something. I'm really not certain; but after that, it looked as if the woman was leading Spica away from the celebration grounds."

"Did you see what the woman looked like?" Laura asked, her pulse quickening. Maybe it was Louise Wang!

The woman shook her head. "I couldn't tell. It was raining so hard. I don't know who it was."

"What was she wearing?"

"It was a dress, a dark-colored one. Could have been blue or green. Maybe gray. The odd thing was she was wearing a black bonnet." She laughed. "Those went out of fashion when my *mother* was a child. Of course, she could have just dug one out of her grandmother's old things so she could keep her head dry."

"I think I might remember seeing a woman with a bonnet," Alcor said.

Laura turned and stared at him. "Do you know who it was?"

"Nope. I only saw the back of her head."

"Darn." Laura paused and then asked the woman, "Which direction was she taking Spica?"

The woman furrowed her brow. "Let me think. Perhaps it was in the direction of the river. Yes. I think it was." Suddenly her face turned pale. "You don't think she could have been *kidnapped*, do you?"

Laura cringed at the sound of that ugly word. "I guess it would be a possibility."

Alcor looked like he was going to be sick. "Oh no..." He put his hands up against the wall and lowered his head, starting to hyperventilate. "She can't have been... She *can't* have been..."

"Try to be calm, son." The old woman grabbed his wrist. "Breathe slowly. My goodness! You have such an unfortunate family. This happened to your little brother too."

Alcor jerked his wrist away from her and sent her a look of pure disgust. "How dare you even mention Procyon, especially at a time like this! You have no idea what my family went through! No idea at all!" He grabbed his head with his hands as if he was going to yank out two fistfuls of hair and bolted.

"I-I'm so sorry," the woman said to Laura as Alcor vanished down the path. "I didn't realize..."

Laura nodded. "Thank you for the information," she said, cutting the woman off abruptly, "but I've got to go."

She could feel mud squishing into her shoes as she ran after Alcor. It was going to take ages to get them clean again, but she could worry about that some other time.

"Alcor!" she shouted. "Stop!"

But the sandy-haired youth kept on running as if he was being pursued by the devil himself. Suddenly, he slipped and fell into the slime that had once been part of a path. Laura caught up with him and helped him to his feet.

"That stupid *witch*!" he exclaimed, wiping globs of mud from his arms. His eyes were red and bloodshot. "Why'd she have to open her big ol' mouth and say something about my brother? Why? What she said was *the* biggest insult. With Spica being…being kidnapped…" His words were choked with tears.

"You don't know that she was kidnapped," Laura said, trying to sound optimistic. "That woman could have just been helping Spica look for her hair ribbon." But in her heart, she had a terrible feeling. What if she *had* been kidnapped?

"No, no. I can feel it." Alcor pounded his chest. "I *know* that something bad must have happened." He paused. "We've got to go and tell the others."

They caught up with Lord Arcturus and Tabitha a few minutes later, and Alcor repeated what he and Laura had just found out from the old woman.

Lord Arcturus looked grim and glanced down at his daughter, who had begun to cry. "We need a bigger search party."

By the early afternoon, the rains had finally ceased and the long-awaited sun broke through the clouds, transforming the waterlogged valley into a natural sauna. It got very, very hot. Laura was glad that it stopped raining; but now her hair was a shambles, her shoes were nearly ruined, and her dress was stained brown halfway up to her knees. And on top of that, she had begun to sweat profusely.

She met up with Rochelle, and they recounted to each other everything they had learned.

"The only thing I was told was that a few people had seen her running after her ribbon," Rochelle said. She shook her head. "I just can't believe that someone would have walked off with her, especially in *this* land. Nobody ever does that kind of thing. But you know, all we can do is pray that she returns home safe and sound."

Laura nodded in agreement. Yes. All they could do was pray. *And not to Litchfield,* she added to herself.

By nightfall, most of the village had joined the hunt for Spica. Dozens of men and women scoured the riverbanks and forests and hiked up into the hills carrying torches, constantly shouting out the little girl's name. A few thoughtful people had employed dogs to help follow the trail of Spica's scent, which mysteriously ended at the water's edge and did not continue on the other side. Some people investigated the waterfall downstream but found no signs that Spica had been down that way.

Laura, Rochelle, and Lady Capella finally grew weary, and the three of them returned home to make certain that Spica hadn't crept in while her grandmother was taking a nap. Unfortunately, the house was silent. At some point, Tara Owens had left to join the search for her granddaughter.

Laura decided to help Rochelle make supper at around nine o'clock. It was late, but a couple of the Owens children had returned home and were hungry. As Laura was rummaging through a cabinet looking for a pot that Rochelle needed, Andrew Walker entered the house, his feet dragging with a mixture of weariness and despair.

"I found this down by the river," he said softly, laying a small object down on the table. And just as quietly, he turned and left.

"What is it?" Rochelle asked, setting down the bowl of berries she had been planning on making into a pie.

"I don't know." Laura went up and picked up what appeared to be a clump of partially dried mud with bits of light green cloth sticking out of it here and there. She flaked the dirt off and felt her heart sink. She held it up so Rochelle could see it. "I think it's Spica's other hair ribbon."

CHAPTER 10

Laura could barely sleep that night from the sound of anguished sobbing emanating from the bedrooms across the hall. It was the most haunting thing she had ever heard.

Someone was walking slowly down the hallway, sniffling as they went. Somewhere, a child coughed; and a soft, female moan drifted in through the gap underneath the bedroom door. How could any person have been cruel enough to cause the family so much pain?

It had to have been at least two o'clock in the morning by now. She had heard the search parties come back only about an hour before, disheartened and empty handed. She had discerned by the muffled voices coming from downstairs that some believed Spica might have run away, as many children sometimes do to escape from their "mean" parents. Others were not nearly as hopeful.

She rolled over and tried jamming a pillow over her head to block out the dismal sounds of weeping. She just couldn't understand why anyone would have tried to abduct the poor little girl, unless they were holding her for ransom. She shuddered and hoped that wherever Spica was she was not being harmed.

A terrible thought happened to cross her mind. She too was a missing person, and her own family, whoever they might be, would be in virtually the same position as the Owenses. Laura couldn't even fathom the grief and pain that a parent would experience if one of their children had disappeared.

She felt an uncomfortable knot forming in her stomach, and warm tears began to run down her cheeks onto her pillow. She started to tremble.

She urged herself to calm down. Now was the time for rest. She could always worry about her problems in the morning.

But a demonic little voice in her head kept saying, *Don't be in denial, Laura. You'll never remember who you are, and you will be stuck in this strange valley for the rest of your life. Your parents will never find out what happened to their darling child and die of broken hearts! And don't forget about Spica. They'll probably just find her broken little body washed up on the riverbank...*

She ordered the imaginary voice to silence itself. Spica had only been missing for half a day. Surely there was still a good chance that she would be found.

Rochelle's voice echoed through her head. *All we can do is pray.*

Rochelle was right. Laura said a Hail Mary and the Lord's Prayer; and as she whispered a groggy, "Amen," she fell fast asleep.

The next day was Sunday. Laura kept experiencing the peculiar urge to dress up nicely and go somewhere—church most likely. But as far as she knew, there was nothing of the sort in the valley. She felt sorry for all the people of Sparkling Falls. Would they automatically go to hell just because nobody had ever taught them about God?

After lunch, Laura went upstairs and found Rochelle kneeling on the floor of her room, praying her rosary again. Laura smiled and quietly ducked back out, not wanting to interrupt such a personal moment.

Laura returned to her own room, shut the door tightly, and kneeled beside her bed. She rested her arms on her mattress and folded her hands together.

"Hi, God," she began, hoping that nobody outside would hear and think she was talking to herself. "It's me again. I kind of need your help. But I guess you'd know that already. Anyway, I really need to find out who I am and get home so I can be with my family. And Spica...please let us be able to find her. And Procyon too. The Owenses are very kind people. They've taken me into their home when I had nowhere else to go. They don't deserve to lose their children.

"I also want to be able to learn more about this place before I leave it. And I want to know who or what Litchfield really is. So basically, I'd just like to know the answers and where to find them."

She stood up and was about to walk out when suddenly three words appeared in her mind as clear as day.

Follow the sunset.

"What?" Laura said aloud. She glanced around the room, making certain that none of the Owens children were sneaking around, playing tricks on her. "What's that supposed to mean?"

Follow the sunset. It is there where the answers lie.

She felt goose bumps rise up on her arms and hastily left the room.

Laura went outside. The sun set in the west, and west was where the portal had been. It had already been a few days since she arrived in what people referred to as "Maribu Clearing," but she was sure she'd be able to find it again without a problem.

Her walk through the woods was more difficult than the last time due to her new dress getting caught up in every fallen branch and bramble. She remembered that the clearing would be somewhere off to the right of the path, but after ten minutes of fruitless wandering, she decided she was lost.

Great. Now what do I do? Laura paused and leaned against a tree to think. She should have brought someone with her who knew the terrain. Mark would have known, but she hadn't thought to go look for him before heading out. Too late now!

Some prickly burrs had adhered to the skirt of her dress, and she bent to pluck them off. As she did so, she noticed that the ground at the base of the tree trunk was overgrown with moss. *Moss!* Someone had told her that the plants grew mostly on the north sides of trees. She couldn't remember who. It might have been in biology class. Had she ever taken a biology class? As much as she strained to call forth the memory from the shadows of her mind, the source of her knowledge of moss continued to elude her.

Oh well, it didn't matter. If moss pointed towards the north, then she had a handy compass growing beneath her feet. But there was one problem: in this forest, the moss had sprung up on *all* sides of the trees. Laura stared at the patches of green for a minute or so. The moss did look a little thicker on one side. Maybe *that* was north. The clearing had been north of the path. Using the thick patch of moss as a guide, she continued along in what felt like the right direction.

Miraculously, this method worked. Laura walked into Maribu Clearing, smiling to herself at her success. The portal had to be close by. It didn't make sense that people couldn't see the portals unless they were in them. Perhaps whoever (or whatever) had made them had designed them to remain hidden.

Laura grabbed a stick to wave in front of her. That way if she found the portal, the stick might vanish first and give her a moment of warning before she followed it back to the basement.

She continued in this fashion for some time, growing anxious. What if she found the portal and went back through only to find that thousands of years had passed? It might not be 2003 anymore, and her family (if she had one) would have been long since dead and gone. And then, if she rushed back through to return to Sparkling Falls, even more centuries could have passed. She would be lost in an even stranger world without a home and without a friend.

She bit her lip. What should she do? *What would Jesus do?* Laura smiled at this latter thought. She pictured herself wearing a blue "WWJD" bracelet that had been popular some years before. Such a pointless memory. But what *would* Jesus do? Jesus wouldn't go running blindly into some bizarre portal ... but he *would* help a grieving family find their daughter.

Follow the sunset!

Not that again! "I can't follow the sunset right now!" she said. "I've got to find Spica!"

Laura threw her stick to the ground.

And, like the Owenses' youngest two children had done, it disappeared.

More search parties went out that afternoon to patrol the riverbanks and the forests. This time, Laura chose to remain home to help out Rochelle and Lady Capella around the house. The older woman was tired and worn and looked about a decade older than she had the day before.

"I found my portal," Laura said to Rochelle at one point when they were alone in the kitchen.

Rochelle was on her hands and knees scrubbing the stone floor with an old rag. "Then why are you still here?"

"Well, you know ..." Laura stopped, for Rochelle was giving her a funny look. "What's the matter?"

"Don't tell me you chickened out." She dipped the rag into a bucket of soapy water that had turned as gray as the floor itself, squeezed out the excess suds, and continued cleaning.

"I didn't chicken out! Well, maybe a little. Did you ever read those Narnia books?"

"A long time ago. Why?"

"Well, those kids were in Narnia and then they went back home through the wardrobe ... but the next time they went to Narnia a huge length of time had passed there. I'm afraid that if I go through that portal it could end up being the year 3000. Then what would I do?"

"You have a point there. But *The Chronicles of Narnia* are a work of fiction. C.S. Lewis couldn't have had any idea that portals really existed. If I were you, I'd try to find the portal again and go back through. I know you're not happy here. You have no reason to stay."

"Who said I'm not happy?" It was true that Laura had her moments of boredom, but she never would have described herself as an unhappy person. "I kind of like this place."

"But you don't *belong* here. Me ... I left nothing behind. I wanted to go home but had no reason to do it. God sent me here to start a new life."

"What if God sent *me* here for some special reason? If I go now, I might not get to do what he wants me to."

"Well, then you'd better get cracking. Just don't forget that you probably have a family out there who's frantically looking for *you*."

Laura nodded. "Trust me. I haven't forgotten."

Once again, the townspeople reported back in the evening, having found no signs of Spica. Alcor and Rotanev seemed to be nauseated each time a person knocked on the door with additional bad news. Finally, Frank Yelton came in carrying a soggy black bonnet that he had found lying in the road about four miles north of town on the way to Upton. Lord Arcturus agreed that in the morning, he would go out and search the area around that town to see if Spica's captors had hidden her in one of the small settlements that many of the valley's inhabitants lived in. But as Laura had suspected, he and his helpers returned without the little girl and with little hope that they would ever see her again.

Most of the Owens family left for Upton Monday morning to interrogate their estranged relatives about Spica's whereabouts in the off chance that she had tagged along with them. Tabitha had decided to stay home to "keep her grandparents company," but Laura saw that the girl shut herself in her bedroom the moment her parents and siblings left.

Laura remembered that she had an initiation to attend up in the cemetery across the river that evening, so she went to ask Rochelle for some last-minute advice.

"Rochelle, what did you take with you during your initiation?" she asked when she found her in the backyard beating a rug over the clothesline.

"My initiation?" The young woman laughed. "I never joined the Woodland Youth!"

"Oh. I figured you had."

"I was invited to join but decided against it. I always thought it sounded creepy camping out in a graveyard. I didn't think it made sense to do that for an initiation, but Yvonne said it was the only thing she and her father could think of when the group first got started. You'd think they'd give you a physical examination, but no! You get to sleep with a bunch of dead people instead."

"Thanks. Now you're making me nervous." In reality, Laura was eager to begin her initiation. Camping anywhere sounded fun as long as nobody tried to sneak up on her. Maybe she had loved going on vacation in the woods before she lost her memory; and if so, maybe her experiences tonight would help bring those memories back!

Rochelle put her hands on her hips. "Hey, if you chicken out on this one, don't blame me!"

"It sounds to me like *you're* the one who chickened out." Laura grinned. "But if you hadn't decided to be a scaredy-cat, what would you have packed?"

Rochelle was kind enough to help Laura find and pack up all of the necessary supplies, including a couple of glowstones and a pitcher for water to keep them charged. Laura left the house at around eight-thirty, laden with two duffel bags and a lantern. Rochelle had made a lot of good suggestions on what to bring, but now she felt like a human pack mule.

About halfway through town, the mysterious message popped rudely into her head again.

Follow the sunset!

The message caught her off guard, and Laura halted in her tracks. She looked over her shoulder and saw that the sun was beginning to dip below the mountaintops in the west.

But I can't follow the sunset right now! Laura thought. *I have an initiation to go to!*

Shaking her head and wondering briefly if she was beginning to lose her mind, she marched onward and crossed the bridge spanning the width of the rushing river. Soon, she was ascending the hill on the eastern side of the valley. It was a difficult climb, especially with the generous amount of luggage weighing her down. It didn't help that the road was still horribly muddy from Saturday's storm. She hoped that she might be able to find a dry patch of earth to set up her camp on but doubted that it would happen.

She arrived at the meetinghouse ten minutes later. Yvonne Harding was waiting for her there, as was Mark Ericson, to Laura's strange delight. For some inexplicable reason, the mere sight of him was enough to further lift her spirits.

Yvonne rose from her chair and greeted Laura with a cheerful smile. "So, you've decided to show up! Very impressive. More than once in the past few years I've had potential members change their minds at the last minute and go running home. Needless to say, they never became members of the Woodland Youth."

"Rotanev Owens was one of them," Mark added with a smirk.

Laura smiled. "Maybe he was afraid of ghosts."

"Could be." He paused. "*You're* not afraid of that kind of thing, are you?"

"Uh…not that I know of. I mean, I never saw a ghost before. Not that I'd remember anyway. I'm mostly just afraid of the *living* creatures that might be out there."

"Don't worry too much about them," Yvonne said. "Just keep a fire going and most animals will keep their distance."

"Yvonne," Mark said, "how is Laura going to be able to *light* a fire? The wood will all be too wet to burn."

Laura could have slapped herself. It hadn't even occurred to her.

"Hmm…" Yvonne bit her lip as if she was racking her brains to figure out a solution. "Well, did you bring any glowstones with you? The light might attract a lot of moths, but it could be enough to frighten away the larger animals."

Mark snorted. "Yeah. Like that worked when that stupid raccoon decided to become friendly with me."

"I did bring a couple," Laura said. She smiled at Mark and patted one of her duffel bags. "Rochelle told me that I should take them. But are you *sure* there aren't any bears or wolves or anything that might be hungry for some nice human meat?"

Yvonne laughed. "Neither of those has been sighted around here for a very long time, and the wolves tend to stick to the western hills. You really have nothing to worry about."

"I hope not." Laura glanced outside and noted that the sky was growing darker. "I guess I should go down there now, shouldn't I?"

"That wouldn't be a bad idea. Mark, could you be a gentleman and escort Laura down to the cemetery? I need to get some things done here this evening."

"Sure. After all, I am *always* a gentleman." Mark gave Laura a sly wink and took one of her duffel bags, which he slung effortlessly over his shoulder. "No sense in you having to carry two of these."

Laura smiled. "Thanks."

They left the meetinghouse and traveled down the road for a few minutes until they reached the cemetery. A crude wooden fence had been erected along the front of the burial ground, and a rotting sign bore the chilling words "The Souls of Sparkling Falls." Laura gave an anxious shiver and her teeth began to chatter, but not from any cold that she could feel. *It's just a campout, just like we did in the old days,* she thought, wishing that she could remember more. In her mind she could imagine sitting around a campfire with two younger girls whose names escaped her. One may have been named Mallory. No, Melody. Wait … it was Melanie! And the other girl was Shannon. The two were twins. Now if only Laura could remember how she knew them!

It was a shame that Melanie and Shannon (whoever they were) couldn't accompany her this time. This was definitely going to be a creepy night.

"Are you nervous?" Mark asked her, setting the bag gently on the ground just inside the gate.

"You bet." Laura scanned the acre-sized area, counting dozens and dozens of headstones. "This place is scary!"

Mark chuckled and put his hand on her shoulder. "Listen, Laura. The scariest thing I had happen during my initiation was when that raccoon got into my face. I'm sure that nothing worse than that will happen to you."

Laura looked up at him. "I'll have to take your word for it, won't I?"

"Of course you don't," he teased. "I could hide in the trees until you fall asleep and then jump out and say 'Boo!'"

"You wouldn't do anything like that to me, would you?" Laura tried to keep a deadpan expression but felt a grin trying to burst through her façade.

"No promises," Mark replied. "But you'll just have to trust that I'm an honest, respectful young man who is too kind to scare the living daylights out of a beautiful young maiden such as yourself."

After he had left, Laura found herself to be in unusually good spirits. She hummed a little tune as she unpacked her duffel bags and laid them out on the ground as a sort of mattress to protect her from the mud. Maybe spending the night here among rows and rows of dead people wouldn't be so bad after all! She kind of wished that Mark would come back and stay to keep her company and talk awhile longer. It was lonely being the only living person around.

She decided to attempt to light a small fire and began to collect sticks and twigs. Unfortunately, most of them were still wet from the rain. But there was no sense in giving up before she'd gotten started. What she needed to do was find the driest twigs of all and arrange them in a teepee shape, all standing up. It would burn better that way.

The woods were now totally immersed in twilight, so Laura went ahead and activated one of the glowstones. Now she could see much better. Eyeing a moderately large tree branch that had to have fallen in the storm, she went to retrieve it and saw that it had landed on top of an old wooden headstone and snapped it in half. Laura moved the branch aside and picked up the wooden slab. It had letters painted on it, but the words were so faded that in that lighting she couldn't tell what it said. She carefully laid the object back down and went to find the lantern, which she easily lit by pressing a metal button on the side. Something mechanical clicked inside and a flame burst into life.

The first word on the headstone had some missing letters, like they had flaked and peeled away long, long ago. It looked like it could have said "Alistair." Laura squinted and turned the headstone in the light, trying to decipher it. Suddenly she felt a pronounced sense of sadness when she realized what it said.

"Alistair Prometheus Owens, beloved son of Sualocin and Tara, loving twin of Arcturus. Born 16 April, 199. Died 7 June, 202." Beneath that, in childish scrawl, were inscribed the words "Rest in peace, brother."

So Lord Arcturus had a twin brother who passed away at the age of three. She wondered if the man could even remember him or if the memory had eventually faded like the old paint she now struggled to read.

Moving down the row, Laura read the next inscriptions.

"Danielle Nevarda Owens, beloved daughter of Sualocin and Tara. Born 19 December, 216. Died 31 December, 216."

"Ronald Aiden Owens, beloved son of Sualocin and Tara. Born 4 March, 204. Died 4 March, 204."

The last headstone in that particular row read, "Cynthia Mimosa Owens, beloved daughter of Sualocin and Tara. Born 10 July, 205. Died 18 August, 205."

Laura blinked back a small tear. How could a mother and father go through so much loss? Of the five children, it appeared that Lord Arcturus was the only one to have survived his infancy. She'd never heard him mention having any siblings. Was infant death really that common among these people?

Strange as it might seem, the monuments of death held Laura captive; and she continued on. The next row of headstones bore the inscriptions of people whose families she did not know; though she did find a few that showed surnames such as Wang, Yelton, and Ericson. The latter headstone was inscribed with the names of two people who had the identical date of death, and Laura assumed that there lay the remains of Mark's mother and father. Someone had placed a bundle of flowers at the base of the grave; but they had wilted and shriveled up, their pink petals dead and lifeless.

Somewhere, an owl hooted.

Wind rustled softly through the ancient trees above, and the sound of a dog howling in the distance rode in on the breeze.

Laura shivered. It really did feel lonely out there.

She returned to her little camp and began constructing her teepee for the fire. She started standing the smallest sticks up in the center and then the larger sticks around the outside. When she finished, she rose and admired her creation. Now all she needed was to figure out how on earth she was going to light it. She chewed her lip. She had no matches and certainly didn't have a lighter. Maybe she could use the lantern! It was fueled with the grease removed from animal lard. She could take some out, smear it on the sticks, and somehow light the fire that way. It just might work.

A sudden, unexpected noise made Laura freeze just as she was about to dump the grease out of the still-burning lantern. At first, she couldn't tell what it had been; but then she heard it again. It was the cracking of sticks underfoot, as if someone was walking toward her.

Laura quickly threw a blanket over the glowstone so nobody would see where she was. Somehow, in her scramble, she kicked over the lantern and made it go out. So much for a fire! But at least now she would be mostly invisible to any unwanted passersby.

A moment later, she could hear a somewhat familiar voice moving past the cemetery gate. Laura's nerves relaxed. It was definitely not someone coming to sneak up on her.

"This is getting ridiculous," she heard the person say. There was a pause and then, "Don't you think this is overkill? Seriously, *Ed*, this is about as low as we can get."

Laura could have sworn that she heard a faint voice angrily mutter something about being disrespected by an ungrateful woman who should know better. At least that's what it sounded like.

The woman's voice spoke again, cruel and condescending. "You are an old fool! You have completely lost your mind!"

Laura was stunned. Louise Wang! There was no mistaking that arrogant tone. But what in the world was she doing out here? And who was she talking to? She had to find out.

Leaving her things behind, she carefully crept out of the dark cemetery and followed the woman at a distance. Louise kept on talking, but she appeared to be unaccompanied by any visible human beings. Yet Laura had heard that soft voice reply to Louise's rant. Was she going insane?

To her surprise, Louise walked right up to the meetinghouse and quietly rapped on the door with a pale, bony fist. Still concealed in the shadows, Laura snuck around the side of the building, just out of sight. She heard the front door open, and Yvonne Harding's voice echoed through the calm night air.

"What are you doing here, Wang?" she demanded, sounding almost angry. "You shouldn't have come. That girl who the Owenses took in is having her initiation tonight in the graveyard. She could have easily seen you walking by."

"Is it a crime for a person to go for a walk in the woods tonight? Nobody will care. I came here because—"

"Shh!" Yvonne interrupted. "Step inside. No sense in having our voices carry."

Luckily for Laura, a window had been left partially open; so she could still hear the unlikely pair's intriguing conversation.

Louise continued. "I think that what you all did is simply *deplorable*," she spat.

Yvonne spoke slowly and firmly. "I did what had to be done."

"You're *sick!*"

Laura peered over the windowsill and saw Louise glaring at Yvonne with her hands planted on her hips. Yvonne stood there coolly, her arms crossed in front of her.

"It is all part of the plan," Yvonne said.

"What *plan?*" Louise looked irritated. "Ever since that boy got himself *lost* all those years ago and Lord Arcturus stumbled across the truth, all you people have talked about is your stupid *plan*. You're all obsessed! I would like to concern myself with my own life for once, not destroying someone else's."

"Do you not agree with what Litchfield has told us to do?"

"You know I don't! I mean, I did in the beginning, but now… I made my feelings clear to him when we were talking a few minutes ago."

Louise had been talking to Litchfield? How could that be?

"And what did he say to you?"

"Among … ahem … other things, he told me to trust him and that my services would be justly rewarded in the end. But this is just absurd! Starting rumors and the like? Just to discredit some fool to keep Litchfield's perfect little world in line? Yvonne, I just want to stay home and take care of my family like any other woman would. We even have a grandchild on the way! I'm tired of this whole ordeal. Aren't you?"

"No. This is the way it should be."

But Louise was adamant. "What I don't understand is why it would be so terrible if everyone knew the truth! I know I swore to secrecy, but sometimes I just want to climb up on a pulpit and shout to the people about the way things truly are. Could it really be that bad? At least I'd be able to end this foolish masquerade. I mean, I never disliked the Owenses. Actually, I always thought they were a decent family. Their son is even courting Nicole!"

"I do not question Litchfield's orders."

"*I'll* question whoever orders I want to. I'm nobody's slave." Louise turned to go but then halted. "Great, it's him again." She paused. "Yes, *sir*, I am talking to Yvonne right now. Yes. She agrees with you. Don't worry. I haven't organized a revolt against you, though you most certainly deserve it."

There was another long pause, and Laura thought she could hear the faint, angry voice again.

"I don't want to argue with you anymore. You know what I think."

Yvonne stood there with a smirk on her face. "He's going to kill you if you keep that up, honey."

Louise snorted and turned to go a second time. "Oh, I meant to ask you. Are you the one who made that Matarna girl go off and break into the storage building?"

"Yes. Why?"

"Because that was incredibly infantile if you ask me." Then, "I hope you can still hear me, Edward Litchfield!"

Yvonne ignored the woman's latter remark. "Infantile or not," she replied, "it was all part of the plan."

Laura was stunned. She was still crouching outside the window, her mind whirling. What in the name of heaven could this sinister-sounding "plan" be all about? She found it hard to believe that Yvonne could be in on whatever it was, especially if it involved hurting the Owens family in any way. But perhaps the most surprising thing of all was that Louise Wang was against it.

She began to feel frightened. What had been the deplorable act that Louise had spoken of? Surely they couldn't have been referring to Spica's disappearance. She forced the terrible thought from her mind.

But one thought remained.

Rochelle had been right. Litchfield was furious with Lord Arcturus and was going to make his life a living hell.

And it seemed as if it had already begun.

CHAPTER 11

Laura cracked open an eyelid. She was lying in a heap of blankets in the middle of the graveyard, with almost no memory of having gone to bed. She did remember spying on Yvonne and Louise. Fortunately, neither of the two women had noticed her hiding outside the meetinghouse. She wondered what would have happened if they did.

She sat up and stretched. With luck, she would have dreamed the whole ordeal.

Who am I kidding? she asked herself.

She began packing up her things, shaking the dirt off before stuffing them back into the duffel bags. The ground was covered in tiny droplets of morning dew. So was the stack of wood she had never burned. The lantern still lay on its side from when she had kicked it over. Just as she bent to pick it up, a voice behind her made her leap about half a foot off the ground.

"Hi there, Laura!"

Laura spun around, coming face-to-face with Yvonne. How had the woman snuck up so quietly? "Oh! It's you," she said. "You just scared the crap out of me."

Yvonne laughed. Her manner seemed to be perfectly normal, as if she wasn't the least bit involved in a plot to harm the Owens family. "I came up here to make sure that you made it through the night. You know, it isn't easy surviving in a forest full of raccoons. Did you happen to see any?"

"Nope."

"Really? That's surprising." Yvonne paused, studying Laura's face. "Are you feeling okay? You look pale."

Laura gulped and tried her best to pretend that nothing unusual had happened the night before. "I'm fine," she said. "Just a little tired."

"I see. Did you have trouble falling asleep?"

"Not really. I'm just not used to camping out in the woods." That was a lie, but Yvonne didn't need to know that.

"I know exactly what you mean. There's nothing better than the comfort of one's own bed. Though, learning how to survive in the wild is never a bad idea. It makes people tougher and better able to withstand the forces of nature."

"Yeah." Laura was beginning to feel frustrated. Why wouldn't Yvonne just leave? After hearing what she and Louise had been discussing, she knew that she could no longer trust the woman. What if Yvonne found out that she'd been eavesdropping and tried to hurt her?

"So, how was last night?"

Laura blinked. "How was what?"

"The initiation, of course."

"Oh!" Laura quickly came up with something to say. "It was ... nice. I, uh, looked around at a bunch of those headstones. I found Lord Arcturus's brothers and sisters. I didn't know he had a twin."

Yvonne nodded. "Alistair died before I was born so I never knew him. Apparently, he died of the influenza. Lord Sualocin and Lady Tara lost so many babies to disease." She sighed, and a wistful gleam appeared in her eye. "Unfortunately, I understand how they felt. My husband and I lost a daughter ourselves. It was very, very sad. But we had to remain strong for our other children. And life went on."

"Don't you just feel sorry for Lord Arcturus and Lady Capella?" Laura asked, testing the woman to see how she would respond. "Spica has been missing since Saturday, and Procyon has been missing for years. They're probably going through the same pain that you did."

To her surprise, Yvonne smirked. Couldn't she even *pretend* to care? "If you ask me, I'd say the lord and lady brought it upon themselves. They don't watch their children closely enough. It's no wonder Spica and Procyon disappeared. Nobody was looking after them! Let it be a lesson to all parents. If you don't have your kids constantly at your side, they're going to get hurt."

Laura decided that this was one of the most heartless women that she would ever meet. "Where are *your* children right now, Yvonne?" she said, feeling proud that she had suddenly mustered the courage to be snide. "It doesn't look like you're watching them closely enough."

Two spots of color appeared on Yvonne's cheeks. "For your information, they are spending time with their grandmother this morning. Not that it's any of your business."

Laura silently gathered the rest of her things and picked up her bags and lantern. "I guess not." She turned to leave.

"Laura..."

She stopped and looked at Yvonne. "What?"

"Members of the Woodland Youth are required to treat their elders with respect. I don't know what's gotten into you, but I expect it to end right now. Do I make myself clear?"

"Uh huh. See you later, Yvonne."

Laura strode out the gate and down the path without looking back, glad to be away from the woman. She was sure that Yvonne was furious with her now, but she didn't really care. If the woman was trying to hurt the Owenses, then she wasn't planning on treating her with the least bit of respect—not now, not ever.

When she reached the eastern edge of town, she immediately sensed that something was wrong. The streets and fields were vacant, save for a few scrawny cats that were crouched down on the ground outside the tavern, munching on table scraps they must have swiped. Where was everybody?

She heard a yell from off in the distance and looked up the road. Gasping at what she saw, she broke into a run.

It looked as if every person in town had formed a mob on Lord Arcturus's front lawn. She could see some people shaking their fists in the air. One man held a pitchfork and was shouting a string of profanities at nobody in particular. Children were crying. Frank Yelton and Andrew Walker stood at the back of the crowd, ordering everyone to please return to their homes. Nobody seemed to pay them any heed. They were too focused on the brawl that was occurring in front of them.

Laura saw Lady Capella shrieking at Adalbert Wang and brandishing a rather large wooden rolling pin at him. The man shouted something back at her, and she swung the utensil with incredible might directly at his face. It made a resounding crunch that made Laura and several others wince. Adalbert clutched his bleeding nose in pain. It was probably broken. She didn't know whether or not to feel sorry for him, since she was uncertain if he shared his wife's rebellious views.

Lord Arcturus was engaged in a heated fistfight with some men Laura didn't recognize. He knocked one of them down but took a heavy blow to the eye in the act. He grimaced in pain and began cursing almost as badly as the man with the pitchfork.

Laura stashed her bags under a tree and carefully approached Andrew, whose voice had gone hoarse. "What the heck is going on?" she said, trying not to draw too much attention to herself. If the lord and lady were being attacked, then she could be at risk as well.

"The village council has placed Lord Arcturus under house arrest for the alleged murder of Spica," he replied. A rather large vein in his forehead was bulging, and his face was crimson.

Laura felt her jaw drop open. "What? You don't mean...They didn't find a *body*, did they?"

"Not yet."

"Then why—?"

"They're keeping him here while the evidence is being reviewed," Frank added bitterly. It looked like he had finally given up trying to send people away. "Lord knows how long that will be. Could be weeks."

"But that's horrible! Why would they even *think* he did something like that? They don't have any proof!"

"According to them, they do." Frank shook his head.

"But we've got to do something!" Laura was enraged. "They can't just lock up an innocent man in his own house!" She wished she could march right up there and join the bloody fight but knew that it would only complicate things.

"You want to help out?" asked Andrew, reading the look in her eyes. "Go find Spica, wherever in the world she might be, and bring her home so this whole mess can be cleared up once and for all."

Again, Laura could sense the otherworldly message in her mind. Only this time it was more urgent than ever.

Follow the sunset!

And for the first time, she understood exactly what she was supposed to do.

"Follow the sunset?" Rochelle repeated, looking perplexed. "I'm not so sure I understand."

Laura had spotted the young woman in the crowd and urged her to come with her so they could talk. Now they were walking down to the riverbank, which was far enough away from the mob that there wasn't a chance of being overheard.

"You told me that the best thing to do would be to pray, so I did. And ever since, I've kept having that message show up in my head. 'Follow the sunset. It is there where the answers lie.'"

Rochelle nodded. "Okay. So what do you plan on doing? Are you actually going to try to 'follow the sunset'?"

"Why not? If it really is a message from God and isn't just me going nuts, I think it would be a good idea."

By this time, they had reached the river. Laura sat herself on a large, mossy boulder; and Rochelle plopped down in the grass.

"The thing is, Laura, virtually nobody travels outside this valley because Litchfield has brainwashed everyone into thinking that it's wrong. And there really are dangerous animals out there. If you really want to go searching for Spica, then you shouldn't go alone. Not by any means. And if I were you, I wouldn't announce where you're going to too many people. You do not want the whole town to know."

"Well, would you want to go with me?" Laura crossed her fingers. If Rochelle went too, she wouldn't be as lonely.

"I don't know. The Owenses might need me at home."

"They might like it better if you helped find Spica."

"True."

"And you said that you used to go hiking."

"I did. That's how I ended up here."

"So you wouldn't have any problem walking for miles and miles out in the mountains."

"Not really. I might get a little sore from having not hiked in about four years, but it wouldn't bother me for long."

"We could be gone for days."

Rochelle sighed. "I know. We'd need to carry a lot of supplies with us: blankets, glowstones, food … I think it would be even better if we found a burly young lad to come with us to help out."

The image of Mark Ericson's smiling face immediately materialized in her mind's eye. "I think I know someone who might want to come with us," she said. "If he agrees, does that mean you'll go too?"

The young woman laughed. "I guess it does! If you're right and we do find Spica, then that would be the most wonderful thing to have ever happened to the lord and lady. When do you think we should leave?"

"Uh..." Laura bit her lip. "What about this evening? I could go try to find Mark right now to see if he's willing to go."

"And if he isn't?"

"Then it will just be you and me."

"I don't like that idea."

"We could ask Andrew."

Rochelle shook her head. "That man is busy enough trying to keep the villagers in line. And now he'll even have to make sure our house is under watch at all times so Lord Arcturus doesn't try to escape."

"What about Rotanev?"

The woman snorted. "As if."

Laura stood up. "Well, I'll go try to find Mark and see what he wants to do. If he says no, then we'll try thinking of alternatives."

"Good luck." Rochelle rose from the ground and brushed the soil off of her dress. "I'll head home and start getting some supplies together. And let me tell you: we are *not* going on an expedition wearing these dresses. We'll have to borrow some of Rotanev's or Alcor's clothes."

Laura was fortunate enough to spot Mark walking down the road into town. The young man looked irritable and was muttering to himself, running his hands nervously over his scalp. She guessed that his behavior had something to do with Lord Arcturus's house arrest.

"Mark!" she called. "I need to ask you something!"

Mark jerked in surprise and stopped. He gave her a slight smile; but she could tell that, in reality, he was far from being happy.

"What is it?" he asked.

Laura glanced around to make sure that no people were within earshot and saw that a few others were now returning from the

Owenses' yard. "Um, can we talk somewhere else? I don't want anyone to hear us."

"Okay…" Mark stared at her with distinct curiosity. "If you'd like, we could go inside the tavern. The only person who will be there right now is the bartender, and he's been deaf for as long as I've known him."

"That should be fine. We need to hurry."

Mark shrugged, obviously confused. Laura followed him inside the cool, dark building and took a seat in one of the booths along the far wall. The elderly bartender sat in a stool at the counter and waved at Mark when he saw them. He held up a small slate and tapped it with a piece of chalk, but Mark waved his hand in dismissal.

Laura hoped that the man was as deaf as Mark claimed.

"What is this all about?" Mark asked after they had sat down. "You look very passionate about something. It suits you well."

Ignoring the compliment, Laura began to explain. "Rochelle and I are going to go hunt for Spica, and we wondered if you'd be willing to help us. She said that we need a burly young man to go too."

Mark chuckled. "I guess that means I'm burly. Sure. I'll go with you. I need to get out of this ignorant village for a while. My grandfather and I were completely livid when Adalbert Wang announced Lord Arcturus's arrest this morning. The Owenses had just gotten back from Upton when Adalbert showed up at their door with his stupid decree. It was awful." His eyes took on a look of sorrow. "It really is too bad about Spica. She's only seven years old. A little mischievous and bratty at times but still an endearing kid. Sometimes I wish I had some siblings like her." He sighed. "Where were you planning on going? I think they've searched the whole valley already."

Laura thought it would be better if she didn't mention the messages she had been receiving. "I think we should explore the mountains west of the valley. If Spica really was kidnapped, then that might be a good place for them to hide her."

To her surprise, Mark blanched. "I'm not so sure that's a good idea," he said.

"Why not? Spica needs to be found and returned to her family. We might as well look there since nobody else has."

"You don't understand." Mark glanced down at the table, avoiding Laura's gaze. "That's where my parents were killed."

"I thought you had come to terms with that."

"I have. But if there are still bears living out there and we just go barging into their domain, they could kill us too. I *don't* want to meet the same fate as my parents. And I don't want you to either."

"Then we should take some weapons with us. Do you have any bows and arrows or maybe a rifle?"

"I don't know what a rifle is. I do have arrows, though."

"Good."

"Have you ever shot an arrow before?"

Laura shook her head. "No, but I could learn how."

He laughed. "It takes a while to get the hang of it, and you need to have some muscle, like this." He held up his arm and flexed his finely toned bicep, which was easily three times as large as Laura's.

Laura smiled. "Nice! So you could protect us. Couldn't you?"

Mark grew somber again. "Laura, ever since I was a child, the adults would tell us this little rhyme: 'Stay safe here in the valley, friend, or you will meet your bitter end!' And after my parents died, I took it to heart."

"But Spica needs us. If she's being held captive out there, we might be her only hope for escape."

Mark sighed. "I suppose you're right. I'll think about it."

"Good!" Laura was delighted. "Come up to the house this evening to let us know what you've decided. Rochelle and I are going to leave tonight. So if you're coming, you need to be ready. And please don't tell your grandfather where we're going."

The crowd around the Owenses' house finally dissipated, and Andrew Walker woefully assigned a grumpy-looking youth to guard the entrance to the home. Laura noticed that Lady Capella's flowers had been trampled to a pulp by the uncaring mob. Tabitha Owens excused herself from dinner; and Laura saw the girl squatting out on the lawn, doing her best to save the poor plants. The guard stood nearby, watching her with a look of disgust.

Everyone else was sitting around the large dining room table, deep in discussion.

"This ordeal has gone way too far," Sualocin Owens stated. His plate of food remained untouched in front of him. "Now that almost every citizen of our valley has been turned against us, what is there for us to do?"

Lord Arcturus sat glowering in his usual spot at the head of the table. His arms were folded tightly across his chest, and his eyes seemed to be boring an invisible hole in the opposite wall. His right eye was swollen and bruised from the fight, giving him a rather rough appearance. "They don't understand," he said hoarsely. "They just don't see that they're making our pain a hundred times worse by doing this."

His wife nodded in silent agreement.

Sualocin spoke again. "It seems to me that someone is deliberately trying to give us a bad name, but I fail to see the reason why."

Lord Arcturus snorted. "Trying? Looks to me like they've already succeeded."

"Arcturus, you've got to think back," his father said. "Is there *any-thing* that you could have done to somebody that would make them try to hurt us like this? Anything at all? Perhaps you inadvertently insulted someone at a town council meeting or wrongfully accused someone of a crime?"

Lord Arcturus didn't answer, and Laura and Rochelle exchanged significant glances. Apparently he hadn't even told his family about whatever he had done to bring Litchfield's wrath upon him.

Rochelle cleared her throat. "Laura and I have a plan that can prove your innocence."

The man looked up, interested. "What might that be?"

"We're going to go out and find Spica," Laura said.

Mark still had not arrived, and she was beginning to wonder if he would show up at all.

"Do you really think anyone is going to find her after all this time? It's been days."

The hopeless look in his eyes drove a nail right through Laura's heart, and she could feel tears forming but hurriedly blinked them away.

"Arcturus, it's worth another try," Lady Capella said. "If they are willing to go out of their way to search for our daughter, then so be it. We must not give up hope."

"That's what you said about Procyon," her husband said softly.

Lady Capella gave a sorrowful nod. "I remember, Arcturus. But this time is different." Then, to Laura, she said, "I would even go with you myself if I wasn't bearing this child. But I cannot risk bringing harm to our infant. Where will you two go?"

"I was thinking that we could start out heading west into the mountains. It seemed—"

"No!"

The room was filled with an echoing silence. All heads turned and stared at Lord Arcturus, whose face had drained of color. His black eye stood out like a violent purple ring.

"No?" his wife repeated coldly. "They're offering to look for our daughter and that's all you can say?"

Lord Arcturus gave his wife a pleading look. "They *can't* go there … *anywhere* but there. Do you even realize what's out in those mountains?"

Laura's pulse quickened. What could the man be so afraid of? "Mark Ericson might be going with us," she said. "He can help protect us from anything dangerous that might be out there."

"You do know that we're going anyway, no matter what you tell us," Rochelle added.

"You could die out there."

Before either Laura or Rochelle had a chance to reply, the front door opened and Tabitha stepped inside. The front of her dress was covered in dirt and pieces of grass.

"Someone's here to see you," she said to Laura.

Mark came in behind her. He was carrying a large, brown canvas sack that was bulging with what Laura assumed was supplies for their journey. He also wore a quiver of arrows slung across his back and had a machete tucked into a sheath in his belt.

"I decided that I'd help you all out," he announced. "So here I am."

Laura found herself beaming. "I knew you'd come!"

"Thank you, Mark," Lady Capella said to the young man. She glanced over at her husband. "It means a lot to us."

Lord Arcturus made no response.

"Oh, it's nothing. Really."

Rochelle stood up. "I'm going to go grab my things. I've been packed for hours. Rotanev, Laura and I need to borrow some of your clothes so we don't have to hike in these dresses. You're just a little bigger than we are, so I think they'll fit just fine."

"Sure. I'll go find some." The somber youth rose from his chair in the corner and trudged up the steps to his room. He came back down a minute later with two brown pairs of wrinkled trousers, two leather belts, and two crumpled-up, short-sleeved cotton shirts. "I found them in the bottom of my dresser," he explained, handing the outfits to Laura and Rochelle.

Laura hurried up to her room and tried changing into the boy's clothing as fast as she could. The shirt was somewhat baggy, and the pants were about two inches too long; but she knew she had no other choice but to wear them. Luckily, Rochelle had lent her a pair of sturdy leather boots so Laura wouldn't wear out her shoes, which had not been designed for hiking.

She grabbed a comb and a new ribbon and quickly redid the braid in her hair. Then she began scooping various last-minute items into her duffel bag, including her pillow and a few spare sets of socks and undergarments. She didn't pack much more than that, since she knew Rochelle had already gathered everything they would need.

Laura slung the bag over her shoulder and went to leave the room. When she opened her bedroom door, she was startled to see Lord Arcturus waiting outside in the hallway for her.

"I wanted to warn you about something before you leave," he said. "It's important that you listen."

Laura blinked. "Okay. What is it?"

The man glanced down the hallway to make sure they were alone and then lowered his voice. "When I was searching for my son, Procyon, seven years ago, I headed deep into the mountains to see if he had wandered along one of the streams that run down into the valley. On my second or third day out, I found … something."

When he didn't elaborate, Laura asked, "What was it?"

Lord Arcturus shook his head. "I can't tell you."

"Why not?"

"Because I could lose my life. Laura, I have never told a single soul about what I found out there, not even Capella. It haunts me to this very day, knowing that the information I now know could harm my family and I."

"It already *is* harming you, isn't it?"

The man nodded. "You are an excellent observer. If I hadn't ever ventured out into the west, none of this would have ever come about. I am almost certain that Spica's kidnapping resulted from it. Of course, I will never tell Capella. She doesn't need to know that everything that's happened is my fault."

"But it isn't your fault. It's Litchfield's fault."

Lord Arcturus gave her a strange look. "I'm not even going to ask how you know that," he said. "But anyway, you three must be prepared to encounter the unexpected and to pay the penalty if you do. I find it very odd that you are going to look for Spica in the very place I wish I'd never gone."

Laura decided to tell him the truth. "Actually, that's where God told me to go. But you probably don't know who that is, do you?"

To her surprise, the man smiled. "I *do* know who God is. He's one of the nicer things I found out there in those mountains."

CHAPTER 12

"Are we all ready?" Rochelle finally asked, having double- and triple-checked the contents of her bag to make sure she had packed all of what she needed.

Laura was filled with nervous anticipation and wanted to get started as soon as possible. It had begun to grow darker outside, and the wind was picking up. She hoped it wouldn't storm again.

"I think so," she said.

"Well, if you've forgotten anything, you'll have to make do without it. We are *not* turning back until we've found her."

"Sounds fine to me," said Mark. "I say we leave now before it gets any darker out there."

They all rose and made their way to the back door so their unwelcome guard would not see them and become curious.

"Wait a minute," Lady Capella said as they were about to leave. She hurried out of the room and returned moments later holding a six-foot-long spear. "This belonged to my father. You can use it to defend yourself against wild animals, and it can also be used as a walking staff." She handed it to Laura. "Use it wisely. I don't want to find out that any of you accidentally impaled yourself with it."

"Thanks!" Laura said, admiring the weapon. The wood of the shaft had been smoothed from years of use, and the point was about three inches long and carved out of brown flint like an Indian arrowhead. The edges were serrated.

Lord Arcturus spoke. "Please be careful, all of you. And good luck." He had a very sorrowful look about him, his face long and forlorn.

"Don't worry," said Rochelle. "We will be."

And with that, they set out into the night.

The edge of the forest grew right along the Owenses' yard and sheep pasture, so the three of them had no trouble slipping undercover. The wind whistled through the trees above them. Laura prayed that a branch wouldn't fall out and crush anyone. They walked in silence for the first few minutes, save for the crunching and snapping of dry sticks and leaves underfoot. That is, until Laura turned her ankle in an unseen hole and stumbled.

"Ouch!' she said, massaging where it hurt. Fortunately, her boots were thick enough to prevent her from seriously injuring herself.

"Are you okay?" Mark asked. He stopped and helped her to her feet.

"Yeah. I'm fine. I just twisted my ankle a little. I really wish I had a flashlight right now."

"I'm not going to bother asking what that is."

Rochelle laughed. "Just think of a glowstone in a tube that you can turn on and off without dousing it with water."

"I see."

"I sure wish *I* could," Laura said. "I don't want to trip and fall on my face out here!"

"But if you did, maybe you'd conk your head hard enough that you'd remember who you are," Mark said with a twinkle in his eye. Then, seeming to realize what he had just said, he sobered. "I hope you know I'm just teasing you."

"That still wasn't very nice," said Rochelle.

Laura grinned. "Actually, I thought it was kind of funny. Maybe if I do hit my head it'll be a good thing!"

She thought back to the week before, when she had first arrived in Sparkling Falls, alone, scared, bewildered... She was surprised by how much she had changed in just a few days' time. Though still confused at the customs and beliefs of the villagers, she was beginning to feel quite at home, as if this was where she was meant to be. She was thankful that the knot on her head had slowly gone away. She had barely given it any thought since Spica had gone missing. Somehow, locating the child had become paramount in her mind.

"I don't see why we can't use the lantern," Mark said a few minutes later after he had gotten caught in a tangle of thorns and Laura and Rochelle had struggled to free him. "Laura's right. One of us could get hurt. Then we'd have to go back home and this would have been one big waste of time."

"We're still too close to the village. If someone sees a light out here, they might get nosy and come see what we're up to. Keep in mind that we're up high enough that anyone in town would be able to see it. So for the time being, we'll have to tread carefully to avoid any accidents."

"Hmm. I guess you're right. So when can we light it?"

"When we're over the first ridge."

"What? That will take hours in the dark! It must be hundreds of feet ahead of us."

"We'll be able to see better with the moon rising. Be tough, Mark. Be tough."

Mark gave a melodramatic sigh, most likely for Laura's amusement; and they pressed on.

Laura was already beginning to feel the strain on her muscles from carrying a heavy bag across her back. Her boots were chafing her feet through her thin socks, and the backs of her legs burned from trudging up the terrain that sloped steeper and steeper as they went. She briefly wondered how long she would hold out before collapsing into an exhausted heap. She stopped a few times and leaned on her spear for support while she caught her breath.

"Feeling tired?" Rochelle asked her a quarter of an hour or so later. The thin crescent moon had finally peeked its face over the eastern mountains behind them, casting a dim twilight upon the forest.

"Uh huh." Laura was panting heavily. "Are we there yet?"

"Nope. But we've made some progress. See?"

"Rochelle, you're killing us," Mark said. He appeared to be in fine condition himself but held a look of concern on his face when he saw how tired Laura was.

"We'll be there soon enough. I tell you what: when we get to the ridge, we can set up camp for the night. Will that make you two happy?"

"Sounds good to me," Laura mumbled. She let out a prolonged yawn. "Wake me when we get there."

An indeterminate amount of time had passed when they came to a rocky outcropping, and Rochelle announced that they would now stop. The land beyond sloped down into a small gully where the wind had blown countless leaves, creating a natural sort of mattress.

"I don't think it could be any later than eleven o'clock," Rochelle said. "But if we get some sleep now, we can set out bright and early in the morning."

"And we'll have to be on the lookout for footprints and things," Laura said. "Maybe there's a road or a trail out here they could have followed."

"It's a shame that both of Spica's hair ribbons were already found," Mark mused. "It would have been nice to find one out here just to make sure we're heading in the right direction."

Laura unpacked her bag and laid her blankets down on the ground. Unfortunately, the land here was not flat and smooth like it had been the previous night up at the cemetery. The leaves did little to cushion the hardness of the ground or the debris lying on top of it. When she lay down to rest, it felt like a miniature mountain range was digging into her spine.

Mark seemed to be experiencing similar discomfort. "Rochelle, you have picked the most magnificent place for us to sleep tonight," he commented, removing several knobby sticks and a rock or two from beneath his sleeping bag.

Rochelle laughed. "Don't mention it! Tomorrow night we should probably set up camp when it's still light out so we can clear all the forest debris away *before* we go to bed."

"That sounds like a plan."

"Can we light the lantern now?" Laura asked. She wasn't certain that she liked the idea of falling asleep in almost total darkness. The trees were growing thick enough on this part of the mountain that the feeble light of the moon barely fell upon them.

"Not if we're going to be sleeping. I don't want to waste the fuel."

"We could use a glowstone instead. That's what I used last night at my initiation."

"Oh fine." Rochelle sprinkled some water over one of the glowstones and laid the object down in the center of their tiny camp. "I didn't know you were afraid of the dark."

"It isn't the dark I'm afraid of. It's the things hiding in the dark that I can't see." Laura closed her eyes. "Like ninjas."

Rochelle let out a snort. "Only you, Laura. Only you."

The wind finally died down to a whisper, and it didn't take long for Laura to fall asleep. At first, her subconscious mind was at peace; but then…

A daggerlike icicle hung from a swaying tree branch. A large snowball sailed through the air and knocked it loose. She watched the icicle fall in slow motion and pierce the chest of the man standing underneath. He collapsed, clutching his chest in agony. People began to shout.

There was blood everywhere.

She woke up gasping. Her face was covered in sweat.

Their camp was immersed in darkness, the glowstone having gone out at some point during her disturbed rest. She stretched her arms out and glanced around for a few moments, unable to see. Why couldn't humans be equipped with night vision like animals were? Then she wouldn't have to keep bothering Rochelle about lighting a glowstone every time it got dark. After minute or two, her eyes adjusted and she could see the dim outline of Rochelle lying across from her.

"Laura, are you okay?" came a whisper from her right.

She jumped, not knowing that Mark had been awake. "I'm fine," she replied. "I was just having a nightmare."

"You were talking and thrashing around in your sleep. It woke me up." He laughed. "Actually, you kicked me pretty hard in the leg."

"Sorry about that. I didn't know." She sat up and looked over at him. "What kind of things was I saying?"

"Some of it was garbled and didn't make a lot of sense, but I did hear you say something like, 'Uncle Tom! Watch out!' and then, 'It was all my fault!'"

His words—or hers, rather—gave her the chills. "I really said that?"

"Yes, you did."

Laura shivered. "Can we go somewhere and talk now that we're both awake? I don't want to bother Rochelle."

"That's fine with me. And I'm sure she won't mind either."

Mark stood up and helped Laura to her feet. He grabbed the lantern and turned it on, being careful not to shine the light in Rochelle's direction. He and Laura strolled farther down the gully until they reached a small stream. Laura sat down on the ground and rested her chin on her hand. "You know how I can't remember who I am?" she said.

"Yes. What about it?"

"Well, I've had this same nightmare or vision or whatever you want to call it a few different times since I lost my memory. I always see a gigantic icicle up in a tree, and then it falls and impales a guy in the chest." She shuddered. "And the scary thing is, I know it must have really happened. Part of my brain is trying to remember it. But the worst part is that I know it was my fault. I must have thrown the snowball that knocked it down." Tears began leaking from her eyes. "I hurt somebody really badly. There was so much blood!"

Mark gently took her hand and gave it a tender squeeze. "Please don't cry, Laura. The man might have been okay. Can you remember anything else about it?"

"No." She sniffled. "He's probably dead."

"You don't know that."

"I know, but I don't see how a person could live after having a two-foot-long hunk of ice plunge into their body."

Mark shrugged. "True, but miracles do happen. If the icicle just pierced his skin and missed his heart and lungs, then he'd have been fine. Right?"

"Maybe. But, Mark, I just don't know what to do! I can't remember who I am. I got whisked here through a portal. I have visions of blood and icicles…"

"But you found me in the middle of all that."

Laura looked up and saw that Mark was smiling at her, and she began to relax. "You're right. If I had never come here, I never would have met such a fine young gentleman, would I?"

"Nope. Not in a million years."

Laura laughed. "Thanks for trying to cheer me up."

"I can do that any time you need me to."

She gazed into his sparkling, almond-shaped eyes. The flickering light from the lantern reflected in his irises and made them appear to be glowing with inner warmth.

"May I kiss you?" he asked.

The question caught Laura by surprise. "I guess so! That is, if you really want to."

"Good! Because I've heard that it can cheer up gloomy young ladies named Laura."

He bent down and kissed her gently on the lips. "How was that?" he asked with a wink.

Laura giggled. "It was lovely. Would it be too bold if I asked you to do that again?"

"Not at all!"

This time, Laura stood up on tiptoe and wrapped her arms around his neck.

"That was fun," Laura said a minute later, brushing Mark's wavy hair back out of his face and tucking it behind his ear. "And you smell good, like oatmeal cookies."

"Thank you." He paused and looked down at her. "If you're ever feeling upset about *anything*, I will always be here to listen. I just want you to know that." He gave her hand a squeeze. "Now we'd better get back to camp and get some sleep!"

"*And* we don't want Rochelle to wake up and think we've been sneaking off together!"

"Wouldn't that just be awful?"

They both laughed, and the two of them walked hand in hand back to their sleeping bags. Much more peaceful and content than she had been, Laura slept soundly for the rest of the night.

"Wake up! Let's get a move on!"

Laura groaned when Rochelle's voice roused her. The sun had not fully risen, so she assumed that it must have been around six o'clock in the morning. She would have preferred to sleep in for a few more hours, but they had a missing child to find.

Rochelle gave her a strip of dried beef jerky, which Laura rinsed down with some water from her canteen. She walked down to the stream to refill it when she had finished. She said a short prayer for Spica's safety as she gazed at her distorted reflection in the flowing water. How would it feel to be a little girl taken away from her family? If Yvonne Harding really was the kidnapper, would Spica even *know* she was being kidnapped?

When she arrived back at the camp, Laura saw that Mark had been a gentleman and packed up her duffel bag for her. Of course, he was acting nonchalant about it, packing up his own bag and whistling a little tune to himself. She smiled.

"Thanks."

Mark jerked his head up, pretending to be startled that she was there. "What?"

"Thanks for packing my bag."

"Hmm. I don't know what you're talking about. It must have been the spirits of the mountain. They've been known to do that kind of thing."

"You can be so odd sometimes."

"You know it."

"Okay, you lovebirds, do we have everything?" Rochelle asked, scanning the ground in case they had missed any of their things.

"Yeah. I think we're good," said Laura.

"And whoever said that we're lovebirds?" asked Mark. "I think Rochelle is imagining things, Laura. Don't you?"

Laura decided to play along. "I think so."

Rochelle laughed. "Don't think you can hide the sparks of young love from wise old Rochelle."

Mark let out a snort. "Since when is twenty-two old?"

"It isn't. The truth is, I was awake during your semi-romantic encounter last night."

"Brilliant."

"Okay!" Embarrassed, Laura decided to change the subject. "It looks like there's a deer trail over there we can follow. It might be easier if we can see a path." She hoisted up her duffel bag and took hold of her spear-tipped walking stick. Why did Rochelle have to witness her kissing Mark?

They continued their ascent up the small, wooded mountain and reached its rounded peak a short time later.

"Laura," Mark said as they sought an easy path downward, "it just occurred to me that the witnesses said they saw Spica down near the river. So why are we heading out this way?"

"Nobody else has looked here. They could have taken a boat up the river for a few miles and then cut through the woods up into the mountains."

"I guess that's possible. It would certainly lead everyone in the opposite direction."

"You know," said Rochelle, "we're lucky that these mountains aren't like the Rockies. We went there once when I was a kid. The peaks were so high up they were covered in snow. These mountains look like anthills compared to them!"

"If these were the Rockies, we'd be in big trouble." Laura couldn't imagine what climbing a snowcapped peak would be like. It sounded like torture.

"It *is* strange, though. This range here looks just like the Appalachians. It's got the same kind of ridge-and-valley landscape."

"Where exactly was it that you went through the portal?"

"I'm not completely sure. I started out in West Virginia, but I was focusing more on the scenery than my location. I think I might have crossed the eastern border into Virginia at some point before I got zapped here." Rochelle sighed and brushed her sweaty hair back out of her eyes. "It was so beautiful there. I had actually considered moving to West Virginia to start a new life for myself. I was even studying to become a US citizen because Canada meant nothing to me anymore. Anyway, I had taken hundreds of pictures on my camera, but I was obviously never able to get them developed. Unfortunately, I didn't have anyone whom I could have shared them with. I was a really lonely person."

"And now you have a crazy teenage girl and a strapping young lad to keep you company," Mark said, throwing both Laura and Rochelle a flirtatious wink.

"Hey now! I am *not* crazy!" Laura protested, laughing.

"Sure you are. You're friends with Rochelle."

"He's right you know," Rochelle said. She stepped around a pile of deer droppings that some inconsiderate animal had left lying in the path. "Ugh. That's lovely."

Mark, who had taken the lead, halted so abruptly that Laura and Rochelle almost smacked into him.

"What's going on?" asked Laura. "Why did you stop?"

"Look at that," Mark said, gesturing at the ground about six yards in front of him.

Just off the side of the narrow path lay a mangled deer carcass. Not much was left of it other than some bones and sinew. A few flies buzzed around like miniature vultures devouring what remained of the flesh.

Laura wrinkled her nose. "That's disgusting."

"I'm not talking about the deer. I'm talking about those animal tracks around it."

"Huh?"

They all stepped closer; and sure enough, there were dozens of paw prints in the dried mud. They looked like they could have been from a large dog or...

"Please don't tell me that those are wolf tracks," said Rochelle, her face growing slightly paler.

Laura knew that there weren't many animals that had feet that large. She turned to look at Mark, whose mouth had formed a straight line.

"I really hope they aren't," he said, "but I don't see what else they could be from. We're going to have to be extra careful from now on, especially at night. I don't want any of us to end our journey as wolf chow."

CHAPTER 13

Laura couldn't have been more grateful for the day's excellent weather. Climbing down the mountainside forced her to use muscles she never even knew she had. She was coated in sweat, and her back ached from the unusual strain. If it had been any hotter, she would have probably passed out.

Hour after hour they hiked. Laura made sure to keep her eyes peeled for anything out of the ordinary. Every once in a while, Mark would stop and examine the ground for footprints; but they usually turned out to be from a deer or a raccoon.

"I don't think any human beings have been out this way," he said some time later. "There just aren't any of the signs you'd expect to see. People leave boot tracks or hoof marks if they're riding on horseback."

"I *know* this is the right direction," Laura insisted. "We just have to keep on going until we've found something."

"Such as Spica?" said Rochelle, who had temporarily taken the lead as they followed the winding deer path. "Don't forget that she's the reason we're out here."

"I haven't forgotten." Laura was thoughtful. "You might think this is strange, but I have this feeling like there's something else out here too, something much bigger than Spica."

"Grizzly bears are bigger than Spica," Mark commented. "And I'm sure there are some out here somewhere."

"That's not what I'm talking about!"

"What *are* you talking about?" asked Rochelle.

"It's kind of hard to explain. I mean, I know that I was sent out here for a reason. That voice in my head told me, 'Follow the sunset. It is there where the answers lie.' So even if we don't find Spica out here, I think we'll be able to find something that will lead us to her."

"We had *better* find her," said Mark, "because I really doubt we're going to find a sign out here that says, 'Spica This Way.'"

"You goof. That isn't what I meant at all! I...never mind."

Laura knew what she wanted to say but was having trouble putting it into words. God was supposed to work in mysterious ways. But how could Mark ever understand when he knew nothing of God?

"Mark, there *has* to be something important out here. Why else would Litchfield keep everybody penned inside the valley like one big flock of sheep when there's all this land out here you could use?"

Mark nodded. "I see your point. Maybe he just wants to keep it all for himself."

They finally reached the bottom of the mountain and began the ascent up the next one a short time later after crossing a narrow valley that was bisected by a meandering stream. Laura wondered how many mountains they would have to conquer before their mission was complete. She knew she would never give up looking for the little girl, even if it meant having to traverse the entire mountain range.

The sun sank lower in the western sky when they made it to the base of the next mountain.

"We should stop here for the night," said Rochelle.

Laura went off to gather some kindling; and with Mark's help, they soon had a small fire burning in the center of their makeshift camp. Laura plopped down on the mossy soil and pulled some jerky out of her bag. Just as she started to take a bite, an eerie howl echoed through the valley.

"Uh, is that what I think it is?" she asked, glancing nervously back and forth between her two companions.

A slightly louder second howl soon followed the first one.

"Unfortunately." Mark anxiously scooted his bow and arrows closer to his side.

As much as she dreaded doing it, Laura unrolled her sleeping bag and lay down. She kept Lady Capella's spear within arm's reach just in case a pack of vicious canines tried to make a snack out of her while she slept. She thought she heard more howling off in the distance once or twice as she dozed off. She was uncertain if the sound was real or if she had just imagined it in her semi-conscious state, but she did say some prayers that the animals would stay far away from them. And to her relief, she did not hear them again for the rest of the night.

Morning broke, and not much was spoken as the trio ate a quick breakfast and embarked on the next leg of their quest.

After several hours, they arrived at the top of the mountain, which was unusually level. The trees here were slightly smaller and more spread out than those in other parts of the forest. Yellow sunlight filtered down through the branches. Its warm rays felt soothing on Laura's skin.

Looking around, she realized that the acres and acres of trees surrounding them grew in almost perfect rows. Had someone planted them like that? Surely it was impossible for such precision to occur naturally.

"I'd like to stop here for a while," she said to Rochelle, rubbing her tired ankles. "My feet are really starting to hurt." It was true. She wasn't used to traipsing around in the mountains wearing a pair of heavy boots, and it was wearing her out.

"That sounds like a good idea to me." Rochelle set down her things and withdrew a pouch of crackers from her pocket. "Want one?" she asked, offering one to Laura.

"Sure. Thanks."

Laura sat on a mushroom-covered log and munched on the crumbly snack. It had looked far better than it tasted. "Does anyone else think it's strange that all of these trees are growing in rows?" she asked.

Rochelle glanced up, as if noticing the forest for the first time. "That *is* strange. It looks kind of like an old orchard. Except these aren't fruit trees."

"Maybe Litchfield found a bald spot on one of his mountains and had it fixed."

"Well, you never know." Laura could tell that Rochelle still wasn't fond of hearing that name. Yes, Litchfield was as mysterious as he was creepy; but she certainly wasn't going to let his name bother her.

Mark dabbed at his forehead with a rag he had been using to wipe off his excessive sweat. "I'm going to go see if there's a stream nearby. My canteen's almost empty. Again."

"Can you take mine too?" Rochelle asked. "I'm going to rest for a bit."

"Fine. If you insist." Mark let out an exaggerated sigh. "The fine young gentleman gets stuck doing all the work yet again."

Laura smirked at him and shook her head.

"Hey, I deserve a little rest sometime," said Rochelle. "I do housework all day."

Mark headed off in search of water, and Rochelle leaned back against a tree trunk to take a short nap. When Laura finished her cracker, she spied some edible-looking berries growing on a vine nearby and picked a handful. One by one, she popped them into her mouth, savoring the sugary flavor. They were very sweet.

A shout echoed through the trees after Mark had been gone for about five minutes. "Laura…Rochelle…you need to come look at this!"

When Rochelle didn't stir, Laura gave her a gentle kick in the side. The woman gave a startled flinch and leapt to her feet. "What in the blazes are you trying to do?" she exclaimed. "Give me a heart attack?"

Laura couldn't help but laugh at Rochelle's look of dismay that her nap had been so rudely disturbed. "Mark said he wants us to come take a look at something."

"Well, I sure hope it's important enough to warrant me waking up." She let out a yawn. "This trip has me exhausted. I was in a heck of a lot better shape when I did this four years ago."

Laura led Rochelle in the direction from which Mark's voice had come and found him crouching low to the ground about fifty or sixty yards down the western face of the mountain. It appeared that there had been some kind of recent mudslide, most likely during the torrential rainstorm on the day of the celebration. Laura could easily tell where a raging deluge of water had washed out part of the slope. A small trickle of water still flowed through the gully. At least Mark had found something to fill the canteens with.

Mark was examining a blackish object, turning it over and over in his hands.

"What *is* that?" Laura asked, coming up beside him. The thing looked just like a rock, but the way Mark studied it told her otherwise.

He shrugged and stood up. "I don't know. It looks like a rock, but I've never seen anything like this one before."

"Is it coal?" Laura knew that coal was black and that it was frequently found in mountainous regions. Then the mining companies would take over, blast the top off of the mountain, scoop out the coal, and then level the place. Was it some strange coincidence that this very mountain had a flat top?

Mark shook his head. "No. It can't be coal. Coal is darker and has a different grain to it. And look where the rain washed all of the dirt away."

"Yeah. That's odd." In the place where there had once been dirt and forest debris, there was a large patch of the peculiar stone. The black substance looked like it had originally been one solid slab but had broken apart into countless pieces over the years. Then it must have slowly been buried with soil and decomposing leaves.

"It looks like part of an old road," said Rochelle. She seemed to have already forgotten about her interrupted nap. "It's a shame that only a small section is uncovered. If it's a road, we could have followed it."

"If *this* is a road," said Laura, "it has to be ancient. Look how much dirt was on top of it! That had to have taken ages to get buried that deep."

Mark frowned, looking rather uneasy. "Why would there be a road out here? Everyone lives in the valley."

"I don't know, Mark." Rochelle gazed at the ground and kicked a piece of stone over with her foot. "None of the roads in the valley have ever been paved as far as I know. This almost looks like old asphalt."

Laura began to scan the ground. Rochelle was right. She could remember seeing an abandoned lane that had been paved in the same way, and it had looked much like this. Obviously, she couldn't recall where she had seen it; but she figured she could worry about all of that later. So what if she had amnesia? She needed to find out where this ancient thoroughfare had once led.

Trees had most likely grown up through the pavement after this length of time so visually pinpointing the route would be next to impossible. She closed her eyes and prayed. *God, I know you intended for us to find this. But how can we continue when we don't even know where it goes?*

All at once, a vision of a sunny hillside appeared in her mind's eye, and she could see a black, freshly paved road angling down the treeless slope into a shallow valley below. *There,* said a voice. *That is the way.*

"We need to go this way," she said, pointing roughly northwest. "Let's get our things and hurry."

Mark and Rochelle gave her questioning looks, but she didn't feel an explanation was necessary.

It didn't take long to reach the small valley. The land here was more even but was choked with vegetation of all sorts: pines, beeches, oaks, briars, and poison ivy, to name a few. The forest grew dimmer; and Laura had to be extra vigilant to avoid entangling herself in the wild, clinging brambles.

"Do you really think there used to be a road *here?*" Rochelle asked. "Some of these trees are enormous!"

Indeed, some of the largest specimens were easily three to four feet in diameter.

"It had to go somewhere, didn't it?" Laura stooped down to prevent herself from smacking into a broken limb dangling haphazardly from a massive oak. "The trees probably started growing up through little cracks in the pavement and just got bigger and bigger over the years."

"Yes, but these big oaks have to be at least two hundred years old," said Mark. "That means the road would have to be even older."

"Obviously. I don't think anyone would build a road with trees already growing here unless they cut them down first." She threw a quick glance over her shoulder to show Mark that she was just teasing him, but he was shaking his head in confusion.

"This just doesn't make sense," he said.

Ten more minutes passed in silence, save for the twittering of the forest wildlife. Here and there, Laura caught a glimpse of an elusive chipmunk or two diving into the undergrowth to hide. The lonesome rattle of a woodpecker echoed from far off in the distance. Occasionally, an acorn would detach itself from its parent and fall to the ground in their path.

Laura stopped for what seemed like the hundredth time to unstick herself from an overly friendly thorn bush. When she finally pulled the last thorn free from the fabric of her pants, she felt an odd sensation wash over her and stood upright, peering nervously around. Suddenly, an unexplainable energy built up within her body like her blood had become charged with a thousand volts of electricity. She broke into a run, and not in the same direction that her friends were headed.

"What in the world are you doing?" she heard Rochelle shout.

She didn't answer. How could she when she herself didn't have the faintest idea what was going on? Her legs were no longer her own as they carried her through the forest, leaping over logs and briars and dodging numerous vines and saplings that stood in her way.

Her legs finally halted at the edge of a small clearing. *You have arrived,* said the divine voice that had led her to the mountains in the first place.

It took Laura a minute to catch her breath. What was so remarkable about this clearing, that God would send her to it? It certainly didn't appear out of the ordinary. She saw a circular open space. Wildflowers. A couple of fallen pine trees. A mourning dove cooing from its perch in a treetop.

That's when she saw it.

"Rochelle!" she bellowed, hardly believing her eyes. "Mark! Get over here!"

The pair arrived forty-five seconds later, gasping from their unexpected jog.

"What is that?" Mark asked in bewilderment.

Laura cleared her throat. "I think it's a house."

Some variety of two-story dwelling stood in front of them like a remnant of a bygone age. It had a dark, sloping roof and tan walls overgrown with a plethora of creeping vines. Some bushy hedges partially obscured the building's façade.

"How were you able to see this thing from all the way back there?" Rochelle looked amazed.

Laura smiled. "I didn't."

"Then how—?"

"I'm going inside."

"We don't have time for that," said Mark. "We've been out here for two days, and we still haven't seen any signs of Spica or her kidnappers."

Go in, the voice urged her.

"I have to see what's in there. It shouldn't take too long."

She trudged through knee-high weeds and began to examine the peculiar building. The door sat squarely in the middle of the front wall and had a dark window on each side. She reached out her hand and found that the walls were quite smooth to touch, like one huge, polished stone. The windows, while clearly transparent, appeared to be made of the same type of substance.

"Have you ever seen any kind of material like this before?" she asked Rochelle.

Rochelle shook her head. "No, but I think it looks like poured cement only shinier."

"That's what I thought." She paused. "So, do either of you want to come inside with me?"

Rochelle wrinkled her nose. "I don't know. It might be full of snakes and spiders. And we don't know how stable it is. We could walk in and fall through the floor."

Laura rapped on the wall with her fist, stinging her knuckles on the virtually unblemished surface where the vines had yet to reach. "Seems sturdy enough to me."

She stepped up onto the leaf-covered flagstone porch and was dismayed to see that the door lacked a knob. Instead, there was some kind of narrow vertical slot in the place where a knob should have been. Was it some kind of keyhole?

"Mark, do you have a little knife I can use?" she asked.

"Yes. Why?"

"I need it to try to pick that lock."

"Oh." He rummaged around in his duffel bag for a moment and withdrew a pocketknife, which he unfolded and handed over to her. "Here you go."

She set her spear and pack down on the porch and stuck the knife blade into the slit. She wiggled it up and down a few times. It sounded like tiny metallic parts were moving around inside. There was a loud click, and the heavy door swung slowly inward.

"That was *way* too easy," Rochelle commented. "Anybody could break into a house that has a lock like that."

"Maybe it wasn't locked." Laura took a deep breath and stepped through the doorway.

Mark was thoughtful enough to light a glowstone with the water that remained in his canteen. Laura took the stone and held it in front of her, and Mark and Rochelle followed her inside.

"Wow. This place is a mess."

Laura was surprised that the room was not empty, as she had previously suspected. Several pieces of furniture, including a love-seat and an armchair, sat around in various states of decay. The air smelled as stale as if it had been locked away for centuries. A slight breeze wafted in from the open doorway, and suddenly the room was filled with swirling tendrils of dust.

"How lovely." Rochelle choked and ducked back outside to have an intense fit of sneezing. When she returned, she had the collar of her shirt pulled up over her nose. "I can breathe now," she said.

Sheets had been hung over the windows like drapes, and Laura went to remove one to let in more light. To her astonishment, it disintegrated into a cloud of dust at her touch. "Oops."

"Nice going, Laura," Mark said with a smirk.

Laura grinned. "I guess I'd better be more careful, huh?"

After destroying the curtain, Laura set about examining the more solid items in the room with utmost fascination. Some paintings hung in tarnished metal frames on the wall, covered in the thickest, blackest cobwebs she had ever seen. One painting portrayed a scene of a peaceful mountain lake. Another showed a family of deer wading through a rocky creek. Whoever had painted them had certainly done a very good job.

The wooden coffee table in the center of the room was warped and cracked across the top. On it sat some coasters and a ceramic mug, along with several paintbrushes. All laid in a quarter of an inch of dust.

"Look," said Mark, pointing across the room. "Glowstones."

Sure enough, two of the mysterious light sources hung from the ceiling, suspended by metal hangers that had been bolted into place. Mark dribbled a small amount of water over each of them to light up the room even more.

The increased lighting revealed a lopsided shelf full of books that lined most of one wall. Unfortunately, it appeared that the books themselves had partially decomposed and could not be touched—lest they meet the same fate as the sheet in the window. The titles on the spines were so faded and peeled that Laura couldn't even guess at what they might have said.

Then she noticed the calendar that had been nailed to the wall.

At first glance, she thought it was made of paper; but closer inspection revealed it to be made of a thick, glossy material.

May 2442 it read at the top in italicized black letters.

Laura felt all of the hairs stand up on her arms and scalp. "Uh, guys? What year did you say it is right now?"

"Two forty-one," said Mark. "Why?"

"This calendar is dated twenty-four forty-two."

"That can't be right."

Mark and Rochelle came over to stare at the old calendar, the latter with a look of extreme concern on her face. She no longer had it covered by her shirt collar. Laura noticed that Rochelle was clutching a dusty book in her hand.

"Look," Laura said, an ominous feeling settling upon her like a black shroud. "Someone crossed out each square, stopping at May seventeenth."

"Then I think you'll find *this* to be very interesting. It's a journal."

Rochelle handed her the slender book. It seemed to be made from the same plasticlike substance as the calendar, so it did not fall apart.

"This was lying on one of those chairs over there. You need to read the very last entry."

Laura carefully opened the navy blue cover, praying that the pages really were durable and wouldn't crumble in her hands. She riffled through the pages until the final heading caught her eye. In frail, shaky handwriting, someone had scrawled:

> 18 May, 2442. I am sorry to say that Rebecca passed on this morning, God rest her weary soul. And yes, I fear that I will not follow far behind her. I grow weaker by the hour. Celine should be by later this evening to check on me again. I hate for the poor dear to see me this way. I can hardly even rise from the chair. I do not know what to do! What is this strange disease which has caught us so rudely by surprise? Every night I pray that it will stop spreading, that they will find a cure. Perhaps it is not meant to be. Even Edward says he has never seen or heard of anything like this, and he of all people should know! I am not so young anymore. I cannot take much more of this. Richard, it has been years since you departed from my life, but I know I will be joining you very soon. Even as I now write I can feel the strength ebbing from my fingers. I look forward to seeing you again, my love. I—

And there, the writing stopped. Laura shivered despite the fact that the air in the house was quite warm. The owner of the journal must have been too weak to complete the entry and scratch the eighteenth of May off of the calendar. Had she died while writing? Or had she collapsed and passed away later? She figured she would never know.

"I think I'll go check out some of the other rooms in here," she said, eager to escape the dismal confines of the front room.

She hurried through an arched doorway holding the dim glow-stone in front of her and got an unexpected face full of cobwebs. Mark should have doused the thing with more water than he had. A dying flashlight would have been more luminous.

She followed a short hallway and found a door standing slightly ajar, so she went inside. The room was dirty and cluttered with boxes, and the walls were completely covered with artwork. She admired the beauty of the paintings and decided that the person who had lived in the house was the artist herself. There was even an easel with a blank canvas sitting over in a corner.

She looked back up at the wall to continue her study of the paintings and froze. It felt like all of the blood had just drained from her face. She began to see colored spots in her vision, and she grabbed onto the doorframe so she wouldn't faint and fall to the floor.

How in the world had she missed it when she first walked in?

She could hear her friends walking down the hallway toward her. She didn't know what they were going to think.

"So, did you find anything interesting in this room?" Rochelle asked.

"Uh huh." Laura felt her entire body shaking, and warm tears began to well up in her eyes.

Mark noticed her condition and took her hand. "Are you all right? What's the matter?"

"I...I...Rochelle, look over at the wall."

The confused woman turned and gasped. She clapped her hand over her mouth. "Oh my God," she breathed. "I don't believe it. I...how..."

The three of them fell silent as Laura and Rochelle were filled with morbid realization.

Hanging on the wall, as clear as day through the shrouds of dust, was a portrait of Jesus Christ. To the right was an equally stunning portrait of Mother Teresa of Calcutta. In fact, most of the paintings on the wall were of famous humanitarians: Mohandas Gandhi, Martin Luther King Jr., Abraham Lincoln. There were also about a half a dozen pictures of people whom Laura did not recognize. Each painting had the individual's birth and death years painted across the bottom in beautiful calligraphy. Some of them said things like "2008–2102" and "2016–2091."

But the most noteworthy portrait of all was that of Litchfield. Beneath the image of his arrogant, stone-cold face were inscribed the words, "Dr. Edward Michael Litchfield, one of my oldest and dearest friends. 2082-"

There was no year of death.

"Rochelle," Laura said in a whisper. Somehow her voice had left her. "Those portals didn't take us to another dimension. They sent us to the future."

CHAPTER 14

"If this is our future, what happened to all the technology? I don't find it likely that people would give up the comforts of life to go live like our ancestors did."

"That woman wrote about some kind of deadly illness in her journal," Laura said, sharing Rochelle's concern. "There could have been a pandemic that killed most of the population in twenty-four forty-two. The people who survived must have banded together and reverted to the way people lived a long time ago because they had no other option." She paused in order to do a quick calculation in her head. "If all that happened in twenty-four forty-two and the survivors started renumbering the years after that, then this isn't really two forty-one. It would have to be twenty-six eighty-three at the earliest."

"Good Lord! I was born almost seven hundred years ago." The young woman grabbed her stomach. "Oh, I feel like I'm going to throw up. All this time I thought I was living in a distant land in some other plane of existence, but I was really in the same place all along. No wonder these mountains look like the Appalachians. They *are* the Appalachians."

"This still doesn't explain why the portals are here or who the heck Litchfield really is."

Mark cleared his throat a few times. Laura could tell by the look of confusion on his face that he had no idea what she and Rochelle were talking about.

"What doesn't make sense," he said, "is that Litchfield is our creator, but the dates on these paintings say that most of these people died before he was born."

"God is our creator, Mark," Rochelle said quietly. "Not Litchfield. The man is just as human as you and I."

"Except for the fact that he has to be at least six hundred years old."

Laura was pensive. Could a man really live that long? It seemed highly doubtful, yet she had seen the image of Litchfield's face with her own eyes. It had even spoken directly to her. The image must have been made by some kind of holographic projector. That would explain why the creepy, disembodied head vanished after lightning struck a nearby pole. The surge of electricity would have shorted it out. And if the image of the head had been some kind of advanced holographic technology, then it had probably been another kind of technology that kept the rain from falling on the celebration grounds. It made so much more sense.

It dawned on Laura that she and her two companions were not the only people who knew that Litchfield was a human.

"Lord Arcturus knows," she said.

"Knows what?"

Laura hurriedly explained how the man had discovered something out in the mountains while searching for Procyon seven years before.

"I already knew that Lord Arcturus was being punished for something," said Rochelle. "We've talked about this before. I guess we have to assume that he found out that Litchfield is just a weird, little, old man and Litchfield got angry about it." She breathed a sigh of relief. "I'm glad to know he's human and not some supernatural demon. He must have some people working for him, though."

"If he does, they could be the ones who kidnapped Spica," said Mark.

"Oh." Laura frowned. "I know who did that."

"What? How?"

Laura went on to tell them about how she listened in on the conversation between Yvonne and Louise and how the two women were arguing about something horrible that Yvonne had done.

"She even admitted to making Eliza Matarna go steal the glowstones," she added. "I think it was part of a plan to make Lord Arcturus look bad since a disabled person got thrown in jail."

Mark had spots of crimson forming on his cheeks. "That evil hag!" he exclaimed. "That woman has practically been a mother to me since I joined the Woodland Youth! How could she steal a little girl just to help Litchfield get revenge on Lord Arcturus?"

"Simple. Because she's an evil hag." Rochelle had a savage look about her. "I can't believe she would gain our trust only to do something so repulsive. I swear if I find out she's hurt Spica in any way, I'll—"

"Did you figure out why Louise was talking to herself?" Mark asked before Rochelle was able to finish describing what she had in store for Yvonne.

"She must have been using a two-way radio," Laura said. "It's something that lets people in two different places talk to each other."

"You know," Rochelle said, "I bet Litchfield had people start the child-killing rumors about Lord Arcturus so they'd think he had gone crazy. Then if he started telling everyone that Litchfield's a fraud, nobody would believe him."

"You're probably right. We've got to get back to town as soon as possible and ask Lord Arcturus about what he found out here," said Laura. "Then we can track Litchfield down to find Spica."

"We should try to gather some of our friends and help Lord Arcturus escape from his house," said Mark. "Then he can show us what he found."

"And we can capture Litchfield and publicly humiliate him. Both of you need to find people we can all trust to do this with us. I'll try to get Lord Arcturus to tell me what really happened all those years ago. When you've found enough people, you need to bring them all back to the house of Owens so we can discuss our plan of action."

Laura smiled. Litchfield was going down.

It only took them about a day to get back to Sparkling Falls since they made as few rest stops as possible and only allowed themselves a few hours to sleep. They arrived in the early afternoon but chose to wait at the edge of the forest until night fell so they could slip into town undetected.

Laura felt on top of the world, more ready than ever to get to the bottom of the mystery surrounding Lord Arcturus's discovery. Her heart was pounding with anticipation. She was full of gratitude for the divine voice that had instructed her to head west into the mountains. Following its advice had allowed her to solve an important piece of the puzzle. Now all she had left to do was interrogate Lord Arcturus and hopefully locate his missing daughter.

"Okay," she said to her companions when the last rays of sunlight finally faded into an inky black canopy of stars. "Mark, you should go find Andrew. And the two of you can tie up that guard who's out in front of the house. Rochelle, you go find as many people as possible to help us. Any questions?"

"I have one," said Rochelle. "How do I know who I can trust?"

The trio disbanded, and Laura tiptoed across the lawn with her spear at the ready. Not that she actually planned on using it. She just wanted to be armed in case of trouble.

Several windows in the house of Owens were dark, save for the faint flicker of a bedside candle or two. Had most of the family already gone to bed? She hoped that nobody had bolted the back door. That would make sneaking in without making a great deal of noise much more tedious.

She glanced around as she stepped onto the back porch to make sure she was alone. It didn't seem logical to leave one entire door unguarded if the house's occupant was under house arrest, but nobody was there to stop her from letting herself in. She turned the knob ever so quietly. To her delight, the door swung open; and she walked inside. She deposited her hiking supplies on a chair just inside the door. She could put them away later.

Lady Capella and Tabitha were both in the living room, crocheting mittens; and they gave a start when Laura strode unexpectedly into the room.

"Did you find her?" Lady Capella asked, a faint ray of hope shining in her eyes.

Laura shook her head. "No, but we found something else. I really need to talk to your husband about something. Where is he?"

The look that Lady Capella gave her nearly broke Laura's heart. "He's alone in his study. I'm sure he's sleeping. It's all he does anymore. I wouldn't disturb him if I were you."

"Well, he needs to be disturbed right now."

If the situation hadn't been so grave, Laura was sure she would have laughed at the shocked expressions that formed on the mother's and daughter's faces.

Laura arrived at the study door and boldly pounded on it with her fist. "Lord Arcturus, it's Laura," she said. "I have something really important to discuss with you."

A bleary-eyed Lord Arcturus opened the door. His hair and clothes were disheveled, and two days of unshaven stubble peppered his chin. "Can it wait until morning?" he asked.

"I'm afraid not. May I come in?"

The man sighed. "Might as well. Close the door behind you."

Laura did as she was instructed and took a seat in a cozy, brown armchair. The study was full of papers and books and had several maps of the village tacked to the walls. A blanket and pillow were laid out on the floor, and next to them lay a large leather-bound tome. Laura could tell even at first glance that it was a Bible.

"What is it that you'd like to talk about?" he asked, taking a seat across from her. It was obvious that he was having a hard time restraining himself from asking anything about Spica.

"Mark and Rochelle and I found an old, abandoned house way out in the mountains," she said. "There were a lot of interesting things in it, like a portrait of Litchfield."

Lord Arcturus blanched at the sound of the name.

"The portrait said he was born in twenty eighty-two. We also found a journal and a calendar in the house that were both dated twenty-four forty-two. If we assume that people started counting the years differently after that, then this year may actually be twenty-six eighty-three. That means that Litchfield is six hundred and one years old. There were a lot of other portraits in that house, and the birth dates on some are much earlier than twenty eighty-two. Therefore, Litchfield cannot possibly be the creator. He's just a creepy old fart who brainwashed everyone into thinking he's a god. That's what you found out when you went searching for Procyon. Right?"

Lord Arcturus gave a slow nod. "You're quite an intelligent girl, Laura. I unfortunately had to find out all of that information the hard way. But you must understand that Litchfield is a cunning devil who will stop at nothing to keep his secrets hidden."

"I kind of figured that since he's trying to ruin your reputation with those nasty rumors about killing children. But I would really like to know what you found out there."

The man was silent for a minute. "I never planned on telling anyone about this. But since you figured most of it out on your own, I'll go ahead and tell you. As I said before, I rode west into the mountains, just me and my horse. After a couple of days, I came across an enormous house built partly into a mountainside that had some gardens planted out in front of it. I had no idea who could be living there. But I thought that if Procyon had made it out that far, he might have gone inside for help. He was such a bright child. I knocked on the door. But nobody ever came to answer it, so I just walked right in. I kept calling Procyon's name in case he was there, but I never heard him and he never came running for me. After a while, I came across a room full of books. There must have been thousands of them. Procyon always loved books, so I went in to see if he had wandered in and fallen asleep. You can probably tell how desperate I was to find him at this point. I half expected to see him sitting on the floor with a pile of books scattered around him.

"I nearly cried when I saw that nobody was there. I did see a stack of books sitting on a writing desk, and a couple of them caught my eye. One said *Holy Bible* and the other said *Journal One Hundred.* I picked up the journal and started flipping through it. And the first thing I knew, I became hooked. I must have sat there reading it for over an hour. And I became angrier and angrier because I realized that everything I had ever been taught about the world was a lie.

"Unfortunately I heard footsteps approaching, and who should walk in but Litchfield and Silas Wang. That's Adalbert Wang's father, in case you didn't know. He died a few years back. Anyway, I stood up and started yelling at Litchfield, telling him that he was a crook and a liar and that he should be ashamed of himself. He told me to get out of his house and not to tell anybody about it or he'd kill me. I grabbed the Bible and the journal and left as fast as I could before either of them could stop me. As I was riding away, I could hear Litchfield shout, 'Arcturus Owens, you'll wish you'd never been born!' I suppose I shouldn't have stolen his books, but it was the only proof I had that Litchfield is a fake. I considered going public with them for years but never worked up the nerve to do it. But now that he's turned my life into a living hell…"

Laura smiled, glad that Lord Arcturus had finally opened up about what happened that day. "Rochelle and I knew you had to have done something to make him angry. May I see the journal?"

"Sure." The man reached over and grabbed a worn black book out of a shelf. "I hope you find it as enlightening as I did."

Laura flipped it open to the first page and began to read.

1 May, 2442. Today marks the beginning of my one hundredth journal. Sometimes I am amazed that I have kept at it for so long; but then again, I am amazed that I have kept at anything for so long.

As I have at the beginnings of my other journals, I will introduce myself for the sake of those who might choose to read this in the future. I am Dr. Edward Michael Litchfield, head of the main research department at the Center of Embryonic Research and Development in Charleston, West Virginia. I was born on 8 April, 2082 in Chicago, Illinois, to poor, working-class parents. I managed to go to college and medical school because of my outstanding grades, which earned me some excellent scholarships.

The reason I have lived for so ridiculously long is because I became wealthy enough to afford the costly Merkelson Procedure, replacing many of my deteriorating organs with artificial ones that take much longer to wear out, thus extending my life by centuries. I had the procedure done when I was a hundred and two years old. I received a bionic heart, kidneys, liver, eardrums, and had special lenses inserted into my eyes to enhance my vision. I get special nutrient injections once a month that strengthen my skin and bones. I even became a strict vegetarian about two hundred years ago so I could keep my arteries cleared of filth.

I live on a huge estate close to the West Virginia-Virginia border, deep in the mountains. I love the peace and solitude here. It's one of the few remaining places that haven't succumbed to urban sprawl. Fortunately for me, the lack of close neighbors allows me to get by with many things that some of my more conservative colleagues would frown upon. I have my own state-of-the-art cloning lab at home as well as hundreds of frozen embryos that I "borrowed" from the freezers at work.

For the past three centuries, I have bought up a lot of property; and now I own a vast ribbon of land containing an entire valley that is forty miles long. I had excavators completely enclose both ends of the valley over the course of twenty years, turning it into an oval bowl tapered at each end. They even rerouted part of the river downstream from the waterfall so it flowed into an underground tunnel before emerging back into civilization on the other side.

I let the government do experimental testing for who-knows-what down at the southern end of my valley. I'll make them leave only if they start harming my precious wildlife. I heard a rumor that they're experimenting with time travel, of all things. Just what we need! I'll believe it when I see it.

Laura stopped reading. "At least now I understand why Litchfield is still alive after all this time," she said to Lord Arcturus. "He's a cyborg."

"Oh? What is that?"

"Well, they didn't actually exist yet in two thousand and three, where I came from. They were just in movies and books. They're supposed to be people who have electronic body parts that work just like real ones only better. I know you don't know what electricity is, but I don't know how else to explain it."

"Never mind, then. Just keep reading."

2 May, 2442. Curse the individual who invented the concept of rumors! According to this morning's newscast, Asian terrorists are "rumored" to have developed some sort of airborne pathogen that will kill off all vegetation and therefore eliminate our oxygen supply. Naturally, the nation is in a panic. Too bad I don't believe one word of it. You see, if I were one of the terrorists, I would simply create a pathogen that would kill people outright without having to sit around and

wait for millions of acres of forest to wither and suffocate us. Fortunately for mankind, I am not a terrorist and I have more important things to do than to make our species become extinct. There will always be death in this world; and as long as a male and female remain to reproduce, there will always be rebirth.

Some of my radical acquaintances think that our planet is suffering from the twenty-five billion souls living on it. I, however, am not greatly concerned. As I said before, there will always be death. The last war left some 170 million people dead. It is a tragedy, but that is the way of things.

10 May, 2442. I am in shock. One of my good friends and colleagues, Sandra Lopez, recently returned from a business trip overseas displaying the symptoms of a mild cold. Three days ago she began to experience extreme fatigue and breathing difficulties. She went to the hospital the night before last when she started having seizures. At around three o'clock in the morning, her heart stopped beating and she passed away in the company of her husband and daughter.

Since Sandra had not shown symptoms that are typical of any known disease, an autopsy was immediately performed on her; and it was found that an unknown virus had first attacked her upper respiratory system and then simultaneously moved into her heart and brain. The disturbance somehow triggered the seizures before paralyzing the muscles in her heart.

Sandra's family has been quarantined inside the hospital in case they are also carrying the disease.

It is times like these when I am grateful that my real heart was removed and incinerated ages ago. Now I pray that my bionic one will be able to keep me going even if I am unlucky enough to be exposed to Sandra's killer.

13 May, 2442. According to the news, about twelve thousand people in Charleston alone have perished in what has become the fastest-spreading epidemic in recorded history. I informed my employer that I will not be coming to work until

the experts classify the virus and develop a vaccine against it. I do not feel the need to place my life into unnecessary danger by traveling to Charleston for work. If any of my underlings need my input on their projects, they are free to give me a call.

14 May, 2442. I decided to be a kind old man today, so I told about thirty of my closest friends and colleagues to come stay in my home while the epidemic passes. I have enough food and water here to last for a very long time. Sarah Yelton and Gertrude Owens were reluctant to leave their houses, but I assured them they would be safer here with me since I know I won't be running out of supplies anytime soon.

23 May, 2442. Another good friend of mine passed away this week: Tatiana Durán, the artist. She was only eighty-seven years old. One of her nieces died right before she did. I invited Tatiana to come stay with us, but she said she had already come into contact with her ailing niece and didn't want to contaminate us.

Her daughter, Celine, had Tatiana's body cremated and the ashes sprinkled throughout the forest surrounding her home. She loved the forest. She always said it inspired her paintings. Her home is only about eleven miles south of my mansion. I used to go over to visit, and she would always show me her latest work. The world has certainly lost a brilliant mind in her passing.

Celine and her husband sealed up Tatiana's house and are forbidding anyone from entering just in case the virus is still there, lying in wait for its next victim.

29 May, 2442. A million souls have perished in North America alone. This deeply troubles me. It reminds me of the apocalyptic films that were popular at the beginning of the twenty-first century. Only this time, it isn't fiction.

I decided to order extra provisions in the event that our supplies do run out. There are thirty-three of us here; and three of the women are pregnant, so we will soon have more mouths to feed. The supplies are going to be delivered via robotic air car directly from the warehouse. Hopefully this will minimize human contamination.

1 June, 2442. All aircraft have been grounded until further notice. Fortunately, our supplies arrived last night, before this order was issued over radio, Net, and video channels. In addition to the food and water, I ordered some reading material, clothing, blankets, diapers for the soon-to-be newborns, and a few hundred of those new glowstones that I've heard so much about this past year.

The government informed me that they have chosen to abandon their project down in my valley, as they have more pressing matters to attend to. They are going to pay me ten million dollars for the use of my land, but what good will that be to me if the entire population is wiped out? Unless there remains an economy controlled by ghosts, all of my accumulated wealth will be worthless.

7 June, 2442. People are dying so quickly that it is nearly impossible to calculate the death toll. In all of my three hundred and sixty years, I haven't seen anything like this. The young people with me are so frightened that they haven't set a foot outside since they arrived here. Sarah and Gertrude have convinced everyone that the disease is the work of God and not the work of man. I am not sure which theory I would prefer to believe— that mankind could be so evil or that our Creator would take it upon himself to purge the earth of all humanity.

A sort of melancholy filled Laura's heart as she continued to leaf through the pages. She couldn't even fathom how terrible it must have been to just sit there and helplessly watch the world fall apart. It chilled her to know what grisly fate mankind had in store. After all that people had lived and died for throughout the ages, had it all been for nothing in the end?

The next several entries mentioned the increased death toll, the birth of a son to somebody named Sheila Ericson, and the wedding of two people named Edmundo Frye and Tasha Li. Litchfield's friend, Ricardo Samaniego, had been the officiant.

As the weeks progressed, the journal entries became increasingly dismal.

2 September, 2442. We are no longer receiving video or radio transmissions. This truly mortifies me. We still have power at the moment because the electric plant is fully automated by androids, though I am uncertain how long it will function without human maintenance. All of our communication systems are down: phone, Net, everything. I hope we don't run out of supplies, because I am unable to order more if we need them.

We all feel empty, like the feeling when you have invited dozens of friends to a party. You've cleaned the house, prepared the meal, and now you eagerly wait by the door for their arrival. Seconds turn into minutes, minutes grow into hours, yet not one soul has darkened your doorstep. With a heavy heart, you draw the curtains to a close and retreat to the dimly lit kitchen, realizing you will be dining alone.

7 September, 2442. Today, Ira Goldman and I went up in my air car (dressed, of course, in full body suits and gas masks) to survey the area out beyond my property. It was a grim sight. In some places, there were human remains on the ground, the bones picked clean by scavengers. Land cars sat abandoned on the streets of East Millersburg, which is a small community about twenty-five miles from my home. Some of the vehicles still had their deceased drivers and passengers sitting in them. I saw a pack of stray dogs roaming the streets. It was almost funny to see poodles and terriers traveling with Dobermans and rottweilers.

We flew out to Charleston, which was in about the same condition as East Millersburg. We did see a couple of living people milling around below us. A few men were busy collecting corpses and putting them in a pile to cremate. They looked up at us when we flew over and gave us a grim salute. Ira thought we should have landed the car and talked to them; but we had no way of knowing if those people were sick, so I ignored his suggestion. The car was running low on power, and I turned it around and flew home.

20 September, 2442. I have been struck by the most terrible of thoughts. For most of my career, I have destroyed human life in the pursuit of scientific knowledge. I now understand the reasons why activists always picketed outside the doors of my workplace. I can't possibly count the number of human embryos—living human embryos—that I cloned and performed experiments on. I had always justified this murder by telling myself that it was for the betterment of mankind. I'm sure that my soul has been eternally damned because of this.

But I might have a chance to redeem myself. I have decided to put the frozen embryos in my lab to good use that does not involve me dismantling their cells and trying to grow new body parts with them. I have counted two hundred and eleven individual human embryos. I do have other varieties, such as horses and pigs; but there is nothing I can do with them at the present moment.

With the help of Alexander Lars, the fertility doctor, I will implant the human embryos into the wombs of my female comrades. We have all discussed the idea of heading down into my valley in the spring so we can build a settlement. There is, of course, still the risk that we might perish from that unknown virus; but it would be far better than spending the rest of our lives indoors.

22 September, 2442. Huluava Villum, Dariya Petrov-Smith, and Juliana Mackenzie each volunteered to become the mothers of some of the embryos. They are now each pregnant with fraternal twins. I am excited and eager to learn what brilliant people I had cryogenically frozen for years. I wonder what the children will look like. White? Black? Asian?

Hispanic? I wonder if this is what God felt like when he created the universe.

I never married nor had any children of my own, so I feel a sort of fatherly attachment to my two hundred and eleven embryos. I am the one who cloned them from the original embryos (I think about half were from Japan or China; someplace like that) that were donated to our lab decades ago. So in a way, I am their creator.

I am the Creator!

CHAPTER 15

Laura read the last passage a few times to allow the reality of Litchfield's statement to sink in. *The Creator.* It was almost true, from a certain perspective. She shuddered.

"I guess this means Litchfield became a little obsessed with his children. No wonder he managed to convince everyone he's a deity."

Lord Arcturus nodded. "By maintaining the illusion that he is divine, he maintains his control over the valley. He's a power-hungry old fool. Now, it's true that he's highly intelligent. But you and I both know he can't live forever. When he finally dies, there will be mass chaos because the 'Creator' will be no more." He let out a hollow laugh. "I've read Litchfield's old Bible from front to back. I can't believe he never taught us about the one true God, Jesus Christ, or the Holy Spirit. I hope that the people of this valley won't be punished in the afterlife for their lack of faith and knowledge."

Laura chewed on her lip. "I tell you what," she said. "If you help us bring Litchfield down and show everyone who he really is, then I will help you teach everyone in the valley about the Gospel. Deal?"

The man sighed. "It's a deal I suppose." He paused. "You haven't gotten to the part about the portals yet, have you?"

"No."

"Then stop your chatting and keep reading!"

"15 October, 2442. Gertrude Owens and Melissa Li asked to be mothers, and they now carry twins. Ten embryos have been implanted so far. Two hundred and one to go. I'm going to wait for several months before we implant more of them so we don't end up raising dozens of infants all at once.

Sheila's son smiled at me for the first time today…

Laura skipped a few more months of entries, searching for any mention of the portals.

1 January, 1. Since this is the dawn of a new era, my friends and I are calling what would have been 2443 'Year 1.' It snowed a lot this week. And do I mean a lot! Snow comes up almost to the first-floor windowsills. I stepped out onto the porch and stabbed a yardstick into the snow, and it measured over two and a half feet deep.

Some of the men are doing research in my library on how to build homes and plant crops. When the snow melts, we're all going to the large valley to begin planning our settlement.

Gertrude thinks we should name the settlement Sparkling Falls after the nearby waterfall; but I prefer the name Upton, which was my mother's maiden name. We got into a huge spat over the matter and had our friends vote on it. The results were in favor of Sparkling Falls. I think that once the settlement is built, I'll get Ira and Alexander and my few other supporters to follow me upriver to build Upton. The Creator will always get his way.

2 February, 1. We hiked over to the valley today. It's about a ten-mile trip through mountainous terrain, so it took most of the day.

The valley is mostly wooded. We're going to have to clear thousands of trees to make room for Sparkling Falls. Ugh! What a name. It sounds like some happy little island paradise with flowers and rabbits and butterflies. Upton, on the other hand, is a practical name, tough, hard-working, enduring.

3 February, 1. In all of my three hundred and sixty years of life, I thought I had seen everything. Today proved that this was not so.

Sarah and Ira and I were following the service road that the government had been using, and we discovered five small buildings built along it that were each spaced about a mile apart from one another. Each building was fenced in and had a sign posted out front that said, "Warning: Authorized Personnel Only. Violators will be Prosecuted," in bold, red letters. Since there are no longer any authorized personnel to care if we intrude, we scaled the fence of one of the buildings and busted down the door. I'm sure it set off an alarm in some off-site facility. We were not concerned.

The building was approximately thirty feet wide and forty feet deep. A bank of screens and control panels lined one wall. A holographic screen displayed glowing green letters reading "Project Nightcrawler Testing Facility 131-C. Please give command for more information."

There was a peculiar chamber toward the back wall. It reminded me of the transporter devices they used in some ancient television show that was popular a century before my birth. I mentioned this to Ira, who laughed and stepped into the chamber. "Beam us up, Mister Scott!" he said.

We had no idea that he would actually vanish into thin air. The room became charged with electricity and Ira dematerialized. Poor Sarah nearly fainted from the shock, but I was quite intrigued.

To my intense relief, Ira returned a few minutes later, visibly shaken.

"What happened?" I asked him.

He said something like, "Do you remember how you said there were rumors that the government was experimenting with time travel?"

I responded that I had. How could I forget?

He went on to explain how he had suddenly appeared in a roped-off corner of a newly dug basement, where several men wearing homespun garments were standing around, talking and laughing. He conversed with them briefly and learned that it was the year 1763. The men told him that scientists had commissioned them to build a dwelling around the wormhole. Ira said that he told them that the scientists were all dead, but to finish building so nobody would accidentally go through while strolling around in the woods.

Wormholes. Apparently this is what the government was splurging our tax dollars on. I remember reading about wormhole theory when I was earning my bachelor's degree. A wormhole is a hole in the space-time continuum that directly links two points that are in different places or in different times. And if this wormhole really does connect 2443 to 1763, shouldn't the scientists have found the wormhole already in its present location *before* they built it? This is not plausible unless the wormholes already existed, created by God for mankind to stumble across and study. This thought has been bothering me all day, so I had better forget about it before I go mad trying to figure it out.

I don't have the faintest idea how scientists managed to manufacture their own wormhole, but I do know one thing: we are going to destroy the wormhole chambers so none of us accidentally zap ourselves into the past.

6 February, 1. Blast it! We began to demolish the first Project Nightcrawler testing facility bit by bit, thinking that it would fill in the hole in the space-time continuum, but the wormhole remained! I discovered this when I stood in the place where the chamber had been and ended up being surrounded by a bright light before entering the basement that Ira had visited. I did not encounter anyone, so I zapped myself home

undetected. I am assuming that once a wormhole has formed, nothing known to man will be sufficient to aid in its destruction. However, we are going to tear down the buildings as planned and salvage some of the parts for our own use.

Once we have built Sparkling Falls and settled in comfortably, I am going to forbid people from leaving the valley unless they are going directly to my home. My friends and I have chosen to never tell the children about the former ways of the world. This is a new beginning, and knowledge of the ugly past will pass away from the minds of mortal men.

Laura had read enough.

"We need to go tell your wife and children about this," she said, closing the book. "The more people who know the truth, the easier it will be for Litchfield to fall."

"I don't know how many people he has working for him. All he would have to do is give the command and they could kill us. I know he's going to take drastic measures to keep his secrets hidden." Lord Arcturus had a look of resigned acceptance about him. "If only the people of this village could follow me in the same way. I have no more power over them than you do. All I am is a figurehead who gives the illusion of authority, when in reality it's all a part of Litchfield's twisted game." He rubbed absentmindedly at the blue circle tattoo on the palm of his hand.

"Mark and Rochelle have already gone out to find someone who can help us. We're going to tell your family, and then we're going to bust you out of here. You're going to take us to Litchfield's house so we can capture him and expose the creep for who he really is. Maybe he'll even tell us where he's hidden Spica."

Lord Arcturus looked hesitant. "I'm not so sure that is going to work. There's no guarantee that *any* of this is going to work."

Laura couldn't believe that this soon-to-be father of six, the one who had practically risked his life to find his missing son seven years before, would be so afraid to cross Litchfield a second time. "You need to stop being such a coward!" she said, not caring that she probably sounded disrespectful. "Spica needs you, and we won't be able to save her unless *you* take us to Litchfield tonight."

To Laura's surprise, Lord Arcturus let out a half-amused chuckle. "Since when did you become so commanding? A week ago, you were almost too shy to carry on a decent conversation with us."

Laura had to stop and think. "It must have been when I realized that God sent me here for a reason." However, she wasn't sure of the exact moment of this realization. "So are you going to help us out, or are you just going to pine away in here, feeling sorry for yourself while your little girl is being held captive in the hands of a bunch of wackos?"

She didn't wait for his reply. Instead, she picked up the journal and marched out of the study, determined to preach the truth.

Lady Capella's normally pale face had turned a peculiar shade of green. Rotanev, Alcor, and Tabitha sat on the sofa, their eyes wide with shock. Sualocin stood fuming in front of the fireplace with his arms folded across his chest. Tara was hunched over in the armchair, sobbing into her hands.

"This is absurd," Sualocin said. "As unbelievable as it sounds, it all makes perfect sense. If Litchfield is not the true Creator, then the real one must be absolutely furious about this crude impersonation. And who knows how many villages rose and fell before Litchfield created his own? We deserve to know our ancestors' history."

"At least now we know why our son has been ridiculed and our own kin turned against us," said Tara.

Suddenly, there came a muffled cry from the direction of the front door, closely followed by a series of bangs and thumps and an occasional curse.

"What was that?" Tabitha whispered, looking fearful.

Laura smiled. "It sounds like Mark and Rochelle might have just arrived with reinforcements. I'll go get the door."

She almost laughed at the scene she beheld out on the lawn. In the light of the waxing crescent moon, she could see Andrew and Frank binding and gagging the guard who had been posted outside to prevent Lord Arcturus from leaving.

"Sorry, Max," she heard Andrew say. "It's for your own good."

They brought the enraged young man into the house and set him down at the dining room table.

"Now you have to promise us that you won't get up and go anywhere," Frank cautioned their captive.

He and Andrew looked at each other and laughed. Max's eyes shot daggers in their direction.

Rochelle and Mark stepped into the dining room from outside, followed by Mark's grandfather; Lord Arcturus's relatives, Leo, Bjorn, and Sedna; Eliza Matarna; and a handful of people whom Laura didn't know.

Eliza gave an energetic wave when she saw Laura. "Hi, Laura!" she said, jumping up and down with sheer excitement. "I'm gonna go help find Spica and kick Litchie's butt!" She demonstrated this latter action, accidentally kicking Max the prisoner in the kneecap.

"That's great, Eliza!" Laura grinned. "We need all the help we can get."

Lady Capella, Lord Arcturus's parents, and the children came out to join the small crowd that had formed in the dining room. Lady Capella burst into tears.

"Thank you all so much for coming to help get my daughter away from that wretched man," she sniffled. "This means so much to us. I'd go out there too, but this little one needs to stay out of harm's way." She patted her abdomen, which showed the slightest bulge through her dress.

"We'd do anything to help our friends, Capella," said Andrew, "including walking straight into the enemy's lair."

He wore a quiver of deadly looking arrows slung over his shoulder. Laura hoped he wouldn't be forced to use them.

"So, where's your husband? He's the one who has to show us the way."

"I'm here, Andrew."

Everyone turned to see the figurehead ruler of Sparkling Falls step into the room. He had ditched his pajamas for a pair of thick, leather riding pants and heavy boots; and he wore a dark brown leather vest over his long-sleeved shirt. He too had chosen to bring along a quiver of arrows, whose points looked large enough to disembowel a grizzly bear. He carried a hunting bow that was almost as tall as himself.

His face was devoid of emotion.

"Let's get this over with," he said.

The group marched single file out the back door, holding several glowstones and lanterns to light the way. Lord Arcturus was in the lead, followed by his father, Frank, and Andrew. Lady Capella and her mother-in-law stayed home.

Laura and Mark brought up the rear of the eighteen-member procession. She still carried Lady Capella's spear as well as her canteen of water.

"Laura," Mark whispered.

"What?"

"I just wanted to let you know that I'm very proud of you. You're one of the bravest people I know."

Laura blushed. "Thanks, Mark. But I'm only doing what I know is right. I don't think bravery has anything to do with it."

"Many people don't have the courage to do the right thing. Heck, I was terrified of leaving the valley just a few days ago. But you pushed me to go anyway. And because of that, we all learned a very important secret." He spread his arms wide. "*All* of these people are out here because of you."

"Are you glad I made you come with me?"

"You bet I am!"

Rochelle, who was walking directly in front of them, glanced over her shoulder and put a finger to her lips. "Shh!" she said. "We want to make as little sound as possible."

Mark let out a snort. "Rochelle, all these lanterns and glowstones we have are going to give us away no matter how quiet we are."

"But if you're busy chattering away like that, you won't be as alert in case Litchfield sends somebody after us."

"Oh." Mark promptly shut his mouth in embarrassment.

Laura couldn't tell how long or how far they had been walking. She had no idea how Lord Arcturus could remember the exact location of Litchfield's abode after having been there only once before. Part of her worried that he would become disoriented and get everyone lost out on the dark, wooded mountain. But the man appeared resolute in his bearing, so she cast her worries aside.

It had said in the journal that the valley was only ten miles away from Litchfield's house. If they were walking at a speed of one mile per hour, they'd arrive in ten hours; but she knew they had to be going much faster than that, so maybe they'd get there in only three or four hours.

She wished they had a bus and a freeway.

Up ahead of her, she could hear Eliza loudly say to no one in particular, "Hey! I hear something walking around over there!"

"I'm sure it's just a little animal scurrying around in the leaves," said one of the women. "Don't worry about it."

"But little animals make little noises. This was a *big* noise."

"Then why didn't I hear anything?"

"Maybe your ears are all broken."

"I didn't hear it either," said Tabitha.

"You people are just silly." Eliza giggled. "Look. I can see it right there. It's just a big doggie."

Lord Arcturus, still in the lead, stopped dead in his tracks and squinted to try to see through the shadows. Sualocin held one of the glowstones above his head in an attempt to illuminate deeper into the surrounding forest. The two of them exchanged significant glances, Lord Arcturus gave a curt nod, and Sualocin lowered the light source back to his side.

Lord Arcturus cleared his throat. "Everybody, hold *very*, very still," he said in a low voice. He carefully drew an arrow out of his quiver and placed it into his bow. He pulled his right arm back, preparing to fire.

Andrew, Mark, and three or four other people did the same.

Laura felt her blood run cold, and she gripped her borrowed spear like it was her greatest friend in the world. Her heart beat furiously against her ribcage. *Please don't be a wolf*, wailed a little voice in her head. *Anything but a wolf!* She tried to see what it was, but too many people were standing in front of her to offer her a decent view. The individuals armed with arrows formed a semicircle around those who had none. Laura snuck forward and positioned herself behind Mark, peering around him to see a pair of gleaming yellow eyes up ahead in the darkness.

A gut-wrenching howl nearly threw Laura off guard. Then there came another and another.

Somewhere to her right, Rochelle swore.

Lord Arcturus let his arrow fly just as the beastly canine leapt into the circle of light. It barely grazed the animal in the side. This only made the wolf madder. It lunged at the man, snarling like a demon straight out of hell.

Something about the animal did not look right. Laura knew that she had seen many photographs of wolves sometime in her forgotten past, yet this one was clearly not the same breed. Its head was thicker and wider, and its fur was rather short. If a wolf and some other kind of dog—say, a pit bull—had puppies, this is what they would probably look like.

And pit bulls weren't exactly known for their gentle, loving nature.

Someone else shot an arrow at the wolf and hit the animal in the leg. Couldn't these people learn to aim any better?

Just when Laura thought things couldn't get much worse, a second and third wolf joined their wounded comrade and took over the fight. Lord Arcturus hurriedly grabbed out another arrow; but before he or anyone else had a chance to release the volley, the two newcomers attacked. Lord Arcturus fell to the ground with an agonizing moan of pain. He kicked and flailed, but the beasts would not let go.

Tabitha screamed and ran forward with a tree branch that had been lying on the forest floor. She started swinging it around like a club and bludgeoning anything in sight that had gray fur and pointy teeth. The branch snapped in half as it made contact with a wolf's head, and the girl whimpered and turned to scramble up a nearby tree to get out of harm's way.

It was chaos. Mark was shooting arrows left and right and taking care to not accidentally wound anyone who wasn't a wolf. Sualocin and Bjorn were trying in vain to pull a particularly brutal wolf off of Lord Arcturus's leg. The animal had its teeth sunk into the man's flesh through his pants and was jerking him around like he was nothing more than a rag doll. Laura could tell that the ground was soaked with warm, crimson blood.

A man lay motionless in the blood-splattered snow...

Laura shook her head to clear it of the intruding thought. She could ponder the vision much later, when nobody was in danger of being eaten.

Much to her chagrin, another pair of wolves appeared; and Eliza started waving her arms in the air, growling as if to frighten the creatures away.

"Go away, you big dumb doggies!" she shouted.

"Eliza, get back!" Rochelle ordered, grabbing her by the collar of her dress and trying to pull her out of the wolves' reach.

The situation did not look good. Only one of the five wolves had been fatally shot; but Lord Arcturus, Leo, and Sedna had all received terrible bites and gashes. And the former was still pinned on the ground by one feral beast who was trying to turn this evening into the man's last. He was no longer moving. Laura prayed that he had only blacked out from the shock, though she didn't understand how he could possibly still be alive.

Suddenly, a gap formed amid all the action, opening up a clear path between Laura and the wolf attacking Lord Arcturus. She carefully aimed the spear and launched it with all of her might. It plunged into the wolf's side like a lethal javelin; and the animal fell over, twitching. At last, Lord Arcturus was free.

The remaining wolves, seeing that two of their kin now lay dead with an assortment of projectiles protruding from their flesh, scampered off into the darkness. They must have decided that their prey were too numerous to defeat.

But Laura felt no relief. She and the others ran to where Lord Arcturus lay and saw that he was indeed still breathing, though his breaths were exceptionally shallow. His face, arms, and hands were bleeding from some minor lacerations that looked like mere scratches compared to the gaping wound on his leg. Mark ripped his shirt off and tied it tightly around the injury to try to stem the thick flow of blood before it was too late.

Lord Arcturus's eyes fluttered open. "Are they gone?" he asked, his voice barely a whisper.

"Yes," said Sualocin. His eyes were red and puffy. "Laura killed the wolf that was attacking them, and the rest ran away."

Lord Arcturus managed to crack a smile that more closely resembled a grimace. "Thank you, Laura."

"You're welcome."

"Daddy, are you going to be okay?" Tabitha asked through her tears.

"I don't know, Tabby. I've lost a lot of blood." He struggled to sit up, but Sualocin shook his head.

"Rest for a while, my son."

Rotanev Owens spoke up. "Father, we need to get you home as soon as possible so we can treat your leg."

"Leo and Sedna are hurt too," Andrew added.

The leader of Sparkling Falls was overcome with a look of despair. "But we can't go back now!" he moaned. "Capella is counting on us to get our daughter back! We have to keep on going until we get to Litchfield—"

"You know you can't travel any farther than this," Rotanev insisted. "You'll die! We've already lost Procyon and Spica. We don't want to lose you too."

His father fell silent.

"The rest of us can go on ahead if you guys go home," said Laura. After all, there was no reason they shouldn't split up the group.

Mark wheeled around and stared at her. "What? We don't even know where Litchfield's house is! How *can* we go on without him?"

"God will lead you there," said Lord Arcturus. "I know it."

It was finally agreed upon that the three wounded persons would journey back to town, with the assistance of Rotanev, Sualocin, Bjorn, Mark's grandfather, and one other man. Everyone else would continue in pursuit of Litchfield and, hopefully, Spica.

Since Lord Arcturus was unable to walk on his own without gasping in agony, he stood between his father and his son, holding onto them for support while hopping along on his good leg.

Laura went over and jerked the spear out of the wolf's cooling hide. She resisted the urge to vomit and wiped the spearhead clean on the ground. She started to turn away but noticed that something was tattooed inside the creature's ear.

"Ezekiel," it said.

Great, she thought. *This must have been one of Litchfield's pets.*

She chose to keep this discovery to herself.

The two groups bade each other farewell and parted ways. Laura led the remainder of the invading party up the side of the mountain and over its peak. Tabitha kept sniffling the whole time. Laura didn't understand why the girl had been permitted to come along with them in the first place since she was only thirteen. Then again, she herself was only a few years older than that.

"It's okay, Tabitha," Rochelle said some time later. "Your dad is a tough guy. I'm sure that once he gets home, your mother and grandmother will be able to fix him up just fine. He'll still have some nasty scarring from all of that, though."

Tabitha dabbed at her eye. "It's not just that! You see, I never liked Eliza because she's weird. But if she hadn't heard the wolves coming before we did, things could have been a whole lot worse."

"I am *not* weird!" Eliza protested. "Why do you think I'm weird?"

Tabitha looked embarrassed. "Well, you act like a child even though you're in your twenties. And you have two pupils in each eye."

"No I don't." Suddenly, the woman clapped a hand over her mouth as if she had just blurted some forbidden secret.

"But you *do* have two pupils in each eye," said Rochelle. "What makes you think otherwise?"

"I'm not supposed to tell. They said I'd get in big trouble."

"What are you talking about? Who said that?"

"My mommy and daddy. They always beat me when I said I was going to tell."

Rochelle frowned. "They're not going to get you into trouble. They died a long time ago. It's okay to tell us."

"You sure?"

"We're positive." Rochelle glanced over at Laura, who shrugged. She didn't have any idea what Eliza could be talking about either.

"Well, if you're sure, I guess I'll tell you. But promise you won't tell anyone else. Okay?"

"We promise," said Laura.

"All right. Mommy and Daddy told me I'm a ... a ... spearmint? No. That's not the right word. Speariment?"

"You mean *experiment?*" Rochelle asked.

"That's it! They said Litchie wanted to do an ex-per-i-ment, and that's why they made me wear these things in my eyes ever since I was a teeny tiny baby. Litchie made them do it. They said he wanted to see how people would treat me if I always wore the things in my eyes. Sometimes, Mommy and Daddy told me that Litchie was ruining our lives with his ex-per-i-ment. One day, they went to go tell him they'd had enough of him and his ex-per-i-ment. But later on, my aunt and uncle said that Mommy and Daddy were dead and I'd have to go live with them."

"Are you saying that your parents ended up dead after talking to Litchfield?" Mark exclaimed. "Everyone said they killed themselves because they were insane!"

"I don't know what happened. I wasn't there, silly."

Mark made a sudden halt.

"What's the matter?" Laura asked.

The young man, now shirtless since he had donated his garment to Lord Arcturus, looked as pale as a ghost in the lamplight. "Her parents died after trying to cross Litchfield. Laura, *my* parents died after leaving the valley on their expedition. Litchfield must have found them and ..." His expression quickly changed to one of rage.

Laura could see the muscles in his arms tighten as if preparing to fight.

"I swear if I find that evil son of a hag I'm going to take my arrows and ram them right down his—"

"What did they put in your eyes, Eliza?" Laura asked before Mark had a chance to finish his gruesome threat. "We don't care if you take them out."

"Fine. I will. They make me itch anyway." Eliza stuck her fingers into her eyes and popped out two lightweight, colored lenses. "That's better. Do you think Litchie will be mad if I throw them away? I always thought they were dumb."

Eliza blinked; and in the light from the glowstones, Laura clearly saw the woman's two perfectly normal, blue eyes.

The other members of their party gasped.

"Go ahead and throw them away," Laura said quietly.

Eliza happily complied and tossed the lenses into a thicket.

"It looks to me like Litchfield is even more twisted than we thought," said Rochelle. "The fact that he would purposely make you look abnormal just so he could do his own bizarre sociological study…"

"And the fact that he *murdered* my parents," Mark added with a note of bitterness.

"We all need to be extra careful when we find him," said Andrew, his voice sounding grim. "It looks like we're dealing with a psychopath."

CHAPTER 16

Hour after hour passed by as the solemn group progressed through the dark forest. Their number had been reduced to a meager ten, and Laura hoped that no more misfortunes would force the remainder of the party to turn back as well.

The lack of sleep began to catch up with her; and every once in a while she found herself nodding off as she walked. She shook her head a few times. As much as she yearned for a blanket and a pillow and a soft place to lie down, she knew that now was not the time for rest.

They came to a cleared, grassy valley just as dawn was breaking in the east. A thick, white fog lingered in the air like a tent, limiting their visibility to about a dozen or so yards.

Mark looked like he was going to collapse. "I can't take it anymore," he moaned. "I haven't slept in more than a day!"

"I know what you mean," said Alcor Owens, who had two rather large dark circles under his bloodshot eyes. "I'm about to fall asleep standing up."

"We really should rest for a while," suggested Frank. He tried unsuccessfully to stifle a yawn. "We want to be as alert as possible if we do find Litchfield."

"I completely agree with that," said Mark. He flopped down in the grass, curled into fetal position, and was asleep instantly.

The others gratefully followed suit, with the exception of Laura, Eliza, and Tabitha. Laura's stomach growled loudly enough that Tabitha gave her an uneasy glance and stepped a few feet away from her. Laura realized that in her haste she had forgotten to bring any food with her. *Nice going*, she said to herself. She began to pace back and forth to keep her mind off of her hunger and fatigue. How long would she have to wait before her friends decided they had gotten their fill of slumber?

The rising sun slowly melted away the fog and revealed the rest of the valley that lay before them. It wasn't as wide as the valley containing Sparkling Falls. There wasn't a river either, just a small, oblong lake covered in lily pads. Only a few scattered pines grew on the valley floor.

"Look at that big house over there!" Eliza said, pointing northwest.

Laura stopped pacing and stared in the direction that Eliza indicated.

Now she knew without a doubt that they had gone the right way. It appeared just as Lord Arcturus had described: a large house built into the side of the mountain. An abundance of shrubs and flowering bushes grew along the front wall. It had three visible floors and an impressive porch whose overhanging roof was supported by four massive pillars. The whole structure was painted a sort of creamy peach color except for the roof, which was black.

Back when dollars still meant something, Litchfield must have indeed been an incredibly wealthy man to have been able to afford a home this big.

Mark and the six others were still sleeping peacefully. Laura didn't have a clue how he could find the comfort to rest after deducing what might have really happened to his unfortunate parents. He had told her that they had been attacked by a bear, which had later been hunted down and killed. Knowing what capabilities Litchfield possessed, he had probably murdered them himself and left them out for animals to eat. The bear might have never even touched them.

She decided she would let Mark sleep while he could.

"What do we do now?" Tabitha asked, eyeing the mansion with trepidation.

"We wait."

Laura gulped. She knew that the longer they waited to sneak inside the greater the chance that Litchfield would discover their presence, if he hadn't already. All the man would need to do was open his curtains and spot ten intruders lurking at the edge of the woods less than a mile away. Approaching the house unnoticed was going to be impossible due to the lack of cover.

"I want to go see the big house, Laura," Eliza said, seemingly unaware of the potential dangers that lay within its pastel walls.

"We will go see it," she said. "But the three of us can't go alone. We have to wait for everyone else to wake up, and then we'll all go together."

"But it's so pretty!"

"Eliza, Litchfield is probably in there," Tabitha cautioned the woman.

A glimmer of something akin to rage flickered for an instant in Eliza's newly normal eyes. "Litchie..." she breathed.

Without warning, the woman began to stride across the valley floor like a soldier going into battle. Her brown hair billowed in the morning wind, and she held her head high in an admirable display of bravery.

Laura swore.

"Eliza! Please come back!" Tabitha pleaded.

But Eliza gave no indication that she even heard the girl.

"Laura, we've got to go after her!"

Laura nodded in agreement. "You should wake everyone up, and I'll go stop her." She immediately began to jog after Eliza; but the woman glanced over her shoulder, saw that she was being pursued, and broke into a sprint.

Laura tried not to panic. Running out into this open field wasn't the greatest of ideas. She envisioned hidden snipers firing upon them from atop the roof, snarling beasts running out to devour her, land mines exploding beneath her feet...

She ordered herself to banish these unlikely scenarios from her thoughts and focused her attention on the fleeing figure in front of her. Eliza must have been in excellent shape, for she was leaving Laura in the dust. Laura pumped her legs as fast as they would go until her muscles burned; but no matter how hard she tried, she could not catch up. She had to slow her pace. Eliza naturally shot ahead.

Minutes later, the blue, brown, and tan speck that was Eliza arrived at the entrance of the formidable structure and slipped through the door. There wasn't anything that Laura could do except go in after her.

At least she still had the spear.

Laura made it to the porch at last and stared at the door with a feeling of dread brewing in her chest. She prayed that her friends would hurry up and come to her aid, but they had yet to budge from their current position. Hopefully they had some other plan.

Fortunately, this door had a knob instead of a slot that needed picked with a knife. She said a quick Hail Mary and pulled it open only to find another door. Litchfield must have reinforced his house to withstand centuries of wear and tear or slow an attack by angry villagers.

The second door opened inward. Laura stepped into a dim entryway lit only by a solitary window built above the door. Tiny motes of dust swirled lazily through the air, fading into the shadows.

It was very quiet.

Laura strained her ears for a minute to determine which way Eliza had gone, but the only thing she heard other than her palpitating heartbeat was a slight creak somewhere above her.

"Eliza," she whispered. "Where are you?"

Hearing no reply, Laura thought it best to venture out of the entryway. In the feeble lighting, she could see a staircase and three corridors leading from the room. She selected the corridor leading straight back from the front door and decided to follow it.

As soon as she set foot in the hallway, a row of overhead lights clicked on.

Motion sensors.

So much for trying to be sneaky.

Several old paintings and photographs hung on the walls, giving the hallway a deceptively welcome touch. All of the doors on each side were closed. The hallway opened out into a spacious parlor, where another set of lights automatically lit themselves. A giant oriental rug that had seen far better days lay on the floor, and various pieces of furniture and potted plants sat about the place. Yet there was no sign of Eliza.

The hall light clicked off.

She was about to call out to Eliza again when suddenly Chopin's "Grande Valse Brillante" began blaring out of an unseen speaker. She jumped about a half a foot off of the floor at the unexpected noise but wasn't going to let it bother her. It was, after all, only a song. She had listened to it many times; *that* she was sure of.

It dawned on her that Litchfield had probably intended to scare her with the recording of the nineteenth-century waltz. Any other person from Sparkling Falls would have run away in terror.

She moved out of the parlor into another hallway that had a number of closed doors along it like the first one. She didn't understand why someone would want a house this huge. This place was like one big, eerie museum. She decided to take a chance and opened one of the doors to see if Eliza was hiding on the other side. Another light blinked on when the door opened, revealing what appeared to be a vacant guest bedroom. There was a bed covered with a dusty quilt, a large wooden bureau, and an assortment of half-burnt candles sitting on a bedside table.

The next two rooms were identical to the first. All of these empty bedrooms must have belonged to the men and women who called this place home during the great pandemic. Laura expected the fourth room to be the same; but when she stepped inside, the automatic lighting illuminated a vast room lined with shelves and shelves of books that reached all the way to the ceiling. One table held an array of dilapidated computer equipment that looked like it came straight out of a science fiction film.

This had to be the library where Lord Arcturus found the Bible and journal. There must have been at least ten thousand books in Litchfield's collection. Most appeared to be in excellent condition compared to the half-decayed ones they found in the abandoned house. There were novels; encyclopedias; dictionaries; religious works; how-to books; and a shelf full of thin, black tomes labeled "Journal 1," "Journal 2," and so on. Laura noted that Journal 101 immediately followed Journal 99.

The center of the room contained four or five mismatched armchairs arranged in a circle around a small table, on which sat an unfinished game of chess. The black side was clearly winning, for almost all of the white pieces were lined up in a neat row along the edge of the board. The white king had only a single pawn and a rook remaining to protect him, and two of the black pieces held the ruler in check. The black king, however, was still in starting position guarded by a trio of obsidian pawns. *Lord Arcturus is the white king,* Laura thought. *It looks like he's about to lose, but by golly I'm going to make sure he wins!*

Laura began to put all of the captured white pieces back on the board.

"Are you a fan of chess, my dear?" inquired a soft voice behind her.

Laura's heart leapt into her throat, and she accidentally dropped her spear.

It was the psychopath himself.

Litchfield turned out to be only an inch or so taller than she was, making him look far less intimidating than he had when he appeared as the giant talking head at the Holy Valley Day Celebration. Laura found herself staring directly into his crystalline blue eyes. The man was dressed entirely in black, everything from his shirt to his boots. His gray hair was thin and wispy, and he had a neatly kept beard that curled into a goatee. His face was emotionless, as Laura had suspected it would be; yet something about those eyes told her that a deadly storm was brewing deep inside.

Laura nervously shook her head. "I don't like chess," she said.

Litchfield tutted. "Such a shame. You look like you might be a worthy opponent."

"I don't play chess at all. I know I used to, but I quit because I always lost." Laura tried to remain calm and focused, not wanting the man to distract her with this useless banter.

"It is an honor to meet you in person," Litchfield continued in his deceivingly soothing voice. "I have been told that you came into my land through a portal, as did your friends, Rochelle Peltier and Andrew Walker. I find it interesting how you bonded so easily with them."

"How could Andrew have come through a portal?" Laura was dubious. "He never said anything to me about it."

Litchfield gave her a condescending smile. "Of course he never told anyone," he said, "for fear of what they would think of him. But I know the names and relations of every single person in this valley, and he has no connection to any of them. But that is irrelevant to the topic at hand. You arrived from a portal, and I would like to know more about you and your time. Tell me, what year was it when you departed?"

"It was two thousand and three. Why do you even care?"

"Two thousand and three…"

A dreamy sort of look came over him, and Laura edged a few steps closer to the fallen spear.

"That was seventy-nine years before my birth, Laura. Seventy-nine years! You're easily ninety-five years older than I am. Do you not find that fascinating?"

Laura, not currently interested in the bizarre paradox, lunged for the spear; but Litchfield had rather fast reflexes for a man so old and stomped on her hand as soon as she wrapped it around the wooden shaft. She cried out in pain and recoiled, clutching her hand close to her side.

"I'd be more careful than that if I were you," he said in an innocent tone as he picked up the spear and tossed it across the room. "You might accidentally hurt yourself."

Laura tried hard not to burst into tears. "Where are Spica and Eliza?" she asked him. Her hand was throbbing with so much pain that she wanted to throw up, but she couldn't allow the demon of a man to see her weakness.

The question seemed to catch Litchfield by surprise. "Eliza?" he said blankly. "Why in the world would I know where Eliza is?"

"Because she came into this house not five minutes before I did, and I haven't found her yet. What did you do with her?"

"I haven't done anything to the girl. I wasn't even aware she was here." Litchfield looked irritated. "I was in my quarters when I heard someone walking around down here, so I turned on my music player to frighten them away. Obviously, it did not have the desired outcome."

Laura decided he was telling the truth. "Fine," she said. "So you don't know where she is. But can you please tell me why you made her look like a freak with those contact lenses? She told us everything so don't pretend you don't know what I'm talking about."

Laura could see the ancient man's hands clench briefly into fists.

"You have to understand that I am a scientist," he said delicately. "I take great delight in studying things. I built this civilization from the ground up. And all this time, I have closely watched how people interact with one another. In Eliza's case, I wished to observe how a primitive culture would respond to a person with an apparent genetic abnormality." He gestured toward the game pieces on the table. "The world is one unending chess match, my dear, and I am the one playing it how I please. I poke and prod to move my pieces to places I find desirable. And the defiant ones who resist me I simply remove from the board." He pulled up his right sleeve, showing Laura a sheathed dagger strapped to his arm. "But you, Laura, are not of this chess match at all. You walked unexpectedly onto my board, scattering my pieces out of the way, the ones that I had worked on so tirelessly to arrange to perfection."

Despite the fact that Litchfield was going on like a madman, his words contained a chilling truth. "But these are *people* you're talking about!" she exclaimed. "Not pawns! You can't keep controlling people's lives like you're some god. You don't even let people out of the valley!"

Litchfield lowered his sleeve back down to re-conceal the knife. "You seem to be of above-average intelligence, and I am going to assume that Arcturus showed you one of the items he stole from me."

Laura nodded. "He did."

"Then you know about the disease that obliterated Earth's human population. Laura, there were twenty-five billion people living on this planet in twenty-four forty-two. As far as I know, the few thousand citizens of my valley are all who remain. I don't know what it was that killed off all those people, and I don't know if it's still lingering out there beyond the mountains waiting for its next prey. The only reason that my friends and I survived the pandemic is because we cut ourselves off from civilization. If my people migrate out of the valley, they could fall ill and die. I cannot allow that to happen. I saved mankind from destruction once, but I simply don't have the resources to do it a second time."

"If you're so concerned about saving lives, why is it that you kill people who do things you don't like?"

Litchfield's face twisted into that awful smile again. "It's a little thing called utilitarianism. I do things that create the greatest good for the greatest number of people. By sacrificing the delinquents, I quench the fires of rebellion before they might spread and wreak havoc on my peaceful valley."

"You're treating people like goldfish in a bowl." *Goldfish who die if they jump out*, she added to herself.

"It's far better to do that than to risk our species going extinct."

Laura decided it was time to change the subject. "Why did you make Yvonne kidnap Spica?" she asked.

The old man actually chuckled. "You're even more intelligent than I thought! In order to remain in control of the valley and prevent people from leaving, I have to make sure that no one knows about my mortal nature. If Arcturus went around blabbing that I'm a human being, then people would ignore my dire warnings, leave the valley, and end up dead. Spica's kidnapping served two purposes: to keep Arcturus's mouth shut and to make him appear insane in case he didn't. Sometimes I think I should have just killed him the moment I found him snooping around in here. It would have saved me a great deal of trouble. But it has been quite beautiful planning this for the past seven years. It took me a while to decide on the precise method of revenge, but it finally dawned on me that I could just start a rumor that he fancied killing children. It was rather convenient that his boy, Procyon, went missing. I could twist people's thoughts into believing that Arcturus had done him in."

Laura blinked in surprise. Subconsciously, she had assumed that Litchfield knew what had become of the child. He acted like he knew everything else. "You really don't know what happened to Procyon?" she asked.

"Nobody knows what happened to Procyon! And goodness, I'm not *that* omnipotent. For all I know, my wolf dogs had him for dinner. I suppose I should feel some sympathy since the Owens family is descended from me, but I don't."

"How can they possibly be descended from you if you never had children?"

"It's all a matter of technology. After Sparkling Falls was constructed, I wanted to start my own 'royal' bloodline. I had frozen some of my sperm cells back during my college days for future experimentation but never got around to it. It's amazing how long the tiniest cells can be frozen and still be revived. My friend, Gertrude, wanted to become the mother of my child, so I thawed out the cells. And without going into more scientific details, a child was conceived. We had a daughter and named her Samantha. The knowledge of the royal bloodline was closely guarded by my descendants for a couple of generations until one of them made me so furious that I forbade them, on pain of death, to pass the secret on to their children. Arcturus has no idea that I'm a distant grandfather of his."

Laura's hand was starting to feel a little better, and she flexed her fingers a few times to make sure they still worked. She didn't dare go after the spear for a second time. It was best to keep Litchfield talking for as long as possible so her friends could have the chance to come rescue her before the old man decided to get nasty with his dagger. "That's really interesting," she said, "but you never did say what you did with Spica."

"She's here, of course. I thought you'd have figured that out by now. I gave her her own bedroom suite and all the old toys she could possibly want, though she's still quite mischievous. I caught her trying to booby-trap the staircase outside of my personal quarters the other night. It was rather endearing. She had building blocks and stuffed animals on every step." He paused. "Spica is never allowed to leave my home. And since you know a bit too much about me, neither are you."

Laura felt her heart sink but did her best to look defiant. "I'm sure I'd be able to find a way out of here," she said.

A wicked gleam shone in the man's eyes. "I could easily arrange a speedy departure for you." In a flash, he had slipped the dagger from its hidden sheath and twirled it around between his wrinkled but agile fingers. Light glinted off of the blade. "I could kill you faster than you can blink, my dear. And then your youthful spirit would be free to roam the far reaches of creation. So what shall it be? An early grave or a lifetime of confinement?"

The sight of the weapon being waved around like some gruesome plaything was enough to make Laura dizzy with fear. "I'd prefer to stay alive."

"I thought you would! I have more empty bedroom suites on the third floor. Feel free to make yourself right at home. But if you and Spica make an attempt to escape, you must understand that I *will* kill you both." Litchfield happily stuffed the knife away.

Laura was about to give some snide response; but suddenly, Eliza charged in through the library door, half-dragging little Spica Owens behind her by the arm.

"Laura!" the woman shouted. "Looky who I found!"

Eliza and Spica sat on the floor, playing with blocks, while Laura drummed her fingers on a table top in deep rumination. She had been there for over an hour; yet there was still no sign of Mark, Rochelle, or the others. What was taking them so long to get here? Were they coming up with an elaborate plan of rescue or had some unforeseen harm fallen upon them?

Litchfield had directed Laura and Eliza to his recreation room on the second floor so they might not become bored and agitated during their permanent stay. But Laura had no interest in fun and games. Maybe if she hadn't been a prisoner she would have been in the mood to try out the old foosball table with Eliza or even throw a few darts.

"So how have you been, Spica?" she asked at last.

The little girl looked up from the tower she and Eliza were building. "I miss my mommy and daddy," she said. "Litchfield won't let me leave to go home. He's so mean." Two tears rolled down the child's cheeks.

"Have you tried to escape when he's asleep?"

"No. He said he would cut me into pieces and feed me to his wolf dogs if I tried to get out. And I think he really means it."

"We saw some wolf dogs during the night," Eliza said, placing another block onto the tower. "They attacked your daddy and chewed his leg all up. Then he went home."

Spica looked like she was going to be sick. "Did that really happen, Laura?"

Laura nodded, feeling a pang of sorrow in her heart. She hadn't planned on telling Spica about her father's injury, at least not yet.

"He lost a lot of blood. But my friend, Mark, tied his shirt around your dad's leg to stop the bleeding. All we can do now is pray he recovers."

Spica blinked and wiped away her tears. "Pray?"

"Yes. Pray to God, our true Creator. Ask him to keep your dad safe and to send his angels to protect him from harm."

"Did God make Litchfield?"

"Uh huh. He made everything."

"But where is he? I've never seen him."

"God is invisible to our eyes. But he's all around us, like the air we breathe. And sometimes if we listen just right, we can hear him speaking to us in our hearts. When we speak to him, he listens. And if we pray to him in earnest, our prayers may be answered. Do you want me to teach you some prayers?"

Spica smiled. "Okay."

"Now, first, you can fold your hands together like this," Laura began, demonstrating to the child, "and bow your head. Then we pray. First, I'll teach you the Lord's Prayer, which goes like this: Our Father, who art in heaven, hallowed be thy name. Thy kingdom come, thy will be done, on Earth as it is in heaven. Give us this day our daily bread and forgive us our trespasses as we forgive those who trespass against us. And lead us not into temptation, but deliver us from evil. Amen."

"Those are strange words," Eliza commented, having completed the block tower and redirected her attention to Laura and Spica.

"Yeah," said Spica. "What do they mean?"

"A lot of those words were used a *long* time ago," Laura said, realizing that Middle English had now been extinct for well over a millennium. "The prayer is basically asking God to nourish us and forgive us for our sins, like we forgive people who sin against us."

"What's a sin?" Eliza asked.

Laura was surprised but pleased to see her two fellow prisoners sitting there with identical expressions of excited curiosity. "A sin is something we do that is bad," she explained, "like lying and hurting other people."

"Litchfield is bad because he won't let me go home," said Spica. "Is that a sin too?"

"It certainly is."

They were silent for some time, until Spica spoke up again. "God," she said, "please get us out of this big, dumb house so I can go home and be with my family. I promise I won't ever put froggies in Alcor's bed again if I get out of here. And I'll stop taking Tabitha's shoes. And, God, please make Litchfield stop sinning. Make him eat lots and lots of asparagus so he won't be bad again."

Laura grinned. "Amen!"

Hours came and went, yet there was still no sign of Laura's companions. A knot of worry formed in her abdomen as she imagined a myriad of horrors that could have prevented them from following her. What would she do if they were all dead? Alcor and Tabitha were much too young to die. And poor Mark, with his warm heart and teasing smile … And Rochelle with her cheerful wittiness …

The only benefit to being a prisoner was that Litchfield's house was equipped with a somewhat primitive plumbing system and running water that was fed by an underground stream. However, the water lines lost pressure each time Laura flushed a toilet; and she had to use a mechanical hand pump to reinflate the lines with air. Litchfield informed her that he normally had to do this at least ten times a day. It was a lot of work; but nevertheless, it was far nicer and less smelly than using an outhouse.

For lunch, Litchfield served the trio rye bread covered in blackberry jam and some fresh apples. Laura couldn't help but wonder if he had laced her food with poison, but she was so hungry that she devoured the meal in an instant.

Laura went upstairs and selected a bedroom suite, which she honestly had no intention to use. The room was spacious and decorated in hideous shades of orange, olive, and pink. She didn't choose it for the color scheme. It offered an extensive view of the mountain just to the east, where she had left her friends. She stood at the window for a half an hour, trying to spot them; but it appeared they had gone.

Despite Litchfield's threats of murder, Laura thought it would be an excellent idea to escape from this ugly monstrosity of a house. She rummaged through the bedroom's large closet to seek out some item that might serve as a weapon. The bottom of the closet contained nothing other than dust and a moth-eaten pair of house slippers that were probably close to three centuries old. Some old suits hung limply from the steel rod spanning the length of the closet. Above that was a shelf on which sat a black plastic case. Laura grabbed it down and found a tarnished piccolo inside.

This didn't look very promising. If Litchfield caught her, what was she going to do, club him over the head with an ancient musical instrument? The thing was barely a foot long. Using this as a weapon would require Laura to come into very close proximity to

Litchfield; and at that distance he would have no trouble disemboweling her with his knife. If only the instrument was bigger!

Laura stepped back and stared at the scant number of items she had to work with. The clothing had no use. The piccolo was too small to inflict any damage upon her captor. An assault with clothes hangers would be ineffective in any fight. The only thing left was … the rod! That might come in handy.

She removed the garments from the closet and piled them in a heap on the floor. To her delight, the rod had been designed to fit any closet and was spring-loaded so she had no trouble popping it from its fittings. It came apart in two sections, and a metal spring slid out of one end. She placed the spring into her pocket in the event she would need it later. She decided that only one half of the rod would be necessary to take with her on her flight to freedom.

She waited until it was dark before slipping out of the ugly room to see if it was possible to get to the front door without being caught. She could sneak outside and find her friends, and then they would all charge into the house together to save the other two captives.

She carried the metal rod over her shoulder, praying she would not have to use it. Litchfield must have shut off his motion sensor lights for the evening, for Laura traveled down the third-floor hallway in almost total darkness. She made it to the stairwell and gripped onto the railing, taking one step at a time. Finally, she reached the dark entryway. The front door was now in sight. It stood there beckoning her, taunting her. This was too easy. She reached out her hand; and when she laid it upon the knob, her body was suddenly filled with excruciating pain. She automatically released her grip on the pipe, and the next thing she knew, she was lying on her back with Litchfield standing over her.

"Lovely evening for a walk, isn't it?" he said, glaring at her.

Laura wet her lips with her tongue and found that doing so required far more effort than normal. All of her muscles were swathed in a burning sensation, and she could barely move. "What did you do to me?" she asked, trying to sit up but only managing to wriggle like a worm.

"I shot you with my electroshock gun," he explained, holding up the pistol-shaped device for her to see. "I've been sitting out here for hours, waiting for you to make your escape."

Laura let her head back down and stared at the ceiling. "I guess you're going to kill me now."

"That was the plan, but I want to see you suffer first." He hit the trigger on his gun, and waves of electricity pulsed through her body anew. Laura writhed on the floor, screaming. She knew that the gun had attached some sort of projectile to her somewhere that allowed the electric current to flow from the gun into her. She was fairly certain it was on her left leg, since that seemed to be the focal point of the pain.

But it didn't matter anymore, did it? She could smell something burning (probably the pants she had borrowed from Rotanev). Dying in this fashion was the last thing she had in mind, but she had run out of ideas and could do nothing but lie there smoldering.

Litchfield released the trigger for a moment to scratch his nose. Laura saw this as an ample opportunity to delay him. "Is this ... what you did ... to Mark's parents?" she hissed through clenched teeth.

Litchfield laughed. "No, I stabbed them to death."

"What about ... the Matarnas?"

"Eliza's parents? I did electrocute them, but I set it up to make it look like they both drowned in the river. Why do you ask?"

"Just wondered ... that's all."

He pulled the trigger again, and Laura thought she felt her heart begin skipping beats. *God, I've failed you,* she said silently. The pain was so great that she had no way to stand up and fight back. Going at this rate she'd be dead within minutes, and Spica and Eliza would still be trapped here at this man's mercy.

"My friends ... are coming ... to save me," she said.

Litchfield laughed. "Friends? Laura, friends don't abandon each other. If you were indeed in the company of friends, why didn't they come in here with you to rescue the Owens girl?"

"I ... don't ... know."

"They must be cowards."

"Not ... cowards ... *You're* a coward ... not telling people the truth ..."

Litchfield's face became angry. He must have bumped up the setting on his gun, because now Laura was hurting *worse* than before. Tears spilled from her eyes, and she struggled to breathe. Every nerve in her body was on fire, and that fire would only be put out when she was dead.

When she was dead ...

Laura was surprised that she had come up with a plan even in the midst of agony. If she could convince Litchfield that he had killed her, he would turn off his weapon.

Laura let out an authentic scream and rolled her eyes up into her head. She let her mouth slack open, but only after inflating her diaphragm so she could hold her breath.

Litchfield released the trigger again. He bent down to examine her, let out a sort of *humph*, and detached the projectile from Laura's leg. He stood back up. Suddenly he swung his own leg and kicked Laura in the side so hard that she felt a couple of ribs pop out of place.

"Pathetic," he muttered. "That wasn't even the highest setting."

Laura felt Litchfield lift her over his shoulder and march her up the stairs out of the entryway. "I'll have to get Adalbert to dispose of you in the morning ... I'm getting too old for this." He dropped Laura onto the floor in the hallway. "There, now you're out of my way; and I won't have to look at you while I wait for your 'friends.'"

Laura heard his footsteps recede. *Thank you, Lord!* She knew her ordeal wasn't over yet, but at least she was no longer in immediate danger. She wished she could move. All she could do now was try to sleep and regain her strength.

Laura lay wide-awake on the olive green carpet, almost at her breaking point. She desperately needed to sleep but could not. She had been in the house for over twelve hours, hoping against hope that Mark and the others would come bursting down the door. Then Mark would bravely ascend the stairs to rescue his damsel in distress. It would have made a great scene in a romantic movie.

But no, she wasn't going to allow herself to be a damsel in distress. She was going to get out of there all by herself, with some guidance from above.

Father, she prayed, *I really need your help right now. I've got to get out of this house with Spica and Eliza as soon as possible. And please don't let anything bad happen to my friends. They don't deserve to die.*

Laura flexed the muscles in her arms and legs, grateful to have them functioning again. She eased herself to her feet and took a few deep breaths.

She then began to develop alternative plans of escape. She could find something heavy and knock out a window, but it would make too much noise. Even if the sound never reached Litchfield's bionic ears, she had no way of scaling the outside wall down to the safety of the ground without falling and breaking her neck.

A sudden noise jarred her from her thoughts. It sounded like the front door opening one floor below. Who could be coming in to visit at this late hour? Was it Mark?

Then she heard a familiar voice call out, "Oh, Edward, look what *we* found!"

CHAPTER 17

The voice belonged to Adalbert Wang. There was no mistaking the showman's lilt in the man's nuances.

That couldn't be a good sign.

Laura crept out onto the second-floor landing and halted when she saw who all had arrived in the entryway.

Below her stood Adalbert and Louise Wang and Yvonne Harding, holding a large collection of weaponry. Laura's missing friends huddled together in a solemn mass behind them. Mark happened to look up and made eye contact with Laura, and he gave her a sorrowful smile.

"We tried, Laura," he said. "We really did."

Laura ran down the steps and gave him a tight squeeze. "It's okay. I'm just glad you're safe."

Litchfield emerged from the shadows. His gun protruded from his pocket. "You're alive?" he said to Laura. His gaze bored into hers, and she huddled closer to Mark.

"Yeah," she said. "You really stink at checking people's pulses. By the way, you were wrong. My friends *didn't* abandon me."

"I can see that. But where were they this whole time? You might have been spared a great deal of suffering if they hadn't left you alone."

"We found them sneaking around outside," Adalbert said, flashing a smile at his boss. "They told us they didn't want to fight, so they surrendered."

"Sorry we took so long," said Rochelle. "We didn't want to walk out into the open field and be seen, so we kept to the edge of the forest and made it around to the side of the house. We waited until it got dark and tried to find a decent way in. Obviously, this wasn't what we had in mind. Though it did work, didn't it?" The poor woman looked exhausted.

"You all will think twice the next time you try to break in here," Yvonne said with a smirk. "Won't you?"

"If Litchfield has his way, there won't even be a next time," Louise countered.

Laura didn't understand why Louise was here with her husband and the woman whom she couldn't stand when, just a few nights before, she'd admitted to being opposed to Litchfield's agendas.

"You've done some excellent work!" Litchfield looked over the captives like a fisherman examining the day's catch. "It must have been perfect timing when I summoned you earlier today. But where are the others?"

"They were too busy to come."

"Oh well. That's understandable. In any case, if you three hadn't arrived when you did, they might have actually gotten in here and freed the young ladies. And you all know what would happen if they got back to town."

"They would tell everyone the truth," said Louise, "which is what our people deserve to know."

Litchfield stared at her blankly. "Excuse me?"

To Laura's immense surprise, Adalbert Wang tossed the stolen weapons aside and lashed out with his fist as if to hit Litchfield squarely in the abdomen. But a millisecond before the fist was able to make contact, Litchfield whipped the dagger out from under his sleeve and slashed it across Adalbert's knuckles. Undeterred, Adalbert moved in for a second punch.

"What are you doing?" Yvonne shrieked, gripping a confiscated arrow like a miniature spear.

Louise swiped the weapon from her hand. "We're claiming what is rightfully ours. Freedom."

Yvonne let out a growl and launched herself into the brawl. Rochelle immediately stooped down and snatched up as many arrows as she could. Mark spotted his machete and quickly tossed it to Laura.

Laura was unsure of what to do with the broad-edged knife, for she had no desire to hurt anybody. Litchfield, still holding the dagger in one hand, pulled out his electroshock gun and aimed it at Adalbert. Nothing happened when it was fired, and Laura guessed that he had used up the charge while trying to kill her. He threw down the useless weapon and kicked Adalbert between the legs. The man let out a yelp and sank to his knees.

Yvonne was putting up an admirable fight considering she had four or five people attempting to force her to the ground but had not yet surrendered. Laura looked up to see Litchfield coming straight at her with his knife. She raised the machete to defend herself; but the next thing she knew, the six-hundred-and-one-year-old man had seized her by the hair and swung her around so her back was pinned against his chest. She could feel a cold metal blade being pressed to the skin of her neck.

"Make one move," he muttered in her ear, "and you're dead for real this time."

Laura's vision began to swim in front of her, and she could see that everyone else in the room had frozen in mid fight to gape at this unexpected move.

"Edward, let her go," Adalbert pleaded as he made an effort to stand. His hand was bleeding, but he didn't seem to care. "She's not a part of this."

"*Oh really?*" Litchfield roared. "If she hadn't barged in here to rescue the Owens brat, then none of this would even be happening!"

Yvonne was glaring at the Wangs. Her face had turned blood red in anger. "You two have been planning to overthrow Edward all along, haven't you?"

Louise straightened up and stared directly into the other woman's eyes. "Clarissa and her husband had their baby last night, a little girl named Angeline. I don't want my granddaughter to live her entire life trapped inside of our valley as the rest of us have been."

"You're all going to die!" Litchfield hissed.

It felt like the dagger was starting to break the skin, and Laura clamped her eyes shut.

"You never saw the horrors that I did. Charleston was a bustling city reduced to nothing more than a steel and concrete grave in a matter of months!"

"My wife and I would like to take our chances," said Adalbert. "I have always been loyal to you and your beliefs. But lately, things have been getting out of hand. Kidnapping an innocent child should never have been part of your agenda."

"So you were just playing along when you ordered Lord Arcturus to be placed under house arrest?" Yvonne asked.

Adalbert bowed his head. "That is correct. I didn't even have Andrew assign a guard to the back door so Lord Arcturus could slip out whenever he wanted to."

Laura could feel the old man quivering with rage, and she opened her eyes. "You don't deserve to live," he said to the Wangs. "After all I have done for you! Louise, I gave you *life*! You wouldn't even exist if I hadn't cloned you from one of the embryos that were originally donated to my lab! And even then I could have easily killed you to study your stem cells like I did with so many others! And if I hadn't implanted you in your mother's womb forty-two years ago, you'd still be in a frozen tube locked away in my laboratory freezer! You were the last embryo I had. I always expected my final one to be somebody special. But apparently, I was quite mistaken."

"How very touching." Louise sighed. "Now put the knife down and let Laura go."

"No."

Laura's pulse jumped up a few dozen beats per minute. Litchfield *was* slowly cutting her neck. She could feel a tiny droplet of blood roll down into her shirt. Such a shame that she couldn't play dead a second time!

Oh, God, please don't let it end like this! she wailed inside her head. *Please send an angel to stop him! You can't let him do this to me!*

She gazed helplessly at her friends. Mark's fists were shaking, and Rochelle and Tabitha looked like they were about to cry.

Laura began to silently recite the Act of Contrition. She knew she had learned it in Sunday school when she was younger. *Oh, my God, I am sorry for my sins and in choosing to sin and failing to do good. I have sinned against you and your church. I firmly intend, with the help of your son, to make up for my sins and to live as I should. Jesus Christ suffered and died for us. In his name, dear God, forgive me. And don't forget to send the angel,* she added.

Suddenly, something shattered right behind her. Litchfield lost his grip on the dagger and crumpled to the floor, pulling Laura with him.

Laura stood up on shaking legs, noting that large chunks of broken pottery were scattered across the floor and Litchfield was in sort of a daze. Standing three feet away was Eliza Matarna, holding what remained of an antique pitcher. She grinned.

"I hope that wasn't a sin," she said, "but something told me that now was a good time to come kick Litchie's butt."

"Now we need to decide what to do with you two pieces of vermin," Louise said after Yvonne had given up the battle following Litchfield's incapacitation. Litchfield sat on the floor, rubbing his head where Eliza had smashed the pitcher over it. Laura didn't feel in the least bit sorry for him.

Thanks for giving me a hand, she said to the divine voice as she pocketed the old man's knife. *Might as well keep it as a morbid souvenir.*

"I say we should chuck them both into a portal," said Mark.

"No," said Rochelle. "That would be too easy for them. Besides, Yvonne has children who don't deserve to lose their mother."

"She's right," said Frank Yelton. "I can't even imagine what it would do to Wade and Natalie if something happened to Evelyn."

Laura had an interesting thought pop into her head. "Rochelle," she said, "do you remember how petty criminals were treated in the Middle Ages?"

Rochelle nodded. "Of course. They were placed in stocks in the center of town so everyone could gawk at them." Her face brightened. "That would be the perfect punishment! The only thing being hurt would be their pride."

"Exactly."

"What should we do with the minions who stayed in town?" Adalbert asked his wife.

Louise shrugged. "Who cares? They aren't my concern, and once they see our 'creator' tied up, they'll probably just run home to their parents anyway. The cowards."

"What's going on down here?" asked a small voice from the direction of the stairs.

Everyone turned to see Spica peering through the bars supporting the banister.

"Spica! You're alive!" Tabitha shouted, running up to her younger sister.

The little girl leapt into her arms, almost knocking the older girl backward down the steps. Alcor burst into tears at the sight of his missing sibling and ran to join Tabitha. Laura found herself becoming misty-eyed as well.

The three Owens children came back down to the entryway, and Spica saw that Litchfield and Yvonne were sitting back to back on the floor with a cord from one of the curtains tied around them. The child got an evil glint in her eye and walked right up to the old man.

"I'm going to make sure you eat *lots* of asparagus," she said.

Since Litchfield and Yvonne were outnumbered eleven to two, it was not difficult to tie their hands behind their backs and herd them out of the mansion like a pair of stubborn cattle. Andrew, Frank, and Mark were more than happy to prevent the psychotic old man from escaping by locating more ropes and attaching them to his bindings to use as leashes. Yvonne's bindings were not so extensive. Louise and Adalbert borrowed some bows and arrows from the invading party and had them at the ready in case Yvonne tried to run off.

Fortunately, no more wolf dogs ran to attack them as they processed through the mountains. They arrived in Sparkling Falls in the early morning and were greeted with curious stares from the townspeople. Litchfield and Yvonne were promptly tied to two separate benches and placed on display in the main thoroughfare of town. Andrew and the Wangs started explaining the truth about Litchfield to anyone willing to listen.

Laura, on the other hand, accompanied Mark and Rochelle to the house of Owens after staring at the two crooks for a few satisfying minutes. There had been a certain beauty in seeing the elderly man brought to justice after two and a half centuries of unnecessary deceit.

The atmosphere within the stone house had transformed into one of immeasurable joy. Lady Capella looked happier than Laura had ever seen her, and the lines of worry in her visage had melted away. Sualocin stood in the living room, playing a jaunty little tune on a fiddle, tapping his foot on the floor to keep time while Spica and Tabitha skipped around in a circle.

Lord Arcturus sat off to one side, beaming at his reunited family. Half of his face was obscured by a thick, white bandage; and his mutilated leg rested on an ottoman. It too was wrapped in layers and layers of cloth that had been tied into place. Laura noticed that the man had a cane close to his side.

"I think," said Lady Capella, "this is the happiest day of my life! The only thing that would make it any more complete is if Procyon suddenly came walking in the door."

June transformed itself into a sunny July, which, in turn, melted into a muggy August. Laura had a promise to keep with Lord Arcturus, so she vowed to not seek out the portal until she had educated everyone about the gospel. She and Rochelle started a Bible class that met three days a week down at the celebration grounds. It turned out to be more popular than she initially expected; and every time the group met, the number of students visibly increased.

Litchfield and Yvonne had been released from humiliation after a mere three days, far less time than Laura thought they deserved. Yvonne went home to her husband and children. Litchfield, on the other hand, was then imprisoned in Eliza's former cell for two weeks after a unanimous vote by the town council. He served his brief sentence and subsequently was required to shovel horse manure off the streets as a punishment for the rest of his life. Every evening, he slunk off into the tavern to start destroying his artificial liver with glass after glass of whiskey. And nobody planned on stopping him.

When she wasn't teaching, Laura spent a lot of time with Mark. Usually, they would stroll along the riverbank, skipping stones, laughing, and talking about any little thing they fancied. It was so relaxing to have someone like him around. He always listened to the silliest of things she had to say and was constantly finding ways to make her smile.

"So, do you think your memory is ever coming back?" he asked her one morning as they lay side by side on a grassy hill, watching the clouds drift by above them.

Laura shrugged. "I have no idea. I've remembered little things here and there, but I don't see how it can all come back. Maybe it just isn't meant to be."

"Aren't you upset about that?"

"Not as much as I was. I haven't even had a flashback in weeks."

"No more bloody icicles?"

"Nope. Something tells me the guy who got stabbed is okay, something in here." She held her fist above her heart, feeling its steady rhythm flow into her fingers.

Mark sat up and gazed over at her with those gentle eyes, pulsating with an inner light. "Did I ever tell you how beautiful I think you are?"

Laura laughed. "I don't think so. Why?"

"I just wanted you to know you're the most beautiful woman I've ever laid eyes upon. And I don't just mean you've got a pretty face. There's something about you that all the other females around here don't have."

Laura raised an eyebrow. "Such as?"

"I'm not sure what you'd call it. It's something unseen, but I can see it. It's like some invisible golden light surrounding you that reached out and touched my heart. I feel stronger and happier inside than I ever have before." He broke off for a moment. "Heck, Laura, I think I love you."

That afternoon, Laura walked down to one of the community gardens with a basket so she could gather some ripe tomatoes for the sauce that Rochelle planned on making that evening. She had a new excited spring in her step. She felt so . . . so alive!

Andrew Walker was hunched over in the garden, digging up some potatoes a few rows over when Laura arrived.

"Hi, Andrew," she said when she saw him. "What's up?"

The man stood upright. "I have great news! I told my wife that she and Joseph should come back from Upton to live with me again," he said with a smile. "They should be here tomorrow evening. I decided I should stock up on some food so we don't have to keep coming down here and leave Joseph unattended."

"That's great! You never know, it might do him some good to be back in his home town." Laura paused. "Does your wife know that you came here through a portal?"

Andrew almost dropped the dirty trowel he was holding. "Yes, she does. But how in the world did *you* know about it?"

"Litchfield told me."

The man snorted. "I should have known. He's got that uncanny ability to figure things out that other people don't. Do you want me to tell you about it?"

"Sure."

"Well, I lived in West Virginia with my abusive father. My mom had run off with some bank executive from Charleston when I was still a toddler. I haven't seen her since. I hated it. Dad drank too much and beat me all the time, so I started sneaking out of the house and finding little places where I could hide. One day, I happened to stumble into a portal way out behind my house and ended up in the woods a few miles north of Sparkling Falls. I was terrified and thought I might be hallucinating, but I managed to get back through and went home. A few days later, I found the courage to try it again. I traveled back and forth many times. I discovered that the portal was invisible unless I was standing within inches of it. Each time I came through, I made exact notes of where the portal was. And then I'd go exploring. I liked to spy on the village from a distance and watch all the people. One day back at home, I got in trouble for forgetting to take out the trash and Dad beat me so hard that he probably would have killed me if I hadn't managed to run away and escape through the portal. I never went back."

"I'm really sorry to hear that." Laura stared at the man, who was always so full of cheer and positive energy even when discussing some tragedy. That Andrew had gone through so much turmoil in his youth but still kept a smile on his face amazed her.

"Goodness, Laura, you don't need to feel sorry for me!" Andrew laughed. "If I hadn't come here, I never would have met my wife or Frank or Arcturus or any of my other good friends. Living here has given me purpose in life. Even if you feel like your world is falling apart and you can't get through a single day without treading through the fires of hell, chances are that some good will come out of it in the end."

Laura nodded, understanding. "You're right. I guess everything has to happen for a reason."

"That it does."

"So, what year was it when you left?"

"Nineteen eighty-nine. I was about thirteen years old. I've forgotten much of my past, but I do remember this really kind older couple who lived just a few miles down the road from us. Sometimes I'd go visit them when Dad was away at work." He smiled. "They always had fresh chocolate chip cookies there for me to eat."

"What were their names?" Laura's heart began to beat faster, but she didn't know why.

"Berger was their last name. I don't remember their first ones since I only ever called them Mr. and Mrs. They had a son who was about five years older than me. His name was Tom. They also had a twenty-something-year-old daughter named Alicia, who'd come over sometimes with her husband and baby girl." He broke off as if he had suddenly lost the ability to speak.

"Are you okay?" she asked.

Andrew shook his head in apparent wonder. "I just remembered the little girl's name. That's all."

"Well, what was it?"

The man glanced down at the hole he had dug. "Her name was Laura Owens."

Laura's jaw dropped. "You're kidding me."

"No. I'm not. That really was her name."

"You … you don't think it was *me*, do you?"

Andrew gave a short nod. "I do see a strong resemblance."

"But how can my last name really be Owens?" Laura was so confused. "That's just too weird to be a coincidence. I mean, it is sort of a common name, but…" She paused. "What was my father's name?"

"Preston."

Laura's mind went numb. Preston. Preston Owens. It kind of sounded like Procyon. It was only a three-letter variation in spelling, a slight alteration that would be more acceptable to the average citizen of the late twentieth century. She gulped. Everything began to click into place like a thousand jigsaw puzzle pieces assembling themselves into a glaringly obvious scene.

On the day she had arrived in Sparkling Falls, Frank Yelton had thought she looked familiar. Mark had said much the same thing. Even Lady Capella had seen a family resemblance when she told Laura to use the Owens surname.

You have the same beautiful eyes that my dear little Procyon once had, the woman had said.

Procyon disappeared without a trace. If he had been killed or died of starvation out in the woods, someone would have come across his remains sooner or later. According to everyone in town, no one ever had.

Death was, of course, not the only explanation for Procyon's disappearance. There was one alternative: a portal.

Laura envisioned a younger version of Lord Arcturus; and suddenly, the image of a warmhearted man with dark hair and hazel eyes presented itself in her mind. He was bundled up in a heavy coat and gloves and was pummeling a man in his early thirties with a steady barrage of snowballs. Two little girls stood nearby, and a blonde woman and her parents watched the fight from the safety of a screened porch.

The girls giggled merrily as the younger man made a dramatic show of being attacked, letting out false cries of pain and jumping from side to side to dodge Preston's shots.

Laura, who was observing the pretend battle from the sidelines, decided to join in on the fun. She bent down, scooped up a chunk of snow, and carefully molded it into a sphere. When the younger man had his back turned, she lobbed it into the air with all of her might.

Unfortunately, she had aimed much too high and the snowball struck a huge icicle that had formed at the end of a sagging tree branch that hung over the yard. It snapped free and plummeted to the earth. She shouted for the man to move out of the way, but it was too late. The spear of ice plunged into his chest through his coat and knocked him to the ground. Blood went everywhere. Children screamed. The man gasped in pain.

"Preston, call an ambulance!" the blonde woman cried as she ran to help the injured man. With the sureness of a skilled nurse, she yanked off her scarf and wrapped it around the icy projectile so it would not shift and cause any more damage.

The ambulance arrived several minutes later, sirens blaring. The man was lifted onto a stretcher by a team of paramedics and placed inside. His grieving parents climbed in to accompany him to the hospital.

"Laura, you should stay here," her father instructed. His expression was very grave. "Try to keep the wood burner and fire going. I'm not sure how long this will take. I'll call you when we find out anything. Okay?"

Laura nodded as tears poured from her eyes. Her mother loaded the little girls into the blue minivan, and her father started the engine. The doors slammed shut, and the vehicle followed the wailing ambulance out of the driveway.

She was alone. She turned and looked at the place where the man had fallen. The ground was splattered with bright red blood that stood out in sharp contrast to the pure white snow. Laura could feel tiny snowflakes stinging her cheeks and nose. They were biting her; punishing her for her crime. She dropped to her knees and covered her face with her hands. Uncle Tom was probably about to die, and it was all her fault.

"Laura, what's wrong?"

She snapped back to the present to see Andrew staring at her with concern. She discovered that she was crying. "Oh, Andrew," she sobbed. "I remember who I am! Thank you so much for telling me about my family! Otherwise I never would have remembered them!" Unashamed, she threw her arms around him.

He patted her awkwardly on the back.

"You're welcome," he said, sounding embarrassed.

Laura stood back and wiped her eyes. "And I know what happened to Procyon! Oh my gosh! I've got to go tell Lord Arcturus!" And without further ado, she raced out of the garden and up the road to the house of Owens.

CHAPTER 18

Preston Owens was a tough man, or so he'd always been told. He was found abandoned in the woods at the age of four, cold, shivering, and crying for his mother and father. Every newspaper in the Virginias reported that a child had been found and asked that his family please come forward.

But no one ever claimed him. Children's services shook their heads in disgust, not understanding why someone would tattoo a blue circle on the palm of their kid's hand before dumping him off near a West Virginia roadside park.

Preston lived in foster care until the Albertson family adopted him two years later. They promptly changed his name to something they deemed more "common." After all, they said, Procyon was the name of a star in the constellation Canis Minor, and they didn't want their new son to be made fun of for it in school.

"But my name is Procyon Owens!" he remembered wailing. "I know it is! Preston Albertson is a stupid name!"

Over the years, he grew to like the name Preston, though when he turned eighteen he chose to change his last name back to Owens. His adoptive parents were upset but understanding; and in the end, he officially became Preston Albertson Owens.

He never did stop wondering about his real family. He could not recall their names, and their faces had slowly faded from his memory. But he did remember being loved and cared for, and he knew deep in his heart that they never would have purposely abandoned him. He had no idea what could have happened to them.

He knew full well the pain they must have experienced when they became separated from him. His oldest daughter had now been missing for over two months. She had stayed at her maternal grandparents' house to keep it heated while everyone else went to the hospital with his brother-in-law. He had tried to call Laura to assure her that Tom Berger would indeed survive, but she never answered her phone.

It snowed so hard that day that even the most heavily traveled roads could not be traversed. Preston and his family were snowed in at the hospital. The roads were finally cleared a few days later, and they made it back to his in-laws' house only to find that Laura was gone. They searched desperately for hours, scouring the house and property for any sign that could have shown what happened to her.

It was all in vain.

A nationwide Amber Alert was issued, and Laura's smiling face appeared on countless news broadcasts for two months. But nobody had seen her, and the news of her disappearance faded from the airwaves.

The snows of January had slowly melted away; and now, in late March, they had been replaced by tiny wildflowers sprouting from the moist earth. The first signs of warmer weather were on their way.

He was at his in-laws' house again, a painful reminder of the last time he had seen his daughter.

He stood at the bathroom sink, scrubbing his hands. He happened to glance up at his grizzled reflection in the mirror and squinted at the stranger he saw staring back at him.

Man, he looked terrible.

Sometime in the past two months, he had developed the most awful-looking bags under his eyes. He looked almost sixty. And was it his imagination, or did his hair look a heck of a lot grayer than it used to?

He sighed and went out into the kitchen to listen to the weather report on the radio. He'd heard they were calling for rain, which would give him a decent excuse to cancel his company picnic this coming weekend.

Clarence Berger, his father-in-law, sat at the table, smoking a cigar and reading over a two-day-old newspaper. He looked up when Preston walked in. "Did you ever hear who won the Opening Day game?" he asked. "Tom must have used the sports section to get the fire going this morning."

Preston shook his head. "I have no idea. You know I don't pay attention to that kind of thing anymore."

He started to switch on the radio, but his wife called to him from the other room. "Preston, can you go see if there are any more paint rollers down in the basement?"

"Yeah. I'll go take a look." His wife was helping her mother repaint the living room walls. Maybe he'd even lend them a hand so he could keep his mind off more upsetting matters.

He grabbed a flashlight out of the junk cabinet and went into the pantry, kicking boxes out of the way so he could get to the basement door. As he descended the staircase, he recalled how the pantry and basement doors had been ajar when they returned from the hospital with a recuperating Tom. He had thought that Laura might have gone down to fetch something, but the basement turned out to be as vacant as the rest of the house.

Preston shined the flashlight back and forth along the storage shelves but did not see any paint rollers. Alicia was out of luck. But wait! Wasn't there supposed to be a really old cellar below the main basement that remained from the original house that had been on the site? Nobody ever went down there. Someone could have stashed some supplies there long ago and forgotten about them.

Praying that there weren't too many spiders lurking around, he crept down the other flight of stairs. He hoped that the wood was sturdy enough to support him. After all, it had to be at least a hundred years old, probably even more than that.

The dark room at the bottom of the stairs looked empty and he turned to go, but some items on the floor caught his eye. There was the skeleton of a rodent, probably a squirrel judging from its size. Some dry leaves skittered across the floor as if caught in a breeze that Preston had not felt. That was odd. Preston looked down at his feet and saw his father-in-law's missing flashlight. He'd been complaining for weeks that he couldn't find it. What was it doing down in this ancient cellar? Unless Laura could have carried it down there. That would explain why the basement door had been left open the day they got back from the hospital. But why would she have just left the flashlight lying on the floor?

Preston began to feel extremely dizzy. He squatted on the floor and lowered his head, which is what his wife frequently prescribed when someone was going to faint. He didn't know what had come over him. The air started shimmering, and he felt like he couldn't breathe. Maybe he was having a heart attack. It wouldn't have come as any great surprise. Excessive stress had been known to do that to people.

He clutched his hand to his racing heart. If he was indeed having a heart attack, he certainly didn't want to die down here alone. He started to call out his wife's name; but as soon as the sound issued from his throat, he became enveloped in a blinding white light. The last thing he remembered before the cellar dissolved into nothingness was the sound of footsteps pounding down the stairs and one bloodcurdling scream.

Preston felt like he was going down one nightmarish water slide, minus the water. The ride must have only lasted for a few seconds. It stopped as suddenly as it had begun, and the white light winked out.

I'm dead, he thought. *I'm dead and in heaven.*

He looked at the forest around him. It was too real to just be a hallucination resulting from a lack of oxygen to the brain. Was that dazzling light the famous pearly gates? If so, where was his Maker?

He held up his right hand. The jagged scar he had received from a broken windshield in a car accident a few years back was still there, as vivid as ever. Weren't people supposed to have glorified bodies in heaven?

So maybe he wasn't really dead.

For some strange reason, this place began to seem familiar to him, like something out of a distant dream. He was struck with a fantastic thought: had this bizarre phenomenon happened to Laura too?

"Laura," he said aloud, "are you here?"

There was no reply, as he had suspected. Preston started walking around the clearing. He cursed the heat. The angle of the sun indicated midsummer, August most likely. No wonder he was sweating like he had just run a marathon.

He spotted a deer path leading into the trees and decided to follow it. It wasn't long before he found his way out of the forest. Before him lay a valley covered in log houses, cow pastures, and fields planted with crops. A river flowed lazily past the town; and about a mile and a half away from him, the mountains continued.

Sparkling Falls, said a small voice within him. *You are home.*

Was it true? The more he took in the sights the more things he recognized, like that big stone house over there. He decided to go knock on the door and ask its occupants if they had ever heard of anybody named Laura Owens. It was worth a try. He just hoped the people spoke English.

He approached the house, admiring the multitude of beautiful flowers that grew across the lawn. His wife would have loved them. He'd tell her all about it, assuming he ever made it home.

Once Preston was on the stone doorstep, he felt a moment of hesitation. These people were going to think he had lost his mind.

He knocked a few times and took a step backward while he waited for someone to come answer it. About ten seconds later, a man roughly his own age peered out the door with apparent caution.

"Can I help you?" the man asked in an unidentifiable accent that was easy enough to understand. He opened the door a little wider, revealing a recently healed scar on his left cheek. It looked like something had tried to take a hefty bite out of his face.

Preston gave a nervous laugh. "You're probably going to think I'm insane."

The man at the door smiled, causing the reddish-purple scar to wrinkle. "Not necessarily. My life has been nothing *but* insanity. I'll know it when I see it."

"Well," Preston began, "I swear I used to live here."

The man laughed. "Live here, in this house?"

Preston shrugged. "I said you'd think I was insane. But this place looks so familiar. I seem to remember playing out here and conking my head on that big sundial."

The scarred man's expression changed to one that Preston couldn't read. "Sir," he said slowly, "may I ask you what your name is?"

Preston paused for a moment before speaking. "I'm Preston Owens."

"I don't know anybody named Preston, but this *is* the Owens residence."

"Well, I wasn't always named Preston. I used to be Procyon. My adoptive parents didn't like it, so they had it changed."

The man's eyes grew round with shock. "You...you can't be. Procyon would be eleven years old now. *You* are a grown man. You're my age, for Litch's sake!"

"That really is my name," Preston insisted. "Some people found me lost in the woods when I was four years old. Nobody ever figured out where I came from."

"Procyon went missing when he was four years old."

Preston cleared his throat, which had become choked with emotion. "How exactly did you know him?" he asked.

The man had tears in his eyes. "He was my son."

Preston was dumbfounded. It was true that they did kind of look alike. They were the same height, had the same nose, the same jaw line...

"Dad?" he said. "You're really my dad?"

"Capella!" the man bellowed, his voice cracking. "Get out here!" He grabbed Preston's arm and yanked him inside. The man limped along with a cane but was still strong enough that he nearly popped Preston's arm out of its socket.

About five or six people rushed into the room.

"Arcturus, who is this?" asked a pregnant, dark-haired woman, eyeing Preston with curiosity.

"Capella, this is Procyon, our son!"

The woman stared blankly at her husband. "But Procyon would be eleven. This man has to be at least thirty-seven or thirty-eight."

"Procyon would *not* be eleven years old if he had wandered into a portal the day he went missing, grew up in the past, and returned here through a different portal," the man named Arcturus explained.

Capella turned back to Preston. "Hold up the palm of your hand," she ordered.

Preston obeyed, showing her the blue tattoo that had been there for as long as he could remember.

And with that, his long-lost mother fainted.

After she had been revived and given a mug of hot tea to sip on, it was explained to Preston that his little sister, Spica, had recently been kidnapped by a mentally disturbed old man and his traitorous henchwoman. Spica had finally been rescued and her abductors brought to justice, but the stress had still worked its damage on Capella Owens.

Then Preston was reintroduced to his "older" siblings, who were now oddly young enough to be his own children.

Speaking of which…

"I was wondering," Preston said, "if any of you know the whereabouts of my daughter, Laura. She has long, brown hair; hazel eyes; is about this tall—" He broke off, noticing that his entire family was gaping at him.

Little Tabitha started cackling.

"You have *got* to be kidding me," said Alcor.

Laura couldn't believe that Procyon was her father. That meant that Lord Arcturus and Lady Capella were her grandparents and their other children were her aunts and uncles! Of course, there was the unpleasant fact that a few drops of Litchfield's "royal" blood ran through her veins; but she was too happy to care.

She almost collided with Mark, who was walking out of the general store with a new pair of pants slung over his shoulder.

"What are you doing?" he asked, laughing. "Running a footrace?"

Laura was barely able to contain her excitement. "I finally remembered who I am!" she exclaimed. "My name really *is* Laura Owens! And you're not going to believe this, but Procyon Owens is my dad!"

Mark cracked up laughing. "Well that certainly explains it! I knew you looked familiar as soon as I laid eyes on you. You look just like the kid."

"Man," Laura corrected. "But hey, come on up to the house with me! I'm going to tell everyone who I am!"

Mark grinned. "Now this is going to be interesting."

Her father was the last person Laura expected to see when she and Mark flew through the front door. But there he was, sitting at the dining room table, talking and laughing with Lord Arcturus just as if they had never been parted.

"Dad!" she shouted, running over and giving her father a gigantic squeeze. "You're here!" She didn't even care to ask how he had found the portal.

"Thank God you're alive!" he cried. "When we came back from the hospital to find that you were gone, I thought I'd never see you again!"

"It just goes to show that miracles do happen," said Lord Arcturus. "I still can't get over the fact that I'm forty-two and my little Procyon is thirty-eight! It almost gives me a headache to think about."

"You're not alone there," said Preston.

Laura marveled at how similar the two men looked sitting side by side. It was a wonder that the sight of Lord Arcturus hadn't triggered the return of her memory months ago.

"How's Uncle Tom?" she asked her father.

"He's doing well. The icicle only sank about two inches into his chest. It didn't hit any major organs, and he had to have about seven stitches. I tried to call you to let you know he'd be fine, but you never answered the phone."

"I know I didn't." Laura paused to wipe the tears of joy from her eyes. "I finally remember what happened that day. I was upstairs when my phone rang, and I ran and fell down the steps. I hit my head so hard on the floor that I couldn't remember who I was. But everything just came back to me about ten minutes ago."

Preston looked at her with eyes full of pity. "You had amnesia?"

"Uh huh. I had a pretty big bump on my head too, but it finally went away."

He sighed. "Your mother is going to have a stroke when she hears about this."

Laura nodded in agreement. He was probably right. Alicia Owens was an emergency room nurse who prided herself in that her own children had never been hurt severely enough to pay the hospital a visit.

"Do you want to come home now?" her father asked. "We've all been missing you."

"What if we can't find the portal?"

"Then we'll have to keep looking! What is a portal, anyway?"

"Technically it's a wormhole," Laura explained. "This is the year twenty-six eighty-three. Some scientists made wormholes to connect different times, and we both ended up stumbling into them."

"Unbelievable."

"I know! I was afraid that if I found the portal again, that it wouldn't be the same year anymore back home. But someone just told me that he went through a portal lots of times, so I guess we don't have to worry about that."

"Well, let's get going!"

Laura found herself to be surprisingly hesitant. "I will, under one condition."

"What's that?"

"You have to let me come back here whenever I want to." She glanced over at Mark. "I've made too many friends here, and I don't want to just leave them all. It wouldn't be right."

Preston laughed. "I'm not going to stop you! Besides, I'd like to come back here and visit my family. Now let's head back to that clearing to see if we can zap ourselves home."

Mark, Rochelle, and the entire Owens family escorted Laura and her father to Maribu Clearing. Laura had changed back into her twenty-first-century garb before leaving her bedroom one last time. How ironic that it had once belonged to her father!

The group arrived at the grassy place among the trees and spent the next hour walking back and forth, trying to determine the precise location of the portal.

"I swear it was about right here," Preston mused, gesturing where he stood.

Laura frowned. "Maybe you're just not standing in the right place."

Five feet to her left, Mark let out a yelp of surprise and dematerialized.

"I think he found it," she said. She approached the place where Mark had been and held out her arm. She could feel an intense field of invisible energy surround it, and she quickly jerked it away before the wormhole dragged it back through time to 2003.

"Don't accidentally give yourself an amputation," Rochelle said with a wink. "It would be kind of hard explaining that one to the doctors!"

"It wouldn't be too hard. I'd just tell them that a wormhole cut it off!"

Lady Capella gave Laura and Preston each a hug. "Be careful, you two," she said. "And don't be gone for too long."

"And don't forget that you're welcome in our home anytime you please," added her husband.

"We know." Preston made his way to the edge of the wormhole. "You ready now?"

Laura nodded. "As ready as I'll ever be."

"Wait, Laura," said Rochelle.

"What?"

"If you ever think about it, bring me back a steaming hot pizza, lots of bacon and onions, no mushrooms. Got it?"

Laura laughed. "Yeah, I will. But you can come with us if you'd like."

"No way! This isn't the portal I came from. I was three years old in the year you came from, and having two of me in the same year would be insane. What if I went back to Ontario and accidentally

ran into my three-year-old self? I'm better off staying where I am."
She smiled. "Besides, this is home."

"Suit yourself, then! I'll be seeing you soon!"

She grabbed Preston's hand; and after one final wave of farewell,
they stepped into the portal.

"That was easily the most bizarre experience of my life," Mark commented the moment he saw Laura.

Everyone had gathered in the kitchen to gawk at the three new
arrivals; and Laura found herself being pounced upon by Melanie
and Shannon, her seven-year-old sisters. Her mother and grandparents were overcome with shock and had to sit down.

"Where in the blazes have you been, Laura?" asked Uncle Tom,
who kept eyeing Mark with something akin to disapproval. "I
thought you ran away after you dang near split me in half with that
hunk of ice!"

"Thomas!" Laura's mother threw Uncle Tom a warning look.

Laura smiled. "It's okay. I just went through a portal."

"A what?"

"A portal. It zapped me six hundred and eighty years into the
future."

"I don't understand." Her mother frowned. "You've been gone for
two entire months, and then Preston went into the basement to look
for paint rollers awhile ago and disappeared... And then this *man*
comes marching up the steps out of nowhere..."

"My name is Mark Ericson," Mark said with a grin. "I haven't
been born yet."

Alicia Owens shook her head in disbelief. "I think I need to go
see a shrink."

"Shall we show them?" Preston asked.

Laura pried her sisters off of her and nodded. "Follow us," she
said.

Everyone rose, giving each other wary looks. Laura led them down into the basement and stopped at the doorway leading into the lower cellar.

"It's in here," she said, "the entrance to the wormhole."

"I'll be darned," her grandfather breathed. "No wonder the people who lived here before us warned us not to go down there. They said it was unstable and haunted."

"Do you all want to come with us?" Laura asked, trying not to laugh at the bewildered expressions on her family's faces.

Her grandparents exchanged glances and shrugged. "Might as well."

Laura pulled the door open, and they all walked down the old set of stairs. She held on tightly to her sisters' hands.

"And now," said Mark with a dramatic wave of his arm, "let us begin the next great adventure!"

Laura watched as Mark and her family vanished one by one in the shimmering air. Finally, only she and her sisters remained.

"Are you ready?" She gave them a reassuring smile.

The twins nodded, looking more curious than frightened.

Laura took a deep breath and stepped forward; and together, they left the musty basement behind to enter that beautiful, mysterious land beyond the portal.